GOODBYE AND EVERYTHING AFTER

GOODBYE AND EVERYTHING AFTER

Mae Coyiuto

FEIWEL AND FRIENDS
New York

Trigger warning: This book covers the death of a parent and many depictions of grief.

A Feiwel and Friends Book
An imprint of Macmillan Publishing Group, LLC
120 Broadway, New York, NY 10271 • fiercereads.com

Our books may be purchased in bulk for promotional, educational, or business use. Please contact your local bookseller or the Macmillan Corporate and Premium Sales Department at (800) 221-7945 ext. 5442 or by email at MacmillanSpecialMarkets@macmillan.com.

Library of Congress Cataloging-in-Publication Data is available.

First edition, 2026
Book design by Mallory Grigg
Feiwel and Friends logo designed by Filomena Tuosto
Printed in the United States of America

ISBN 978-1-250-29309-1
10 9 8 7 6 5 4 3 2 1

To the daughters who try their
best to take care of their families.
I see you and please take care of yourself too.

And to my dad, Peter.
Out of all the dad characters I write,
you'll always be my favorite one.

We invite you to explore the glossary at the end of the book as you enjoy *Goodbye and Everything After*.

1

I'M WEARING BLACK TO MY MOM'S ENGAGEMENT CEREMONY BECAUSE I'm mourning my mother's lost potential.

This is a statement, a protest if you will.

For the past month, our world has revolved around *the* Lilibeth and Derrick ting hun. The soundtrack of our lives has been my mom's and sister's calls to people about jewelry, medallions, the perfect noodle recipe.

Ever since Auntie Baby told Ma that women enter the ceremony walking backward to fend off negativity, I'd catch Ma practicing in the kitchen. My mom is already the most superstitious person I know—it's no surprise that she'd feng shui the shit out of her engagement.

All this fuss for a guy who talks to the moon.

No joke. I once caught Dr. Derrick outside our condo having a full-blown conversation with the sky. I rushed inside to tell Ma, naturally thinking this would be a clear sign that she should stay away from this man, but all she said was, "Derrick is very spiritual."

Ma has always been superstitious, but at least her beliefs are always grounded by some sense and culture. With Dr. Derrick's influence, Ma adopted his woo-woo stuff—rambling about the phases of the moon and wearing all the random jade jewelry that Dr. Derrick gets from Ongpin.

I wouldn't be surprised if they plan on getting the moon to officiate their wedding.

Since Dr. Derrick is his family's precious only son, his mom insists on the whole traditional Chinese Filipino engagement.

Which, honestly, I don't get why Ma has to go through since she's already been *married*. Every time I bring that up with my sister, Jackie, she sighs at me like I'm a little kid and says, "That's beside the point, Nika."

So, I played the role of good daughter and let go of all my very valid points during the whole engagement prep. My sister has outlined the ting hun program for me an ungodly number of times.

Step one: Dr. Derrick enters with his family. I, the dutiful daughter, guide them to their seats like they're toddlers who aren't familiar with the concept of sitting down yet.

Step two: My sister and I are supposed to serve Dr. Derrick's family orange juice and candy for god knows what reason. Probably some Chinese Filipino tradition that says higher sugar levels mean higher happiness.

Step three: My mom finally graces us with her presence as Auntie Baby escorts her to the living room, walking backward for good luck (unclear if this is luckier than juice and candy).

Step four: Ma comes face-to-face with Dr. Derrick, where they exchange gifts, rings, and have a tea ceremony—practically sealing her fate with the dentist till death do them part.

"Oh, Nika! Hello!" Dr. Derrick stumbles into the apartment carrying a giant bouquet of flowers when I open the door. No surprise that the man shows up to his engagement wearing his same striped purple tie that I've seen in every dentist appointment. If he really were a medical expert, he would have observed by now that a striped purple tie clashes with everything—even his dental scrubs.

He wastes more of my time with another attempt at small talk. "What an . . . interesting dress. They do say that black jade stones can ward off negative energies."

Too bad it's not enough to ward off *his* negative energy.

While staring at the floor, I gesture to where Dr. Derrick is supposed to go. Achi told me I had to guide Dr. Derrick, she didn't say I had to make eye contact with him.

For the record, I've been civil to Dr. Derrick. This was the same dentist who suggested I get braces back in seventh grade, and I was mature enough to not hold *that* against him. When Ma canceled my dental cleaning after we lost Pa, Dr. Derrick sent over a care package with condolences. Ma immediately prepared to send him her own care package as a thank-you. I wish I would've stopped their care-package flirting right then and there.

Just like a dentist-size toxic mold wearing a striped purple tie, Dr. Derrick continued to seep into our lives. He started popping up during family dinners, Sunday Mass. One time, Ma and Achi were stuck at work when I needed a guardian to sign my report card. Ma had the audacity to suggest I get Dr. Derrick's signature. Naturally, I forged her signature instead.

Ma didn't need to tell me they were dating—that report card defined their relationship for me.

And maybe I could've lived with that. If Dr. Derrick kept intruding into our lives, I could try to make an effort to hold my tongue, semi-acknowledge his presence when I was in a good mood. But Dr. Derrick ruined all chances of peace when he proposed to my mother.

Achi started calling him Uncle Derrick, but he's firmly Dr. Derrick to me. Scratch that. From this day forward, I refuse to patronize any of his teeth-cleaning services. I stand by my belief that it's a huge red flag that a dentist would romantically pursue any of his patients, especially his patients' parents. Like, whenever he was cleaning my molars and filling my cavities, was he thinking, *Ooh, I'd love to shove my tongue down her mom's molars one day.*

Seeing how Ma went through all this trouble to celebrate being engaged to the dentist? This definitely warrants a day of mourning.

Meanwhile, my sister has decided to become the clear front-runner for ting hun MVP. The rest of the Go family starts filing into the living room, and Achi is playing the role of perfect hostess. Every time she bows at one of Dr. Derrick's relatives, I sneak a piece from the giant candy box. Achi doesn't even bat an eye when his family keeps calling her Jacqueline (which I know she hates) instead of Jackie.

I had to do a double take when she arrived in a dress, heels, and *lipstick*. My sister has always been naturally beautiful but refuses to do anything to accentuate her beauty. Like, a few years ago, someone stopped us at the mall and asked Achi if she wanted to compete in a beauty pageant to be the next Ms. Chinatown.

She refused to do Ms. Chinatown, but *this* she was willing to get made-up for.

"Nika," she scolds when she catches me sneaking another piece of candy.

I gasp and cover my mouth. "This is bad luck too?"

She snatches the candy box from me and slams it shut. "Don't you think dressing like *that* is enough?"

"I wanted to wear my nicest dress," I say, pretending like we didn't already have a five-hour long argument about my outfit this morning.

When one turns eighteen, some say that marks a girl turning into a woman. When Achi turned eighteen, she switched from human to robot. Five years later, she still only cares about following Ma's rules, being on our "best behavior," and showing society that the Ilagan women are doing A-OK. Of course, she can't resist lecturing me about my "impulsive tendencies."

"Nika, when you put on that dress this morning, did you stop and think about the consequences of your actions?"

Of course I did. The consequences were my main motivation for executing said action. Contrary to her opinion, I'm fine with other people thinking, *Nika's being the bitchy sister again.* At least I'm the bitchy sister who looks good.

Mourning purposes aside, it's also very satisfying that black is my color. In her bright red dress with gold circles all over it, Achi looks like a walking red envelope.

Achi skims Ma's notebook of superstitions one more time. Ever since she took over ting hun planning, Ma's "book of superstitions" became her bible. "When you serve juice to Uncle Derrick's relatives, remember you're supposed to say, *Tshia dimmmmmm.*" Achi enunciates the words as if she hasn't been telling me how to say "Please drink" in Hokkien every single waking moment of the past month.

"How come you never teach me how to say bad words in Hokkien?"

Achi grumbles and tells me to let her handle the talking. She goes back to studying Ma's notebook again and blocks my view when I try peeking. "The notebook is reserved for the planning committee."

"There are four people planning this ting hun, so we're *all* on the planning committee." I try grabbing Ma's notebook and she dangles it above her head so I can't reach. Ugh. I *hate* it when she uses my height against me.

When Dr. Derrick mentioned that his family wanted to hire a ting hun coordinator to plan the engagement ceremony, my type A sister couldn't resist volunteering for the job. For the record, no one asked her—and no one asked me if I was okay with getting grouped into "committees" with my aunties.

Auntie Grace and Auntie Baby have been friends with Ma

since high school, and they grew even closer when they all had babies at the same time. They joke that they were always fated to find one another since all their names started with Marie: Marie Beth, Marie Grace, and Marie Francesca (side note: People call Auntie Baby "Baby" because she's the youngest in her family, not because it's short for Francesca). Together, they call their friend group the Marie-tres.

They're not only Ma's best friends, they're Ma's number one enablers. The reason why it took forever to schedule this ting hun is because Auntie Baby kept finding new ways why every single date of the year was bad luck. When Ma told her Marie-tres that she wanted to get engaged on a "lucky" date, Auntie Baby went on and consulted all the feng shui experts around the country. The only date that Auntie Baby's several sources agreed on was August 8, 2088 (I was fine with putting off this whole wedding idea for another few decades, but of course, my sister had to butt in and ruin the fun).

I love my aunties. Ma doesn't have any sisters, so Auntie Baby and Auntie Grace have always filled that void. Auntie Grace's daughter, Kayla, even became my best friend.

It's Auntie Baby's son who I could use less of.

My theory is that his ego was built in from the genesis of his actual name, Moseph. Like, naming him after one biblical name wasn't enough. Apparently, his parents couldn't decide between Moses and Joseph, so they decided to squish them together—hence giving him double the biblical superiority complex.

"Auntie Baby mentioned that Seph needed help setting up. Told her that you would be the point person."

Achi waves at Auntie Baby, who's standing by the kitchen, and gestures that I'm coming over. To my misfortune, Seph is right next to her and waves right back.

"Oh, I really don't like you right now."

"Go on," Achi says, pushing me forward.

I grumble, "Can't believe this is how you treat your only sister."

As I make my way past the couch toward the dining area, I can feel the stares and even gawking from Derrick's family. When they become harder to ignore, I hold on to the hair tie on my wrist, straighten my posture, and walk with even more confidence in my dress.

"Annika!" Auntie Baby lights up when she sees me. There's a slight crack in her cheeriness when she eyes me from head to toe. "What a . . . dress."

"Thanks, Auntie," I deadpan, ending the window for small talk. "Achi said you needed help?"

"Oh, yes. Jackie put me in charge of the entertainment committee!"

I hold my tongue from pointing out that she's the lone member of said committee.

She turns to Seph. "Can you show Seph where to set up? Your mom agreed that it'd be wonderful if he can play some background music when she enters the room."

Not even the occasion of my mom's engagement can stop the star of Moseph King from shining.

"What if the two of you do a duet? That would be such a great shot for the ting hun video!" She beams at me and adds, "You know, Nika, they also give awards to couples at prom too."

It's not enough that I have to put up with this guy's presence—I also have to tolerate Auntie Baby's not-so-subtle hints about going to prom with him. As president of the Saint Agnes Alumni Association, Auntie Baby is also very active in the parents' prom committee. She's made it her mission to secure my attendance, and to hint that I should bring her son along with me.

Based on our history, I'm pretty sure Seph isn't a fan of going to prom with "Bad Luck" Ilagan.

During the summer after Pa passed away, I was supposed to be Gabriella to Seph's Troy for *High School Musical.* I never made it to the show. Ma and Achi were already in the car, ready to take me to the theater, but I couldn't budge from the bathroom floor. It was like every time I thought about my lines, or singing in front of a whole audience, my chest squeezed tighter and tighter—to the point that I had to cling to the edges of my sink so I could remember how to breathe. My head still felt like it was floating when I lied to Ma and said I was sick. Achi insisted I go to the theater the next week to explain why I didn't show up. As I made my way to the entrance, I saw Moseph talking to the other Trumpets theater kids. They were saying how my surname Ilagan actually means "to avoid" in Tagalog. I heard someone laugh and say that it made sense since I choked on opening night. Then another guy made some joke about how they should avoid saying my name so it doesn't bring bad luck to the show.

It was so incredibly obvious that Moseph was the one who started the whole thing. I mean, he's the only person who calls me Ilagan. And it's not like I'm holding a grudge. I'm great at letting things go! The reason why I didn't join Trumpets again was because I got busy with more important things. Plus, why should I even care what Seph thinks about me? His opinions are the least of my concerns.

Once Auntie Baby leaves us, Seph unfortunately opens his mouth. "Nice dress, Ilagan."

To an uninformed outsider, Seph's comment might be misconstrued as a compliment. I, however, an insider with tons of experience, know it's an opening to what he really wants to say.

"Maybe you can get a prom date at this ting hun."

See?

"Not going to prom, Moseph," I tell him. "Based on all the shameless selfies you've been posting, I'm guessing *you* don't have a date yet." I tsk and tilt my head. "Couldn't get anyone to say yes?"

"Taking my time with my options. Did you notice all the moms who have been visiting the condo? A lot of them were asking Ma if I'm free to take their daughters to your prom."

"Makes sense," I say, nodding. "Even hell has lots of visitors."

The sides of his eyes crinkle and his nose scrunches when his lips quirk up. Every time he gloats or shows off, he always adds in an obnoxious smile.

"So where should I set up?"

I gesture to where he's standing. "Knock yourself out."

His brow furrows. "How are the acoustics in this area? I'm playing the *dying every day* song and I don't want anyone to miss the buildup to the chorus."

"Do you mean 'A Thousand Years'?"

He's always been the worst at song titles.

"I'm sure the 'famous' Seph King can play in any environment."

"Ilagan." Seph clutches his chest, matching my sarcasm. "You think I'm famous?"

He smiles.

I smile.

Having a conversation with Seph King actually makes me grateful when Achi calls me to get the pitcher of orange juice from the kitchen.

Yet when I budge open the kitchen door, I see that Auntie Grace and Auntie Baby are already huddled by the ref. Another reason why Ma's barkada is called Marie-tres: The three of them are pro-gossipers, Marites personified. Even when Ma refuses to sign up for any form of social media, she's still up to date because of my aunties' network. Auntie Baby has sources far and wide, so she allegedly knew that Prince Harry and Meghan Markle got engaged, even before it was announced to the public.

As soon as they're looking away from the door, I sneak inside and crouch down by the kitchen island. Achi always scolds me for eavesdropping, but I'm pretty sure she'd want to get first updates about the Royal Family too.

My ears suddenly perk up when I hear my name in their conversation.

"Does Beth know that Annika was going to be wearing that dress?"

I hear Auntie Baby sigh. "Hay, you know naman Annika. Didn't Beth say that she wishes Nika could act more like Jackie?"

My fingers fiddle with the hair tie on my wrist while I keep listening. Granted, I enjoy chismis way more when it doesn't involve me, but this is old news. I've always known that Achi was Ma's favorite—no surprises there.

Then the gossip gets more interesting.

"I made excuses for her in front of Derrick's relatives," Auntie Grace says. "Told them that the girl's been through a lot and they should pray for her."

"Beh khan tshiu pa tapos ang judgy na," Auntie Baby scoffs. "The amah was telling Derrick that she hopes the girls would look proper for the ting hun. She's worried about Jackie and Nika when she's the one with a single fifty-year-old son."

Knew it! I *knew* that Derrick and the whole Go family was sketchy. This is the kind of chismis that's healthy for the soul.

"But Beth does look happy, doesn't she? It reminds me of Beth and Ton back then."

“Grace, you can’t compare. That was first love and iba naman ang glow ng prom king and queen.”

Wait. My parents went to prom together?

. . . My parents were prom king and queen?

“Nika!”

My body knocks over a stool when Achi bursts into the kitchen. “What’s taking you so long?”

Auntie Baby comes over and bends to check my hiding spot. “Why are you crawling on the floor?”

“Uh . . .” I stand and smooth my dress. “I was looking for the orange juice.”

“You mean this one?” Auntie Grace points at the pitcher directly on the countertop.

“Ah, there it is!” I quickly grab the pitcher before this looks any more incriminating. Walking past Achi and my aunties, I push open the kitchen door. “Proud member of the juice committee. Tshia dim, tshia dim!”

Once I get through the difficult ordeal of serving people juice (and dodging Achi’s accusations that I was eavesdropping again), Auntie Grace tells everyone to settle down and get ready for Ma’s entrance.

Moments later, Ma emerges from the bedroom in the red dress her Marie-tres helped her pick out. I sometimes forget how utterly stunning my mom is—and her shoes accentuate her leg muscles even more. Ma has such toned legs that her calf muscles already pop when she’s wearing flats.

I shouldn’t be shocked that she was prom queen in a past life.

The music starts as Ma begins her grand entrance. Even if Seph always makes his weird smoldering face when he plays the guitar, I hate to admit that he isn’t totally out of tune. Auntie Baby is extra careful when she guides Ma backward down the steps leading to our living room. I can practically hear Ma muttering a prayer under her breath.

"Why aren't you Ma's lucky lady?" I ask Achi.

"Auntie Baby knows more about these things."

According to tradition, the woman who assists you in this ting hun entrance is supposed to be a "lucky" lady. Meaning: married, has kids, and ideally has parents who are still alive. So I guess with that criteria, Achi and I are zero for three.

And while Auntie Baby had the misfortune of having Seph for a son, she frequently mentions how "magical" her whole ting hun experience was with Uncle Francis.

Ma keeps walking until she reaches the center of the living room that has the prepared gift table covered with a red satin cloth. Auntie Baby spins my mom around three times and finally faces her in front of Dr. Derrick. While all this is happening, Dr. Derrick's auntie keeps sneaking glances at me.

"Bo le so," she mutters, very loudly so everyone within the vicinity can hear.

I expected better, to be honest. When Auntie Baby and Auntie Grace were gossiping about Dr. Derrick's judgy family, I envisioned getting way more lethal comments from them than "She has no manners." God, this family can't even come up with good insults. The Gos are becoming an endless cycle of disappointment.

Although, I do wish she didn't say it while I'm right next to Achi. It's like having an annoying life-size angel on my shoulder when I only want to listen to the devil. All the comebacks I have in my head unfortunately have to go to waste.

I keep expecting Achi to lecture me about the dress or read off another superstition listed in Ma's notebook that I've broken, but she remains completely quiet while Derrick's parents go on with the gift ceremony. It's only when Ma and Derrick exchange gold bangles and wear them on their wrists that she says something.

"Ma didn't think this would happen," I hear her say.

"What?" I scoff. "Her marrying our dentist?"

She shakes her head and pauses. "Feeling happy again."

It takes all my willpower to hold back from screaming that this is not Ma's happily ever after. Believe me—I really, really tried to be mature, be the kind of daughter Ma wants me to be. When Dr. Derrick proposed to Ma, her first question to Achi and me was, "Are you okay with this?"

What was I supposed to do? Say no when she and my sister were jumping for joy?

The tea ceremony begins with Dr. Derrick carrying the tray of teacups. Ma pours the tea and serves a cup to each of Dr. Derrick's parents. Auntie Baby mentioned that this action symbolizes Ma communicating that she sees them as her parents too. Serving tea translates to: *Now I call you Mom and Dad.*

When his parents call for photo taking, Dr. Derrick's family is all smiles and laughing like we're witnessing some Disney fairy-tale wedding.

My wrist has marks from how hard I'm gripping my hair tie, but none of it calms me down. I can't—I can't do this. I can't sit around here and pretend like I'm okay with Ma settling for this. That this is the life she wanted, that this is the guy she's using to replace Pa?

Before they call Ma's family for pictures, I get up from my seat and bolt straight to my room. I don't care how many bo le sos get thrown my way again.

Like what Auntie Baby said, Dr. Derrick will never compare to my dad.

2

I DON'T KNOW HOW THE WORLD EXPECTS ME TO GO THROUGH MA'S ting hun and then sit through chemistry class on a Wednesday morning.

After graduating summa cum laude from Ateneo, Achi was offered jobs at all the top companies in the country. What did my sister decide? She chose to go back to high school and be the senior high guidance counselor. It's not enough that she monitors my every move at home—with her job, she can spy on me during school too! She gave me an emergency key to her office during the times she'd have to stay late after dismissal so I can still be productive and catch up on homework.

I'd argue that this alternative to chem class also counts as being productive.

"This movie always makes me cry." Kayla hugs the couch cushion tighter while the couple on-screen starts having a dramatic conversation in the rain.

"Ky, every movie makes you cry."

You know what I love most about Kayla? She always supports me 100 percent. Whenever I declare someone my new nemesis, I don't even have to explain myself, they automatically become Kayla's nemesis too. She even did something that's totally out of character and agreed to skip class with me, and it only took *slight* persuasion. I mean, we're nearly halfway through senior year and it's just a few weeks until Christmas break. Realistically, are we even capable of retaining information at this point?

What sold Kayla on my brilliant idea is my suggestion that

we could use the projector in Achi's office. Kayla is obsessed with movies. Her lifelong goal is to watch every movie that's ever been made. She fell in love watching the actress Kathryn Bernardo when we were kids and has watched every movie of hers since. Kathryn and her on-screen partner, Daniel Padilla, broke up years ago, but Kayla still hasn't moved on.

"And what makes that sorry different from all your other sorrys before?" Kayla chokes up when she recites Kathryn's line along with her.

While Kayla and Kathryn Bernardo are having a moment, I focus back on my achi's evaluation reports. When I was setting up the projector, the midyear student evaluations for Ms. Jacqueline Ilagan were on her desk, ready for anyone to take them!

Every time I see a student score my sister with less than a five, I cross it out and circle the higher score she deserves.

Ms. Ilagan can be pretty intense.

Can't believe Dani Bautista had the nerve to write this and rate Achi a two in classroom engagement. Maybe my sister would be more *engaged* if Dani wasn't bothering her so much about whatever's going on with student council.

I mimic Dani's handwriting and improve on her comment.

*Ms. Ilagan can be pretty intense**ly helpful**!*

"Nooooo!"

I look up to see a black screen and a code that it's having trouble playing the current title. Kayla tries reloading the movie, but it keeps on flashing the same error message.

"Ugh." Kayla slumps on the couch. "And they were on their way to getting back together."

"They should've stayed broken up."

Kayla gawks at me like I just slapped her in the face.

"Kathryn wasted so much time on the guy! She could've

been a doctor already without her boyfriend getting in the way. It's just like how Dr. Derrick keeps getting in the way of Ma's life."

"Auntie Beth wanted to be a doctor?"

"No . . . But she could've! Maybe she would've discovered more options without Dr. freaking Derrick."

"True," Kayla says, grumbling along with me. "Dr. freaking Derrick."

Love it. One hundred percent support.

"What're you busy with?" Kayla looks over at Achi's desk and I cover the folder with my arm. Skipping class was already a stretch for Kayla's conscience. She might spiral into an existential crisis if she becomes a witness to me forging evaluation forms (albeit, forging them for the better).

Thankfully, she gives me the easy way out. "Are those club registration forms?"

"Yes, yes they are," I say, lying my butt off.

Kayla's whole face lights up. "Which clubs are you signing up for?"

Another factor that bonds Kayla and me: I have no interest in joining any extracurricular activities, while her *parents* don't let her join any extracurricular activities. Auntie Grace and Uncle Walter are super religious and super active in their church. Kayla once asked if she could join the school paper and Auntie Grace asked, "Isn't it more important to spread the word of God?"

"When Achi Jackie gave us that talk about how we only have a few months left to be involved in the Saint Agnes community, I started thinking," Kayla says.

"As a student who's been going here for twelve years, you're already involved in the community."

"It's senior year and I don't want to feel like I've missed out. There's a chance my mom might allow me if we join together."

I groan when I see how much this means to her. "Which club?"

Ever since Dani became student council president, our high school has exploded with the most random clubs. Since her whole agenda has been getting everyone to "participate," the apparent solution has been creating a club or organization for every possible niche interest. Saint Agnes now has a karaoke committee, manga appreciation organization, a Taylor Swift crochet club (the Swifties Who Crochet apparently have two-hour-long meetings discussing which stitch matches which Taylor Swift song).

"The prom committee is looking for people—"

"No," I cut her off before she continues.

"If you're in charge of music, then you get to dictate the playlist!"

"Ky, what are the things I'll do before going to prom?"

She sighs. "You would rather get braces all over again."

"And?"

"You would rather wear a bikini, take a bath in your own blood, then go swimming in a pool of sharks before setting foot inside prom."

I smile. "Exactly."

"Maybe I should listen to Ma and volunteer for the socials at church . . ."

My heart twists when I see Kayla's face drop. "Hey, what if you start a movie club? I'd join that."

Still doesn't lighten up.

"Every meeting can be devoted to a movie and you explaining the lore behind Kathryn Bernardo."

This makes her slightly intrigued.

"If you can get another movie to work, we still have time to watch the beginning."

Kayla's already scrolling through the movie catalog. To my misfortune, the only KathNiel title that plays is *Pagpag: Nine Lives,* otherwise known as Moseph King's claim to fame.

Back when we were eight, Seph had a minuscule, teeny-weeny stint as a child actor. Seph's dad is an executive at a media company, and one of their film projects was scouting for a Chinese Filipino boy. Long story short, Seph ended up booking the gig as a guest supporting actor for the horror movie *Pagpag: Nine Lives.* The horrific part of it all? Some people actually treat Seph as if he is an artista, and he loves every minute of it.

But since I already rejected Kayla's prom committee proposal, I've lost any right to reject her movie choice.

The movie opens with a girl walking into her boyfriend's funeral. But once the boyfriend's mom sees her, the mom kicks her out, blaming the girl for his death. Humiliated, the girl then runs straight home.

When the girl gets scolded by her roommate for wearing red and breaking superstitions, it reminds me of how Ma lectures me about stuff like pagpag.

Pagpag is this Filipino superstition that says you're not supposed to go home immediately after a wake. To prevent spirits from following you home, people are supposed to make a pit stop, like at a McDonald's or a convenience store. Maybe the goal is to bribe the spirits with chicken nuggets or pancakes so your house looks way less tempting. Either way, I never really bought into the whole superstition. Like all my mom's sayings, I learned it's easier to follow along and give up finding the logic in her beliefs.

"Oh no," Kayla whispers, and grabs the cushion. "She didn't pagpag."

She covers her eyes when the eerie music starts to play.

Come on. Anyone can predict that a ghost is about to show up.

The door mysteriously creaks open, the girl slowly turns around, and a picture frame with her dead ex crashes to the floor. When she picks it up, his expression changes from smiling to glaring. It's *so* obvious that . . .

"Ahhhhhhh!"

Kayla yells out when a corpse appears, and the school bell rings to signal the next period.

I quickly hit pause on Achi's computer before more dead bodies appear on-screen and Kayla passes out. "Achi has office hours next period. She's going to kill me if she finds out I sneaked in here again."

While we're busy covering up evidence, Kayla quizzes me on the whole history of the movie. "True or false. *Pagpag* was one of Kathryn's first film projects. It is also one of the highest grossing Filipino horror films in history."

This is how Kayla fangirls over things—she gives true-or-false quizzes.

"Could the first sentence be true and the second be false?" I clarify. "Or am I supposed to give one answer for both statements?"

She quizzes me more while I make sure all the evaluation papers are filed neatly in the folder I found them in.

"Later on, Kathryn's character doesn't pagpag, so another ghost named Roman ends up haunting her and her family. But the big twist is—it's Roman's wife who's behind the whole thing! She made a deal with the devil so she can bring her dead husband back to life."

Kayla suddenly yelps when the office window flies open.

"Relax, it's the wind," I tell her, and shut it closed. "Maybe we should stick to the romance movies instead of the horror ones."

"You really don't find any of that ghost stuff scary?"

I shrug. "It's all fake."

"Still. That doesn't stop your mind from wondering about possibilities."

"Guess my mind works differently."

Before Kayla can grill me with more questions, I ask her to make sure the projector is off and the screen is rolled up.

I'm not sure if I can ever tell anyone the real reason why ghosts don't really scare me. If you've been wishing for so long that your dead dad can come back, it kind of cancels out the horror factor. But I know better now. When someone's gone, they're gone—no matter how much you wish things were different.

It's a fact that my family has been trying to tell me about Pa for years.

THE WALK FROM THE SENIOR HIGH BUILDING TO THE SCHOOL GATE takes about fifteen minutes, which means I have fifteen minutes to rant more about Dr. Derrick before I meet my sister.

"You know I heard from Auntie Baby that Dr. Derrick took a break from dental school? How do we even know he got his license? Based on his record, he doesn't sound so professional."

Kayla shakes her head and walks by my side. "Unprofessional."

"Do you know his mom calls him every day? That's a huge sign he's a mama's boy."

"Such a mama's boy."

"Then all those years he kept visiting the bakery, checking in on Ma . . . I'm pretty sure he was already plotting on how to brainwash her into falling for him," I say. "Sobrang abangers."

Kayla takes a moment to respond. "Yeah . . . Such a banger."

I pause. "You don't know what abangers means, do you?"

"Of course I do." She pauses and says, "It's someone who . . . bangs a lot."

"Ew, no." I quickly try to shake away that mental picture. "Someone who's abangers is someone who waits for their crush to be single so they can make a move. They're people who pretend to be your friend, but in reality, they're just getting close to you because they're interested in you romantically."

"But what about friends who naturally develop into something more?"

"Ky, if Dr. Derrick was Ma's genuine friend, he would've stayed a friend. Everything that happened reveals his true character. He's no better than your dog who kept humping everything when she was in heat."

"Speaking of animals in heat . . ."

Once we get closer to the school exit, we see at least ten guys waiting outside the Saint Agnes school gate with posters, balloons, even a giant red panda stuffed toy. You can tell what school they're from based on the uniform. The brown slacks signal they're from Holy Cross; black pants means they're from the all-boys school next door, Saint Francis. Achi gave our whole class a lecture that our last year in high school is about zoning in on our goals. Well, *their* goal is securing a hot prom date.

Five guys from Saint Francis clear a space on the already crowded area by the crosswalk and start blasting a BTS song from a portable speaker. After doing a poor imitation of the choreography, they all unbutton their uniform polos to show their undershirts that spell out the question: *PROM?*

The most appalling dancer of the bunch then calls out to our classmate Julia. He raises a cutout of his face with a sign that says: *Julia, I know Jungkook might be your bias, but prom with me wouldn't be a minus!—Sean*

Julia says yes, even with the questionable rhyme on Sean's sign, then she and Sean proceed to have sex up against the school gate in broad daylight.

Okay, fine, the two of them are just hugging, but a hug that tight could be counted as sex in some countries, maybe even some areas in the Philippines.

People around the gate clap as if the two horny teenagers are newlyweds while Sean's friends slap his back and tell him versions of "Go, bro!" "Lakas mo, bro!"

Even Kayla is looking at them with googly eyes.

"Please don't tell me you got kilig over that," I tell her.

Kayla lets out a sigh, unfortunately dripping with kilig. "Kathryn also did a public dance to show her love for DJ in *She's Dating the Gangster*."

I take back my romance movies comment. I prefer horrified Kayla over delusional Kayla.

"Is Seph also asking someone to prom?"

I check to see where Kayla's looking, and Seph is indeed waiting by the gate—another boy probably infected by prom hysteria. No surprise, his uniform is unbuttoned so the whole world can see his sando undershirt again. He always leaves the top buttons of his shirts open to show off that he hit puberty and gained man cleavage. I feel sorry for the poor girl destined for the misfortune of a Seph King promposal.

And then he says my name.

"Pssst, Annika. Nika! Ilagaaaaaan!"

Kayla shoots me a knowing look.

"No, *no* way."

"Ooh! Can you ask him what it's like in show business?"

Ugh. Unfortunately, Kayla is one of the people who gets blinded by "former child actor Moseph King."

"Maybe Seph is a banger for you."

I quickly shut down the possibility and go find out what in the world Seph wants.

Moseph rebranded himself to Seph when he grew five inches and girls in our grade discovered he could play the guitar. Outside of Auntie Baby's Facebook page and Viber blasts, no one cared that Seph was a one-time child actor. But then sophomore year happened.

During the Saint Agnes–Saint Francis interaction party, he volunteered for the talent portion and played "Tenerife Sea" by Ed Sheeran. Someone in our grade took a video, which got spread around our all-girls-school network. The top comment on the post: *It's like ed sheeran turned into a cute fil-chi boy!*

Suddenly, people started piecing together that Fil-Chi Ed Sheeran is the same cute zombie boy from that one horror movie.

The occasion sadly proves the fact that my generation has a weakness for discount K-pop performances *and* discount Ed Sheeran guitar playing.

"Happy to see me?" Seph asks when I get closer to the exit.

I groan. "What are you doing here?"

"Auntie Beth asked me to walk you to the bakery."

Seph then pulls out his phone and shows his conversation with Ma.

Can you walk Nika to the bakery? –Beth

Ugh. That's definitely Ma. She's the only person I know who signs off every message with her name.

"I'm not a dog. I don't need to be walked."

"Yeah, you can actually train a dog," Seph adds, and I shoot him a glare.

"I don't need a chaperone," I emphasize. "And I'm already going home with Achi."

It's bad enough that my mom doesn't trust me to brave the daunting *five*-minute walk from school to Buns by Beth, she also linked my school ID to my sister's so I can't even leave the Saint Agnes premises without her.

"Oo nga pala. Achi Jackie said she was going to be late and gave me this . . . ," he says, reaching for his pocket. "You need this to get out, right?" He pulls out my sister's ID and slips the lanyard around his neck. "I guess this makes me your chaperone."

He grins at me and I resist the urge to rip the lanyard off his body.

3

MAYBE SEPH CAUGHT A COLD FROM HIS EXPOSED CHEST. IT'S THE ONLY rational explanation for why he's acting super suspicious today. First of all, he paid for my food.

As soon as we step outside the school grounds, we're greeted by Mang Willie's famous "Tahoooooooo!" Mang Willie is a staple across all batches for being the Saint Agnes and Saint Francis go-to taho vendor. Ever since I was in kindergarten, he'd be outside the school gate every dismissal carrying two aluminum buckets filled with soybean custard.

As Mang Willie starts pouring the pearls and syrup into plastic cups, Seph hands him enough cash for two orders.

"Libre ko," he says when I try paying him back. "Chaperone's treat."

The second red flag in Seph's behavior is when he starts complimenting me.

"Did you get a haircut?"

"Uh yeah, by a few inches." I hold on to the ends so it doesn't look so short. "The hairdresser I usually go to isn't free until the weekend, but Ma insisted I get my hair cut on Monday since Mondays symbolize 'new beginnings.'"

Then he says, "It's nice."

I'm already brainstorming possible comebacks for his inevitable teasing, but Seph doesn't say anything else.

"Like, nice for a Shih Tzu?"

"No."

"A Chow Chow?"

"It's nice for a girl . . . person." Seph doesn't take the bait and confuses me further. "Your hair looks nice."

I study him and hold him off before he scoops another spoonful of his taho. "Why are you being weird?"

"I just complimented you."

"Yeah," I point out. "Weird."

"Aren't compliments supposed to be nice?"

"You being nice is *weird*," I emphasize, and suddenly question the free food in my hand.

Seph avoids eye contact and fidgets with his plastic cup. "I figured you had a lot going on with . . . Sunday coming up," he says, and my insides freeze. "Didn't want to put you in a worse mood."

"How do you know about Sunday?"

"Overheard Achi Jackie talking about your dad to my mom."

This Sunday is the fifth anniversary of Pa's death, but no one in my family has spoken about it. I always thought my sister never liked talking about our dad. I guess she just never wanted to talk about him with me.

My brain has already tuned out Seph when I realize he's asking me a question.

"So . . . how are you . . . doing?" The boy's looking at me like I'm a bomb about to detonate.

"Please, stop," I tell him. "This is painful."

"Me being thoughtful isn't lifting up your mood?"

"Sadly, I think my mood's better when you're being the usual annoying Moseph."

He scoffs. "You know you're the only person in the world who calls me Moseph, Ilagan."

"And you're the only person who calls me Ilagan," I say, and repeat, "Annoying."

His nose scrunches at my comment. "That means I put you in a good mood then."

Seph laughs when I mime throwing my taho cup at his face.

"By the way," he adds. "You definitely give off Chihuahua energy."

"I identify as a Shiba Inu."

He shakes his head. "You're four feet tall. How in the world are you a Shiba Inu?"

"Excuse you, the doctor said I was five *one* during my last checkup."

"Exactly the height for a human Chihuahua."

Seph goes on to roast me about being my chaperone and I reply that he reminds me of Kayla's Pomeranian that humps everything in sight. It unfortunately doesn't stop thoughts about Sunday and Pa roaring in my head.

THE BAKERY IS WAY MORE CHAOTIC, SO I'M PRETTY SURE DR. DERRICK decided to "volunteer" again. When Paolo, the regular barista, called in sick earlier this week, Dr. Derrick said he could take some time off his clinic hours to help out.

When he offered, Ma looked like she had a female boner and Achi kept saying it was very "thoughtful" of him. Thoughtful?! Come on. It's another way Dr. Derrick is sucking up to Ma. Like, we get it already! She already said yes to marrying you! God.

Knowing he's a dentist, too, I see his ulterior motive. He wants to give people more coffee so their teeth get stained, coincidentally, giving him more patients. It's a despicable, deceitful plan.

"Sir!" A customer waves at Dr. Derrick from the pickup queue. "Matagal pa? I ordered my latte an hour ago."

"Almost done, ma'am!" Dr. Derrick yells back. From the way he's inspecting the milk he's pouring, he's obviously more focused on his latte art than the urgency of the situation.

Another thing I learned about Dr. Derrick against my will: He's probably the world's slowest barista.

More people from the line start complaining while Dr. Derrick is still perfecting the one latte order.

"Should we help him?" Seph asks me.

"We're not miracle workers, Moseph." I sigh and tell Seph that he can go and I promise him I'll tell Ma I survived the deadly walk from school. As much as I would enjoy seeing Dr. Derrick crash and burn, this is Ma's business on the line.

I start checking out food orders at the register to placate the hungry clients who have been waiting in the queue.

But not even shouldering Dr. Derrick's customers can dampen the thrill I get when walking into the Buns by Beth store. The bakery always has the same warm wonderful greeting, the sweet smell of freshly baked bread and an overwhelming display of pastries. You're offered a tray and tongs at the entrance, then you can pick from rows of pastries enclosed in their own plastic casing. But the Buns by Beth treasure, the one that has propelled the bakery to be one of *Manila's must-try pastry shops,* is the nationwide famous siopao. It's the dish that started Ma's whole career.

Growing up, I always had Ma's steamed buns filled with pork asado for merienda. During Pa's wake, she went overboard and made probably a hundred siopaos—which made people inquire who our caterer was. Ma used to sell her siopaos in bazaars back in her high school and college days but didn't pursue it when she started a family. So when people still kept asking Ma about her siopao supplier after the wake, Ma started a business where she'd bake from home and Achi would help arrange the deliveries.

Two years later, Ma decided to convert one of the warehouses Pa used to manage into her own bakery. She started trying new recipes, baking all kinds of pastries and desserts.

If you check the Buns by Beth menu, Ma's siopaos come in different flavors, from the classic asado and bola-bola to her salted egg twists.

Buns by Beth would be even bigger if Ma wasn't so paranoid about social media. The country's biggest supermarket chain approached her about a partnership, but Ma freaked out when she saw their proposed marketing plan. She said being featured that much "around the internet" is a huge security risk.

Once the line finally dwindles down, Dr. Derrick makes another attempt at small talk.

"Your mom and sister are in a meeting, but they'll be here soon."

Aside from her job as a counselor at Saint Agnes, my sister also somehow finds time to help Ma manage Buns by Beth. She was already gone to check on today's kitchen prep when I woke up this morning.

Dr. Derrick then offers me a Flat White. "Your favorite, right?" It even has the most symmetrical-looking heart at the center. This must have taken him hours to make.

I accept the mug and place it on the side, still avoiding eye contact with Dr. Derrick. Maybe he can buy Ma and Achi with his fake selfless barista volunteering, but I know better. My willpower is stronger than simply being tempted by coffee.

Although . . .

It's so tempting.

Dr. Derrick goes to refill some of the pastry displays and has his back turned. Maybe he wouldn't notice if there's slightly, very minuscule, less drink in the mug.

I pour a little in a separate cup and take a sip.

Shit, it's good.

The smooth feel of the drink and its perfect amount of sweetness makes me close my eyes so I can savor every taste. My self-respect goes down a notch with each sip.

But the Flat White suddenly turns sour in my mouth when I see Ma walk in and greet Dr. Derrick. He pecks her on the cheek, rubbing their relationship further in my face.

"Thanks for taking over this afternoon," Ma says.

"You should thank Nika." Dr. Derrick gestures in my direction and smooths his striped purple tie that hurts my eyes. "She saved the day."

Ugh. Suck-up.

Ma's eyes widen. "You and Nika worked together?"

"He should get barista training before you leave him alone."

Before they inflict me with more of their PDA, I excuse myself and tell Ma that I left something in the kitchen.

With the pork asado and chopped egg slices laid out on the counter, I can tell Ma is preparing puto pao again. The soft and fluffy rice cake filled with savory pork filling was my dad's favorite snack. Ma always makes puto pao leading up to Pa's anniversary, insisting on some superstition that preparing food for my dad would help sustain him in life after death. As if death doesn't cancel out the whole being alive thing.

Ma's superstitiousness went to a whole other level when Pa died. She keeps a little red notebook where she jots down superstitions, pamahiins, and some other practices that originate from who knows where. Our condominium used to have a small staircase with four steps leading from our living room to the bedrooms. Since the number four in Mandarin also sounds like the word for death, Ma chopped off a step. When she heard a Filipino superstition that having staircases divisible by three also meant attracting death, she shaved off another one. These days, I have to risk a pulled hamstring every time I have to leap through our botched staircase.

Seeing that my mom is prepping way more puto paos this year gets me thinking. If Ma is readying this whole feast, could Achi be preparing something too? She *did* go to Auntie Baby . . . Does Pa's fifth anniversary mean our family is going to *talk* about Pa for once?

I sneak into Ma's office, glancing behind my shoulder every few seconds to make sure no one's watching me. My eyes roll to the back of my head when I open a drawer and see Ma's collection of Dr. Derrick greeting cards. Every Valentine's Day, birthday, monthsary (what grown man celebrates monthsaries?!), Ma always gets a card from Dr. Derrick.

Happy birthday! Yours, Derrick
Happy Valentine's Day! Yours, Derrick
Happy monthsary! Yours, Derrick

No pickup line, no joke, no cute designs. He also chooses the world's most boring sign-off: *yours*. Considering there's a wide selection of greeting cards with template greetings, Dr. Derrick always sends cards with dedications that can put me to sleep.

I'm looking through the corner where Achi usually stores her things (I previously found advanced copies of our report cards here) when I see the key hanging from the bottom filing cabinet. I once tried opening that drawer, but my sister said it's always been broken.

When I turn the key, I find a folder of bank documents and

investment fund applications. I go through the other envelopes filled with recommendation letters for Jackie Ilagan, copies of her résumé and transcripts, flyers from college fairs.

What the hell?

They're all brochures for master's and PhD programs.

Master's in School Counseling

Master's in Clinical Psychology

PhD in Child Psychology

Each one details programs and schools miles and countries away. While I'm leafing through a University of Florida brochure, I take note of the highlighted text, the comments added in the margins. All of them are in my sister's scratchy handwriting.

I'm still calculating the distance from Manila to some place called Gainesville, Florida, when I hear footsteps approaching outside. Midway through stashing the evidence, my sister walks in.

"What are you doing?"

The drawer is hanging open, brochures scattered on the floor, and I still have one in my hand. Really painting the picture for the worst crime ever committed.

Although, the best way of explaining away sketchy behavior is pointing out others' sketchy behavior.

"You're moving to *Florida*?"

My sister stiffens. "You went through my drawer? My *locked* drawer?!"

"When were you going to tell us? Once you landed in Florida?" The thought of Achi being that far away triggers this hot feeling at the back of my throat. I rack my brain for any reason to convince her not to go.

"Do you know that Disney World is in Florida?" I remind her. "Why would you go there when you're scared of roller coasters?"

Achi's mind is still on the stupid drawer. "Didn't you see

the lock?" she yells. "A lock means boundaries, off-limits, no trespassing!"

"You left the key *inside* the lock!"

"That doesn't mean you have permission to open the drawer! If I left a gun next to me, does that mean you can shoot it?"

"No, Ach," I deadpan at her ridiculous question. "I won't be able to kill you if your body is all the way in *Florida.*"

We both go quiet when we hear Ma's voice from the kitchen. "Where did those two go?"

Achi switches on the room's loud ceiling fan as if the whirring can retroactively mask our yelling. She signals for me to zip my mouth, our cue to hit pause on our argument.

Our ceasefire kicks in when we step outside the office and find Ma packing some of the puto paos. Although seeing Dr. Derrick right next to her doesn't help that my blood's still boiling about my sister's secret move.

"The client from Marikina called that their bulk order didn't get delivered to their party," Ma tells Achi. "Can you be the one to take Nika home?"

"You're going to Marikina *now*? That'll take forever during rush hour."

Ma waves Achi off. "It's okay. I like the drive. It clears my head."

Achi and I share a look when Ma goes on about the million errands she was able to do today. During Pa's death anniversary two years ago, Ma actually passed out from pulling multiple all-nighters at the bakery.

Then Dr. Derrick inserts himself yet again. "I can drop you off there too."

"It's okay, I'll do it," Achi volunteers. "I promised this client that I was going to take a meeting with them too."

Buns by Beth is a *family* business, after all.

"Then who's going to go with Nika?" Ma asks.

"Hi." I cut in when everyone seems to forget I'm in the same room. "No one needs to go with Nika. It's a miracle, but Nika figured out how to walk—all on her own!"

As usual, my joke falls flat with my family.

"Speaking of . . ." Ma turns to me. "Remind me to give Seph some siopaos for looking after you."

"Ma, he did not look after me. All he did was walk by my side, which I'm capable of doing *alone*!" I groan. "Also, between Moseph and me, I'm the one who's more responsible and mature."

"Yeah, Ma, Nika is responsible."

We all stop short when my sister suddenly compliments me out of nowhere. This is even weirder than when Seph was doing it.

"When you say Nika . . . you're referring to me, right?"

Achi nods and the smug gleam in her eyes makes me nervous. "*Super* responsible. I was really impressed when you volunteered to handle the dish station today."

I peek at the washing station and it's overflowing with a tower of pans, trays, bowls. I don't know how she pulled it off, but every single dish there looks greasier than usual. I'm also 100 percent sure that dish duty is payback for me opening her stupid drawer. Yet, I hold my tongue and save all my comebacks for later. If I make a fuss about this now, Ma might enlist Seph for Nika-walking duty until I'm forty.

Fine, I will swallow my pride. I will *continue* to be the bigger person and wash the dumb dishes.

"Did you see the email with the supermarket's latest offer?" Achi asks Ma. "They even tagged Buns by Beth in their post about brands to watch."

Ma's gaze hardens. "I don't want them tagging us. If they start posting about us, then people will know where we are."

"Ma, that's the whole point of marketing," my sister says, still trying to reason with her.

Ma drops the subject and hands Achi a puto pao. "How do you like the texture of this? I tried steaming the bun for a bit longer than usual."

Maybe I was distracted by Dr. Derrick's presence or Achi's dishwashing scheme. Or maybe it was hearing Ma talk about Pa's favorite food. I'm not really sure what compelled me to break the rules.

"Do you remember Pa's birthday when he got sick from eating too much puto pao?" I ask, smiling at the memory. "Can't believe he still managed to eat more the next day."

As soon as I bring it up, I already feel myself holding my breath.

"Ah, Annika." Ma doesn't look at me when she answers. "Let's not talk about those things."

Achi swiftly swoops in and brings up how sales have increased this week. When Ma excuses herself to check on the register, Achi eyes me with an expression that screams, *What the hell was that?*

Because of course, I should know better. Ma can talk about Pa when she reminds us to include Pa in our prayers, when it's about replacing the flowers by his grave, when she tells us not to harm any butterflies because it might be our dead father visiting. But when we think about memories with Pa, the happy stuff, the times when he felt *real*—Ma hasn't been able to handle that.

That's why Achi tells me to adjust. Keep mentions of Pa to a minimum, shove it all in during the days when Pa is all I can think about. I mean, what right do I have when Achi and Ma are able to keep it together? Achi had Pa until she was eighteen, Ma fell in love and built a family with him. Twelve years is all I had.

What right do I have to grieve when their loss is way bigger than mine?

When Ma returns and Achi does damage control by chatting more about the puto pao texture, I turn on the faucet and start rinsing. I blink away my tears as I turn up the water pressure and soak the pans with surfaces that make the loudest noise.

Pull yourself together. Like what Achi says, if Ma sees that you're okay, then she'll be okay.

But, god.

Sometimes, being around my family makes me feel so lonely.

4

BY MY FAMILY'S TWISTED LOGIC, GETTING FORCED INTO DISHWASHING duty grants me solo-walking privileges. Ma stays back to close the bakery, Achi is probably stuck in traffic on the way to Marikina, and I have the condo all to myself.

This rare moment of peace means I have a small window for chilimansi pancit canton.

My sister does regular "deep cleans" of our kitchen and that means throwing out any chips, candy, soft drinks—basically, anything with flavor. During Achi's last birthday, Auntie Baby and Auntie Grace sent over a cake each and Achi immediately gave one away. If my sister wins the lottery, she would be the only person in the world who'd turn down the jackpot and say, "No, thank you. We don't want to have *too* much fun."

I can live without the cake, the chips, the soft drinks, but my sister's vendetta against instant noodles? It's downright deprivation.

For my pancit canton stash, I have to regularly switch the hiding place just so my sister doesn't throw away my noodles. I climb on top of the stool to reach for the broken kettle stored in the highest cupboard.

Aha! Noodles secured and found.

I've memorized Achi's sermon about how instant noodles have dangerous amounts of sodium and are bad for my heart, but you know what? Pancit canton is good for my *soul*. After a day like today, nothing sounds better than a hot serving of spicy, savory noodles.

As I wait for the water to boil, I hear footsteps approaching the front door.

Shit shit shit.

I quickly stuff the sauce packets and noodles in my pockets.

"Nika?" Ma enters the condo, carrying two paper bags. "Kumain ka na? Ordered some food for dinner."

She pauses when she sees me by the kitchen counter. "Why is the pot out?"

My face remains stoic, my voice calm. "Just needed hot water."

". . . From the pot?"

"Yeah, my throat was feeling weird, so I needed hot water." I pat my neck for emphasis. "Lots of hot water."

Ma then stares me down. "Are you making pancit canton?"

I'm about to counter when she asks, "What flavor?"

"Uh . . . chilimansi."

She places her takeout on the table and tells me to help unpack the containers. "Make sure you throw the wrapper outside so Jackie doesn't see."

A moment passes and she adds, "And make sure you have enough for two."

PANCIT CANTON, RICE, FISH, DUMPLINGS, AND BOK CHOY. IT REALLY IS A perfect dinner—fit for fine dining if you ask me.

"Nika." Ma scolds me when I stick my chopsticks in my bowl of rice to prepare the noodles. "Leaving your chopsticks like that is bad luck. They look like incense at a funeral."

I'm about to ask Ma how in the world she goes from looking at chopsticks to thinking about funerals, but I decide to leave it be. If Achi's really going to Florida, having meals together would be a permanent thing—just Ma and me.

So I remove the chopsticks from the rice, leave them next to the bowl, and serve my mother noodles.

“This is sinful,” Ma mutters as she stares at the pancit canton.

I grab the plate of bok choy and place some pieces on top of Ma’s bowl of noodles. “Look, the vegetables make it healthy. God should forgive you now.”

A slight smirk crosses her face. “I’m starting to question the quality of your Saint Agnes education.”

“Unhealthy noodles plus healthy vegetables means the vegetables cancel out the noodles,” I say, laying it out for her. “That’s great math.”

Ma shakes her head, laughing. She tells me to add more vegetables to my plate while she checks her phone that’s been buzzing nonstop with her work group chats.

If every day could be like our dinner tonight, I guess that wouldn’t be so bad. Look, Ma and I are capable of bonding, having dinner alone without things exploding. Maybe the next time Ma talks to her friends about me, she’ll rave about how fun I am instead of how I’m hard to deal with.

“Are you giving any of your teachers trouble?”

I shake my head, trying to focus on my noodles instead of taking Ma’s accusation too seriously.

Then she asks, “You’re passing all your classes?”

“Think so.”

“Does that mean yes or no?”

“It means I think so,” I repeat.

“So you’re not failing anything?”

“You never ask Achi these questions.”

“I used to ask her about school too,” Ma points out.

“No, you would ask her about what honor she got or what awards they were giving her.”

“Your sister gets lots of awards. Why wouldn’t I ask about them?”

I sigh and drop it. Maybe Ma doesn’t do it on purpose, but

I'm not sure if it's sadder her subconscious already expects the worst of me.

That's when all hell breaks loose.

"You skipped chemistry period?"

"Mmm?" I respond, my mouth still busy chewing.

"I got an email from school about your attendance."

Her chopsticks drop to the bowl when she scrolls through her phone. "Annika, you've missed nine classes this quarter?!"

I think about making a chemistry-related pun that the subject isn't really in my *element* . . . but something tells me Ma isn't in the mood.

"How do you expect to graduate if you miss that much school?" Ma demands. "During your sister's graduation, she had to go onstage five times to accept all her awards. Don't you want that too?"

"Not a big fan of stairs."

I can practically see the smoke steaming above Ma's face. Yeah, not a great time for jokes.

She pinches the bridge of her nose, taking a deep breath. "I know you've been having a hard time adjusting to the situation . . ."

By situation, she means her getting engaged to my dentist.

"And I've tried to be more patient with you. I tried letting how you acted at the ting hun go, but this can't go on forever." She clasps her hands together. "I want you to get back on track. Apply yourself in school, graduate, and get to college.

"Niks, we need to move on."

My body stiffens at Ma's words.

"I'm not going to graduation."

"It's still early in the school year. Of course, you can still graduate. I'm going to talk to your teachers. You know what, I'm going to have Jackie talk to them—"

"No, *I* don't want to."

Ma pulls back at this. Her mouth opens and closes multiple times, like she has no idea where to start.

"I don't feel like going," I explain, filling the silence. "Lots of successful people don't finish high school and I already saw Achi do it—"

"You don't *feel* like going?" Ma repeats, her voice growing louder. "Nika, you know how many things I do every day that I don't *feel* like doing? Do you think I *feel* like waking up at five in the morning or staying in the bakery until midnight? Do you think I *feel* like constantly worrying about how I'm going to pay your tuition and then find out that you don't even go to class?"

My eyes stay firmly on the table when I feel the hard lump in my throat.

"I don't, okay? But I still show up even when I don't feel like it," she says. "You wonder why I don't trust you to be responsible yet? This is why."

There are a million things I want to tell Ma. I want to tell her that I don't mean to make her life harder, that I don't mean to make her feel like I'm wasting all her hard work.

I want to tell her that the real reason I don't want to go to graduation is because I always thought I'd have Pa there in the audience watching me.

But I have no idea how to let any of these words out without bursting into tears.

The two of us sit in silence until Ma dismisses me from the table. "You should get started on your homework."

She waves me off when I try putting the dishes in the sink. "Ako na. I'll handle it."

Maybe it's for the best. I'll probably just make everything worse, like I always do.

Following Ma's orders, I let her be and retreat to my bedroom.

5

YOU CAN HIDE ALL THE PICTURES, AVOID TALKING ABOUT THEM, BUT you know what you can't do? Delete someone's digital footprint.

I'm very, very grateful that my dad had a few glimmers of internet fame.

If you search *happy piano man philippines mall,* the top result is a video of my pa playing Mariah Carey's "We Belong Together." Seeing an unplayed piano was Pa's weakness. When we went to the mall in our area on Sundays, he couldn't resist playing at least one song on the piano down on the first level.

At the start of the video, my dad asks the crowd around the piano for song requests, then he points to the person who shouts out, "'We Belong Together'!"

"Of course I'm going with Mariah Carey," Pa says as he takes a seat on the piano bench.

Pa *loved* Mariah Carey. Even though his voice could never reach her high notes, he always belted out her songs during our drives to school. Achi once teased Pa that listening to Mariah Carey was a "girlie" thing.

"If appreciating talent is girlie, then I'll be girlie," Pa replied. He then continued playing Mariah on repeat while educating us about which scales she's able to hit and how she writes all her songs.

Singing was something Pa and I bonded over. Achi called me the "queen of unsolicited singing" since I used to sing everywhere—in the shower, while doing homework, during car rides. My sister gave me time-outs and placed her hand over my mouth when she needed moments of peace and quiet. But Pa was the one person who always wanted to hear my voice.

I make a mental note that there have been twenty more views on the video in the past week. Even if I watch the video every day, it still doesn't explain the rising view count. I like thinking that there's some aspiring piano player out there who gets inspired by watching Pa.

My dad was always the happiest when he was playing the piano. And it's not the classy, cool smile singers have once they finish a mind-blowing performance and grin to the crowd implicitly communicating, *Yeah, I did THAT.* No, even in this video, Antonio Ilagan looks like some happy-go-lucky dorky dude who got high from playing the piano.

Pa always embraced whatever made me happy, no matter how ridiculous. It's the reason why I still have snowflake stickers glued to my ceiling. I had this *Frozen* phase when I was younger and kept telling my family that I wanted to see snow.

Achi and Ma were on the same page and tried educating me about geography and climate conditions. "Nika, we live very close to the equator. See?" Achi said, pointing to the Philippines on the map. "That means we have a tropical climate and if we do have snow, it'd be a nightmare for agriculture, livelihood, infrastructure."

But that night, Pa went into my room, knelt before my bed, and said he had a surprise. "Guess what?" he whispered to me. "I found you snow."

I remember I was confused and said, "But it doesn't snow in the Philippines."

"Dinala ko dito. Special delivery for my bunso."

"But Ma and Achi said it was impossible."

"Superstar." Pa used to call me that all the time. "That's why we dream bigger."

So Pa took out these snowflake stickers and spent the night decorating the ceiling on my part of the bedroom. Achi asked me once if I wanted to have our ceiling repainted since cracks began to form, but I hated the idea of not having those faded, tattered snowflakes looking down on me.

I count the patterns on each snowflake while I wait for the moment some higher being finally grants me the gift of slumber. *If I fall asleep right now, I'll get a respectable seven hours of sleep.* Every time I get bouts of insomnia, my sister always suggests that I try some guided meditation videos that make false promises like: *Fall asleep instantly, fall into deep sleep in FIVE minutes!*

Fun fact about me: Meditating makes me want to stab my eyes out.

I usually end up spending an hour, still *wide* awake, feeling even more frustrated after a voice instructs me with bullshit like "find your center of gravity and become aware of your pinkie toes."

How can I find peace when my brain is suddenly confused about what my toes are supposed to feel like?!

Sleeping is already hard enough on most days, but it's basically impossible after the whole pancit canton debacle with Ma. Not to mention Pa's impending anniversary.

In the middle of the lady's meditation video offering more vague instructions, I pull out the other phone hidden in a carved-out book tucked in my drawer. It's a miracle that my sister hasn't found Pa's phone yet.

When my sister was cleaning out everything Pa owned in the condo, I found his phone in one of his bags.

I open his messages and type out Miss you, Superstar.

Moments later, my phone lights up with an alert that I got a message from Pa.

Ugh. My family would *so* judge me if they knew about this. For the record, I'm fully aware that I'm using two phones to continue a conversation with myself—but . . . I like seeing Pa's name on my phone. For some moments, I think I trick my brain into believing that *he's* the one messaging.

I put back Pa's phone and give this dumb meditation another shot.

Okay, Nika. Calming thoughts. If you knock out right now, that gives you six full hours of restful sleep. Find your center of gravity. Be aware of your ankles or whatever the meditation lady is going on about.

Although my attempts at peace and deep breathing get rudely interrupted when Achi intrudes into my room.

"My eyes, my eyes!" I cry out when Achi flips on the lights. "I was *sleeping*!"

She scoffs. "You seem awake."

Achi dismisses my very valid sleep problems and rudely pulls the blanket off my body.

"I hate you," I grumble, and wrap my arms around my pillow before Achi takes that too.

Even though my sister already got her own apartment when she started working, she sleeps over so much that it feels like we still share a bedroom. I remove my earphones and try rolling to the other side when she taps my head.

"Were you going to sleep with your hair wet?"

I groan. "I'm not going to go blind."

In my mom's eyes, one of the most dangerous things you could ever do is sleep without drying your hair. According to her belief system, sleeping with wet hair equals waking up blind. The threat used to terrify me as a kid until I fell asleep after a shower—and ended up with eyesight on both sides still intact.

I'm pretty sure my sister doesn't buy into all of Ma's beliefs either. She just can't help switching to de facto parent mode with me—and that includes implementing our mother's superstitions.

Achi doesn't stop goading me until I groggily get up to blow-dry. By the time I get back, she's already hogged most of the bed.

Before I can even settle under the covers, Achi asks, "Are you going to stop sneaking into my office now that Ma found out you've been skipping class?"

"How did you . . ."

Achi tilts her head at me—in Jackie-speak, this means, *How do you not get that I'm incredibly smart?!*

So I thump my head back on the pillow. "Can you please make the lecture short? Ma already told me how I'm a disappointment over dinner."

She pauses and studies me. "You do know if you miss ten classes you wouldn't be credited for the class."

I nod.

"And that you need that chemistry course credit to graduate."

I nod again.

"And just because I work at the school, that doesn't mean I'm going to help you. Your actions have consequences, Nika."

I'm about to nod when a realization hits me. "Why didn't you tell Ma that I was skipping?"

"What?"

"You knew I was skipping and you didn't rat me out."

"This isn't about you, Nika. I didn't want to stress Ma."

"You were protecting me." I beam at her. "You were saving me from a consequence of my actions."

Achi bristles with the accusation. "Well, don't expect me to do it again. If you don't get your act together, I'm not defending you in front of the faculty." I keep teasing her that I'm her soft spot as she flips open her iPad and places it on top of the comforter.

I lean closer to her while she scrolls through Netflix. Once again, she ignores all my critically acclaimed suggestions. "The new K-drama I've been watching is pretty good."

Achi makes a face. "Aren't the episodes, like, three hours long?"

"Remember when you gave a talk at school about my generation's short attention span?" I ask. "That's you. You're the problem."

She ignores me and angles the iPad away from me so I can't see. "Why is this *Pagpag* movie on my recently watched list?"

"I don't know. You have weird taste, Ach." I shrug, avoiding suspicion.

She still tilts her head at me, and pretty soon, I start hearing the film's opening credits.

"*This* is what you're watching?" I ask.

"I've never watched Seph's movie before."

My eyes roll to the top of my head. "This isn't Seph's movie." Regardless, Achi still pressed play, so I ask her to turn up the volume.

Achi rewinds the movie to the beginning, and I pay more attention once we pick up where Kayla and I left off. After a group of teenagers break superstitions that should be observed during a wake, a ghost suddenly comes back to haunt and kill them.

When one of the girls sees a shadow lurking through her home, she assumes it's her boyfriend surprising her instead of the actual ghost murderer on the loose. The girl proceeds to follow the ghost around the dark on her own.

"Stupid," Achi and I mutter at the same time.

Eerie music builds until the ghost appears and gouges out the girl's eyes.

"She wouldn't die instantly from the ghost ripping out her eyes," Achi says. "She would be blinded, but she would have to lose forty percent of her blood to die."

"You know way too much about murder."

Two more dead bodies (and two more death probability analyses from Jackie Ilagan) later, the movie reveals the truth about Roman the ghost. When Roman passed away in a fire, his wife made a pact with the devil to bring him back to life. The devil's condition for his resurrection: Ghost Roman has to murder nine people.

And that's where Celebrity Moseph King comes into the picture. When ghost Roman tracks down Kathryn's character and threatens to stab her heart, a little Seph shields her and cries in tears, "My heart is yours!"

Cue very extra-dramatic music when Seph's heart gets pierced and Kathryn Bernardo sobs while cradling his body as the light in his eyes goes out.

For an eight-year-old, it's pretty decent acting—but there's no way in hell I'll ever admit that to Seph's face.

"Hey, what if you were Roman's wife in the movie? Would you do the same thing?"

Achi side-eyes me. "Are you asking me if I'd make a deal with the devil?"

"Hypothetically," I stress. "Would you exchange murder to bring your dead husband back to life?"

"I don't even have a husband."

I groan. "You're the worst at this game."

While more people die and Roman's wife defends her actions by saying all she wanted was to bring her family back together, I ask Achi about Ma.

". . . How is she?"

"Good," she answers, eyes still glued to the screen. "She was thinking about going back to the bakery to sign off on some things, but I talked her out of it. The lights were off when I checked her room."

I don't know how my sister does it. Whenever I try talking to Ma, it's like I'm incapable of finding the right words.

"And about Florida . . ."

Achi only mumbles a very vague, "Mm-hmm?"

My mind starts spiraling again at the thought of Achi being so far away.

"Did you know that Florida has lots of alligators?" I mention. "I saw this video where an alligator was running after a golf cart. If they can chase after a golf cart, you'd never make it. You're so slow."

My sister lets out a snort and meets my eye. "You're going to miss me, 'no?"

"No," I quickly retort.

She chuckles and pokes me. "I'm *your* soft spot. Admit it. You're *so* going to miss me."

"This is me protecting you from getting eaten by an alligator."

I'm about to give her statistics about alligator chases when Achi says, "I'm not leaving."

"Oh."

"I applied to those programs as a joke," she explains. "I was never going to actually go."

My body's working overtime to stop my face from smiling. *If you don't act cool, Achi might change her mind and leave you for the alligators!*

Then she starts poking my ticklish side again.

"Achi!" I squirm and hold in my laugh.

She continues tickling me until I grab her hands to stop. "I thought you moving out meant I could have my own bedroom," I tell her when I catch my breath.

"But then you'd miss me too much," she teases, and loops her arm through mine.

"Whatever." I sigh and rest my head on hers.

The other thing I'm too stubborn to admit—the only time I get a good night's sleep is when my sister is sleeping beside me.

6

MY SISTER AND I HAVE ANOTHER UNSPOKEN RULE DURING MY DAD'S death anniversary.

I've been waiting outside the bathroom for almost half an hour, but I don't knock on the door.

When Achi eventually comes out, I don't ask her if everything is okay. I've learned a long time ago to pretend.

When we lost Pa, Achi helped Ma sort out the hospital bills, plan the funeral, thank everyone for their condolences. That whole time, my sister's pleasant hosting demeanor didn't break *once*. I'm pretty sure she's the one least affected by grief.

But I give her space when today comes. I know that our bathroom is one of the rare places where Achi allows herself to be sad.

Once my sister steps out and we make our way to the car, I don't point out that her eyes are puffy. I also hold in all my comments when she wears her oversize Kardashian-esque sunglasses even though the shades are bigger than her face. We get in the car and the whole ride is silent except for Ma's monologue about today's itinerary.

Her red notebook is laid out open on the dashboard, but Ma has already memorized our routine by heart. I try not to get nervous when I notice her knee bouncing each time we reach a stoplight. "Nika leads the novena prayer, Jackie takes care of the incense, I handle the altar, rice, and the ang paos . . ."

There are superstitions that are supposed to be for funerals or wakes that Ma insists we still practice every time we visit the cemetery. The one that she's extra, extra careful about is—

"Pagpag. Already checked," Ma mumbles to herself. "Called Gloria Maris and made sure we could get the big table."

Unlike the movie, there aren't any murderous ghosts or deals with the devil for how we practice pagpag. Even though I've explained to Ma multiple times that pagpag is a superstition that's practiced during wakes, she applies it to every visit to Pa. It simply became routine that we never go straight home after the cemetery. We always pass by the nearest McDonald's, Jollibee, or convenience store after seeing Pa. If my dad's friends visit, we go to Gloria Maris.

The sun finally shows when Ma pulls up to the road leading to the Memorial Park. Ever since I can remember, there have been the same flower vendor stalls lined up outside, with names like Lily's Flower Shop, Cesar's Flower Shop. We enter the park and drive through the sprawling lawn covered with graves and flowers until we turn the corner toward Pa's lot.

Pa's old coworkers from the warehouse business usually arrive a little before noon, but this quiet time early in the morning—we save this moment for our family.

Ma sets up the altar in front of the grave while Achi and I prepare the flowers and the incense. Once we're ready and take our places around Pa, I start leading the rosary prayer. Mere seconds in, my sister can't resist butting in. "You recited the Joyful Mysteries."

"Yes, and you're interrupting."

She interjects again. "It's a Sunday. We should be praying the Glorious ones."

"No," I argue, not giving in. "It should be Joyful."

"Where'd you get that information from?"

"Jesus," I deadpan.

Ma sighs and urges us, "Let's just get on with the prayer."

By Achi's head tilt, though, she's for sure thinking I'm wrong. It really pisses me off that my sister thinks I'm incapable of doing anything right.

I carry on with my prayer leading, while Achi shoves her phone in my face. My stomach sinks when I read that Joyful Mysteries *are* designated for Saturdays.

God. Why does she have to be right every single time?!

"Achi, you're ruining the mood for the prayer."

"I just want to make sure you're leading it right," she argues back.

"Well, it's hard to lead people who never follow."

Ma then snatches away my pamphlet and consequently my duty as prayer leader. Achi and I resume standing there on our best behavior through the whole rosary while Ma leads the novena. Even in her silence, I can still feel Achi gloating that she caught me being wrong *again*.

We finish the prayer and Achi lights the candles on the altar while Ma passes me three incense sticks. When Ma showed us how to use incense years ago, I overheard Achi ask if it was ironic that our family attended Catholic Mass and used incense. I didn't know what ironic meant so I chimed in that we weren't ironic, we were just Chinese Filipino.

I light the sticks and bow three times toward Pa. His date of birth and death are written in golden script with his name: *Antonio Simon T. Ilagan.*

This part always makes me nervous. When Achi and Ma bow and do their prayers, they always linger in front of Pa's grave, looking like they have so much to say. I don't even know the whole story about the day Pa died.

When Ma picked me up from school instead of Pa that day, I asked where Pa was. My mind still remembers how Ma's knee was shaking and how her knuckles looked pale as she gripped the wheel. Ma took a long time to answer. Even back then, I was scared to ask more questions. She stayed quiet until a butterfly with black wings landed on the hood of the car.

"Nika, did I ever tell you why butterflies are so special?"

Ma continued explaining. "Some believe that butterflies are actually the souls of our departed loved ones. So whenever you see a butterfly, that means someone you love from heaven is saying hello."

Later on, Achi was the one who broke the news to me that Pa was gone. She said he got sick—and that it was fast so it wasn't painful. She and Ma were so busy afterward that they didn't have time to explain further.

Ma wipes the corner of her eye, then meets my gaze. "You doing okay?" she asks, gently rubbing my arm.

I lie and nod.

She sighs and does the sign of the cross before tapping Pa's photo on top of the altar. "I thank God every day that I have you and Jackie."

It makes the heat rise in the back of my throat. "Yeah, it could've been so much worse," I joke. "You could've had sons."

Ma keeps pushing her agenda to make me cry. "I mean it," she insists. "You two always come first."

It was a nice moment.

And it could've stayed a nice moment if we weren't interrupted. We look up when a car drives by and parks on the road across from us.

Is that . . .

You've got to be fucking kidding me.

My hair tie's starting to fray from how hard I'm pulling on it.

With literally no shame, my mom lets go of my arm and

It's what she said when she broke the news to me the first time.

It's what she said when I went back to school and expected Pa to be in the driver's seat.

It's what I've been hearing over and over again for the past five years . . .

But why does it still make time stop and the rest of the world fade into background noise?

Why does the truth crush every single thing inside me all the time?

"Nika!" Achi calls out to me when I start running.

I wipe the tears that slide down my cheeks and hug Pa's picture to my chest as my feet pound on the concrete harder. There's a sharp tug at my throat and a hitch at my sides, but I push myself to go faster—hoping there's something, anything I can do to stop feeling this much hurt again.

7

"DR. DERRICK HAD NO RIGHT TO BE THERE. AND MA SHOULD'VE AT least asked us before inviting him! I'm sure he's the last person you'd want to see on your death anniversary!"

I'm pacing around my room and rambling to the picture of my dead father on my bed.

The upside of my meltdown: I finally figured out how to talk to Pa. It turns out, all I need is to become completely unhinged.

I fold my hands above my head while my phone keeps buzzing with notifications from Achi and Ma.

Ma: Annika, where are you? —Beth

Ma: We reserved for lunch at 12 if you want to go straight there. —Beth

Ma: Remember, don't go straight home! —Beth

Ma: Please answer so I know that you're safe. —Beth

Achi: HOY!!!!! ANSWER!!!! DO YOU ENJOY SHOOTING UP MA'S BLOOD PRESSURE?!

The image of Dr. Derrick showing up at the cemetery kept replaying in my head, and all I wanted was revenge. So I didn't drop by a McDo or a Chinese restaurant—I went straight home, daring the whole universe to let the spirits into our condo.

I still stand by being in the right and that Dr. Derrick was *way* out of line. But now that my blood has cooled down, other things are going through my mind. God. Ma looked so crushed when I shouted at her.

"You're on my side, right?" I ask, turning to Pa's picture.

His stern, stone-faced eyes stare back at me. I really hate that Achi picked out this photo for Pa's display. It's the headshot he used for his warehouse business. Unlike the Piano Man in the

YouTube videos, Boss Antonio Ilagan is always in corporate attire, arms folded, signifying that he commands the room and always means business. And what I hate most about the picture is how edited it is. Achi said that Pa's company wanted his profile to look "presentable," but it looks like the photo flattened and brushed off features that made Pa . . . Pa.

The photo completely edited out the scar on top of Pa's left eye. Whenever I asked him about his scar, Pa always joked that it was his "magical scar" that made him see better. Achi only told me the real story years later—that Pa got the scar when I was a baby. She said that he dove and grabbed me when a ceiling fan almost fell on my stroller.

After more check-in messages from Ma, I quickly send her an I'm ok message with a thumbs-up emoji.

Ma heart-reacts it while Achi messages: i'm ok?!?!?!?! that's all you're going to say???

I groan and grab Pa's picture to mope in the kitchen. Aside from the gnawing guilt eating up my insides, my stomach's also been rumbling from skipping lunch. Pa's eyes keep following me while I search through the kitchen for something to heat up.

That's when I find the six-pack box of siopaos. These were the ones I was supposed to give Seph for walking with me from school.

I can already feel the judgment from Pa's picture frame.

"If I eat these, then I can give Seph a fresh batch," I argue. "And you know how Ma hates it when people don't eat her siopaos right away."

The judginess continues to exude from the photo.

While I rip the tape sealing the box, I also flip Pa's picture so he's facing away from me.

I've officially reached a new low. My morals have completely gone out of the window, and all it took was an annoying dentist and an empty stomach.

As I'm about to reach for the first siopao, I jump when the bathroom door slams open out of nowhere. I carefully walk through the corridor and find the room empty.

My heart thumps faster when the ceiling lights start flickering.

Seeing Ma obsess over these superstitions made me anxious around them too. Even when my rational mind picks away at the missing logic, I still get paranoid when I don't follow Ma's pamahiin properly.

Come on, Nika. The lights blink all the time. It's just the electricity.

But to be safe, I check the living room, the bedroom, and the bathroom again. Despite confirming many times that I'm alone in the condo, that feeling of being followed never lifts.

The front door is locked, the windows are shut, there's nothing under the beds. Once I return to the kitchen, I reach for my siopao and accidentally knock Pa's portrait off the table. My heart stops when I pick it up and stare at the slightly cracked picture frame.

. . .

. . .

Why is Pa smiling?!

I rub my eyes and it doesn't change. I've looked at this photo for years and Pa was always frowning in this picture every single time.

Shit. Isn't this what happened to the girl at the beginning of the *Pagpag* movie . . . right before her dead boyfriend popped up?

Then I remember the whole reason for the pagpag pamahiin: *If you don't make a pit stop, spirits will follow you home.*

I quickly go inside my room and plug in Pa's old phone.

When it comes to life, I check its activity: recent messages, calls, Google searches. There's nothing new.

Opening his messages app, I type: are you here?

My finger hovers before I send it—almost expecting a text bubble to appear, signaling that someone else is typing.

...

What. is. wrong. with me.

I am a woman of science, a woman who stands by research! These are all side effects of hunger and guilt. Slapping myself out of this nonsense, I leave the phone, the picture frame, and quickly wrap the siopao back up and stuff it inside the box. When I leave the unit and head to the elevator, I resist the urge to check over my shoulder. I don't think about the constant feeling that someone's still following me all the way to Unit 3H.

"Auntie!" I say when Auntie Baby opens the door. I've never been so relieved to see another human being.

"Annika?" Auntie Baby steps out. "Di ho se bo? Why aren't you at the memorial?"

"I'm good, I'm good! I was just going to drop off something for Seph." I lift the siopao box for evidence.

A huge smile lights up her face at the mention of her son's name. "Wow, how sweet naman! You're giving gifts to each other!"

"Actually, this is from Ma—"

Auntie Baby is already hurrying me inside her unit where I see Auntie Grace sitting at the kitchen table. When Auntie Grace waves me over to join her, I have to walk past the "Moseph King" shrine. Auntie Baby's condo unit has an entire shelf that's dedicated to all of Seph's achievements. There are soccer medals, framed report cards, his blown-up elementary school graduation photo.

Just in case you ever forget that Seph was once a child actor, the top shelf is decorated with pictures from his plays, the jersey he wore from the *High School Musical* Trumpets production, and a signed movie poster of *Pagpag: Nine Lives*.

Auntie Baby offers me a chair and then hands me water in a mug with Seph's signature line: "My heart is yours!"

"Seph just came home from rehearsal, but he'll be ready soon. Grace and I were just looking through our old yearbook." Auntie Baby then purses her lips. "I keep telling your mom to pick hers up since it's been collecting dust in the alumni office for years."

"Auntie, is that you?" My eyes widen when I see a younger Auntie Grace look-alike in a leotard posing on top of a six-person pyramid.

"Grace was dance captain," Auntie Baby chimes in.

Auntie Grace frowns when we flip through the dance troupe pages. "For an all-girls Catholic school, they really shouldn't have allowed us to dress like that."

"It's good to flaunt the Lord's creation," Auntie Baby says, shimmying her shoulders. "We're still sexy and desirable, Grace! You should take out some of the old dance troupe outfits. Kasya pa kaya sa akin? Maybe I can wear it to Homecoming."

While Auntie Baby tells Auntie Grace that they're too young to be dressing like grandmothers, I go through the yearbook searching for signs of Ma. My heart then stops when I stumble upon the prom section.

It's a picture of my parents smiling and holding hands with the caption underneath: *Soiree before the big day!*

"Wow, look how totoy Ton was before." Auntie Baby points at the picture.

"Can you imagine if I married the boy I went to prom with? Have you heard the news about Grant Sy?"

"That he has a mistress?" Auntie Grace's gaze flickers to the ceiling and she does the sign of the cross. "He even brought the woman to church! There were pictures of them kissing in front of Father Melvin!"

Auntie Grace shows her phone with a blurry photo of a man pecking another woman on the cheek during Mass.

"Imagine!" Auntie Grace says, outraged. "Offering the sign of peace to your *mistress*!"

Auntie Baby shakes her head. "You know, that's why his hairline keeps receding—karma! Grant used to have such good hair. I remember I used to brush my fingers through his hair and it felt so soft."

Auntie Baby then turns to me. "Don't be like me and get swayed by good hair, Nika. Just because a boy's head has good hair on the outside, doesn't mean he has a good mind on the inside. Thank goodness your Uncle Francis has both!"

My own mind is too caught up with my parents to digest Auntie Baby's dating advice.

"Were my parents already together here?"

"I think this is when they first met." Auntie Baby looks to Auntie Grace for confirmation.

"Ah yes, I remember it was the soiree that Beth hosted before prom with the Saint Francis boys."

"And we had to play this ridiculous game. We had to pair up with a Saint Francis boy, hold an ice cube in between our hands, and keep talking until the ice melted."

"Beth didn't find it ridiculous, though," Auntie Grace adds.

Auntie Baby scoffs. "Those two kept talking long after the ice cube melted. They really were in their own world back then." Auntie Baby sighs and squeezes my arm before standing up. "Don't bring this up with your mother, okay? It's hard for her to remember the past."

I nod as if my sister doesn't give me the same kind of lecture weekly.

Auntie Grace mentions that they should head out before rush hour traffic. "Nika, do you want to ride with us to the memorial?"

"Oh, I'm okay."

"Is anyone bringing you there?" Auntie Grace asks.

"No need to worry about me, Auntie."

"What do you mean we don't have to worry?"

I should have expected this. When I went over to Kayla's last week and said no to Auntie Grace's offer to stay for dinner, it turned into a full-blown interrogation. Instead of withstanding a thousand questions about my diet and food preferences, it was easier to give in and eat.

When I make up an excuse that I have to stay back to wait for a delivery, Auntie Baby suddenly beams at me. "Why doesn't Seph take you?"

"Um."

"We can take Grace's car and Seph can drive mine."

"But—"

"The car ride should be enough time for you to give your gift . . . and enough time to talk about prom too." Auntie Baby pushes the siopao box closer to me with a wink.

I turn to Auntie Grace and she doesn't object to the idea. For someone so strict, you would think Auntie Grace would frown upon an unsupervised car ride between the opposite sexes. This is more unholy than your sleeveless dance troupe outfits, Auntie!

Suddenly, Auntie Grace asks, "Should we call your mom to let her know?"

"No!"

If Ma finds out that I'm with the aunties, she'll tell them everything I did this morning, then force me to go back to the memorial and say sorry to Dr. Derrick.

"I'll do it." I recover and tell my aunties calmly, "I'm sure she'll be all right with Seph taking me. She always says you raised him really well, Auntie Baby."

This automatically relaxes her. Tip I've learned through the years: Flattering an auntie will get you places. Flattering an auntie's *son*? That'll get you even further!

When the aunties finally head out and leave me in peace, I go back to browsing through Auntie Baby's old yearbook.

By the time I reach the actual prom spread, I spot Ma with Pa again. This time, the two of them have glittery sashes across their bodies that spell out *Prom King & Queen*. It's a perfect candid photo of Ma laughing at whatever Pa was telling her. It doesn't even look like they were aware that someone was taking their picture.

"Ma!" Seph steps out of his room in shorts and a towel draped around his neck.

His hands immediately cover his chest area when he sees me. "You're not my mother."

"Nice boobs."

I laugh when his face flushes and he quickly grabs a shirt. "Auntie Baby and Auntie Grace went ahead!" I call out.

Once he's decent and fully clothed, he takes the seat across from me at the table. His hair is still wet so there are strands that fall right above his eyes. I suddenly remember what Auntie Baby said about running her fingers through a boy's hair. I wonder how soft Seph's would feel if I reach over and touch . . .

"This is for you." I offer Seph the siopao box, distracting my mind from impure thoughts.

His face does his annoying nose scrunch again. "You brought me gifts?"

"They're from my mom," I clarify.

Seph opens the box. "Must have done a really great job as

your chaperone—" He suddenly frowns. "What happened to this one?" he asks, pointing to the sad-looking siopao I carried the whole time I was searching my condo for some mystery stalker.

"Maybe you were a bad chaperone," I say with a shrug.

I laugh when he scowls and eats the half-eaten siopao anyway. When his phone lights up, he says, "My mom is checking if we've left already."

"You don't have to bring me."

"How are you getting to the memorial then?"

"I'll find a way."

"Why aren't you with your family?"

"I was with them this morning," I point out.

"But you came back here . . . ?"

"Yes." I nod and gesture toward the box. ". . . Because I had to give you the siopaos."

Ugh. His interrogations are worse than his mother's.

Seph narrows his eyes at me. "You're not planning on going back to the cemetery, are you?"

"I *am*. I have . . . other ways of getting there."

"Got it." He nods slowly. "You were going to fly."

"Seph."

"Wait, you were going to walk." He checks his watch. "If you start now, you should get there by midnight."

I groan.

"Teleportation? Should we alert the scientific community that you've made this breakthrough?"

"If I admit I'm not going, will that make you stop?"

He finally goes quiet and a moment of silence stretches between us until Seph's phone lights up with a call from Auntie Baby.

"You should really get going," I tell him.

"What about you?"

"I'll probably reflect on how I can achieve teleportation."

Seph still watches me closely.

"I'll hang with you then."

Before I can argue, he checks my mug and carries it to the sink for a refill. "You want coffee? I made some this morning."

I say yes, then wait a moment to check. "You're not staying because of me, right?"

"Of course not," Seph replies with a scoff.

"Because I'm totally fine on my own."

"I know." He pours coffee into two mugs and sets them down on the table. The mug he got for himself also has *My heart is yours* printed on it.

"Does every mug you own have your catchphrase?"

"Ilagan." His face lights up. "Did you watch my movie?"

"First of all, it's not *your* movie—"

"But you watched it."

"And you only had one scene."

"But you watched it," he repeats again.

His grin is so freaking huge that I have to sip my coffee to stop myself from secondhand smiling too.

"Moseph?" I say after a beat.

His eyebrows raise in response.

"Thanks." I lift the mug. "For th-the coffee."

And for keeping me company.

"Hopefully, this earns me more of Auntie Beth's siopaos."

"Meh." I purse my lips. "Don't think you earned it yet."

"Gotta work on being a better chaperone then."

I roll my eyes and drink my coffee, making sure that Seph doesn't see me smiling behind the mug.

8

ONE OF THE WORST FEELINGS IN THE WORLD: WAKING UP BEFORE MY alarm.

I groan when my phone screen reads five thirty AM. My body is supposed to have thirty more minutes of blissful sleep . . . Why does my body not want that for me?!

It also doesn't help that I didn't fall asleep until two in the morning. I mean, late nights aren't unusual for me, but this wasn't a case of my regular insomnia. The reason I forsook hours of valuable sleep was Ma's silent treatment.

When Ma's upset with me, I'm used to the sermons, her favorite line: *Why can't you be more like your sister?*

Yesterday, though? I got nothing.

She came home after their Gloria Maris lunch and asked me if I had eaten already. I said yes and she proceeded to go to her room to make some calls. Achi joined us for dinner and they only talked about bakery-related topics—not one word about how I was rude, immature, no comments from Achi that I probably turned out the way I did because kid-me once bumped my head on my crib.

They're not going to sway me into thinking I was wrong for calling out Dr. Derrick yesterday. All those things I said to Ma? I was upset about Dr. Derrick, not her! Just because he tricked Ma into saying yes to his proposal doesn't mean he can weasel his way into my family.

Although, it's way easier to defend that I was right if Ma actually brings up what had happened.

If we can't articulate ourselves through words, maybe we can do it through food. Hence, me waking up extra early to make breakfast for Ma before going to school. It's a great strategy: I'll make Ma breakfast, open up about my side of why Derrick shouldn't have been there yesterday, then she'll see the error of her ways and cancel the whole wedding!

I kick off my blanket and set my plan into action.

But someone already got to the kitchen before me.

"Why do you even pay rent for your apartment?" I ask Achi, who's already in the middle of heating up corned beef. She's also giving me the silent treatment, but I can tell hers is out of pettiness.

"I need the kitchen," I say when Achi pretends like I don't exist.

She still doesn't look at me. "For what?"

"To make breakfast."

Achi scoffs and checks the rice cooker while still stirring onions in the pan. "What are you going to make? Eggs na naman?"

"Eggs are a worldwide breakfast staple!" I insist.

For Mother's Day, we usually make Ma breakfast in bed where I take my time preparing my scrambled eggs with the perfect runny texture. While I'm focused on my specialty, Achi does a hundred things at once and makes longganisa, bangus, tocino, and every other breakfast food ever invented. It's not my fault that I prefer quality over quantity.

"Don't use my pan," I warn her before going to the bathroom. I can deal with reclaiming the kitchen more effectively after I brush my teeth.

Shutting the bathroom door behind me, I turn on the faucet and splash my face with water. I try to focus on anything else instead of the feelings that are lighting my head on fire.

Shut it down, Nika. Ignore it, ignore it.

Still, all the things I'm angry at keep cycling through my mind.

I am pissed at Achi for hogging the kitchen and insulting my eggs.

I am pissed at my stupid body clock that doesn't let me sleep.

I am pissed that I have to wear retainers for the rest of my life.

Most of all, I am still incredibly pissed that Ma is moving on with Dr. freaking Derrick.

The mirror fogs up as I'm trying my hardest to wash away everything I'm pissed at. None of this is productive! I have to move on and figure out how Nika Ilagan will thrive on this given Monday.

As I'm fixing my mindset, the window by the shower slowly creaks open.

Hasn't that window always been locked?

. . . Isn't this also what happens before the ghost murderer shows up in the *Pagpag* movie?

A window opening is normal! My brain tries to scream at my quickening heart rate. I'm paranoid because of sleep deprivation. On the very slim chance that there's truth to the pagpag superstition, a ghost should've appeared yesterday! Ghosts are known to be very punctual! Even in the movies, ghosts never wait a whole *day* to show up.

My heart comes to a full stop when a butterfly suddenly flies into the bathroom . . . and I hold my breath when it lands on the sink.

Ma's words ring in my head: *Butterflies are the souls of the departed.*

Shit. Am I staring at the soul of the departed?

I put up my hands in case this soul has murderer tendencies too. "I come in peace," I declare.

"Kumain ka na?" I ask, remembering how Ma always welcomes guests in our home by offering food. Maybe the departed soul will be hesitant to kill me if it thinks I can cook.

"Have you already eaten?" I give the English translation in case this butterfly is a foreigner.

The butterfly stays completely still. Its black wings don't even budge when I try blowing on them.

If I paid more attention during Chinese class, maybe I would know how to ask the question in Mandarin too.

When I take a closer look, it still doesn't move. No budge in its legs, its wings, antennae. Would a dead person be reincarnated into a dead butterfly?

I empty the cup that carries all the toothbrushes and hold my breath when I carefully place it on top of the butterfly. "Hello?" I ask and wait for some spiritual reply.

Nothing.

But I do feel better that I'm staring at a cup instead of a possible departed soul. Hiding my problems can sometimes solve them, right?

Maybe there's a superstition about how covering a butterfly with a cup can protect people from ghosts! Yes, yes, I like that a lot better. Let's go with that.

Okay, back to planning out my Monday.

Step one: Cook Ma the best eggs in the world and bask in her revelation that *I'm* the one who's on the right side of things.

Step two: Ask Kayla what in the world is going on in class.

Step three.

AAHHHHHHHHH.

I jump when I see a figure in all white next to me in the mirror. Oh god. It's the departed soul!

Fuck. This is how people die, right? The ones who see the ghost first always die in the movies!

Squeezing my eyes shut, I try my best to stay calm. If the ghost wanted to kill me, I should be dead by now. A non-supernatural being would've killed me faster.

Okay, Nika. Remember, hiding from your problems can work. When I open my eyes, I will just see my regular, normal reflection. Not a man who I think looks exactly like . . .

The mirror shows the same man patting down his head and squinting as he checks his reflection. The squarish face, the graying hair, left eye slightly smaller than the right . . . *Why the fuck does he look exactly like my dad?*

His eyes widen when he turns to me. "Nika?" The sound of his voice makes me knock my head on the towel rack. *How the fuck does he know my name too?!*

Then I hear Achi from the outside yell out my name. "What was that noise?"

"N-nothing!" I yell back, and cover my eyes again.

What if this isn't a ghost? What if you're hallucinating?

Didn't your ninth-grade assessment say you have an overactive imagination?! Lots of renowned geniuses suffer from hallucinations: Vincent van Gogh, Isaac Newton, even Olivia Rodrigo thinks everyone in her party has her face in one music video. Maybe I'm not seeing a ghost, maybe I'm just exceptionally intelligent!

When you open your eyes, you will be fine. He will be . . .

Standing in front of me.

"I can't believe I'm back," the hallucination's voice chokes out as he marvels at his hands like he's just now noticing that they're the color of the baby powder on the sink. The hallucination lights up even more when he flexes his fingers and stretches his legs. My heart then freezes when the hallucination faces me again. "Sorry nabigla 'ata kita. Been a long time and it took me a while to recognize my bunso." I momentarily forget the striking Pa resemblance and notice that his feet aren't touching the floor. Does Olivia Rodrigo also see levitating dead people?!

He floats closer and I hurl myself into the shower, pulling the curtain closed. I crank on the faucet and let the water soak through my pajamas. "This is a dream, this is a dream," I mutter to myself while turning the knob to the coldest setting.

But I'm wide awake and I still hear his voice.

"Nika, are you okay?"

There are about a million layers to that question.

"I know this might be a lot to process, but everything's going to be fine," the hallucination assures me while I'm still praying for the shower to wake me up. This happens in horror movies, too, right? Demonic evil spirits pose as your loved ones so they can trick you into trusting them! I'm racking my brain for any superstition about driving ghosts away. Didn't Ma once say that holy water purifies a space? My hand goes through all the bottles and containers lined up on the shower rack. Great. We have two tubes of anti-dandruff shampoo but no holy water. If I get possessed by a demonic spirit, at least I'll be dandruff-free. "Hello?" I hear the demon's voice again.

I'm not going to answer. I may be delusional enough to see dead people, but I haven't gone so far as to *talk to* dead people. I'll let my sanity have that.

After more unanswered questions, I start hoping that the hallucination has disappeared and left me alone. But then I see a chalk-white hand poke through the shower curtain—and based on my extensive science education, NORMAL HANDS SHOULDN'T GO THROUGH SOLID THINGS!!!

"Ahhh!" we both yelp, and someone barges through the doorway.

"Niks!" Achi pushes the shower curtain so fast that it rips. "What happened?"

She gapes as I'm sprawled in the bathtub, her expression screaming the same lines of *There is something seriously wrong with my sister.*

My eyes immediately land on the hallucination beside her . . . that Achi doesn't pay attention to.

Or is it because I'm the only one who sees Pa?

Wait, no. *That is not your father! It's a hallucination!*

He/she/they/it (I don't know what pronouns hallucinations use!) looks at me, then turns to my sister. "Jackie?" The hallucination tries talking to Achi, but she never turns his/her/their/its way.

"I, uh . . ." I try to steady my voice while blinking away the water still hitting my eyes. "I forgot to take off my clothes before going in the shower."

"You . . . forgot?" Achi asks, rightfully bewildered.

"Yeah, so I got surprised when I turned on the water and I wasn't naked," I casually explain while grabbing the towel. No matter how much I wipe my eyes, the hallucination is still there, peering at me.

I drown out the hallucination's voice in the background that still sounds eerily like Pa's.

"You know, I never realized how big this bathroom is." I stretch and move my arms so I'm gesturing in the hallucination's direction. "Did you ever realize that we can fit *three* people in this bathroom? Wouldn't that be cool if we had *three* people here right now?"

Achi pauses and frowns. "Why would you need to fit three people in one bathroom?"

Oh god. She really doesn't see the Pa clone literally hovering in the bathroom. Maybe it's for the best. Better to have a family with one lone delusional person versus a family with two.

"Nika? Jackie?" We suddenly hear Ma's voice.

Achi stops me when I reach for the door. "Don't let Ma see you like that."

I wriggle out of her grip and rush out of there. Maybe my hallucinations are location-specific. It's like when my phone malfunctions whenever I leave Manila. Leaving the bathroom might be like a factory reset that will revert my mind to normal functioning.

"Why are you all wet?" Ma says when she sees me walk out in my soaked pajamas.

I'm too stressed to even make a joke.

"Baka mapasma ka niyan," Ma scolds me. "Go change before you get sick!"

My heart almost jumps out of my chest when the hallucination pops up beside me again. I shoot he/she/they/it daggers when Ma's distracted. *Get away from me, demonic spirit!*

Ma keeps on listing all the ways I can get sick from wearing wet clothes, so I guess it's safe to say that she doesn't see the ghostlike figure either.

Then I hear the hallucination's voice again.

"Your mom got so mad at me when I convinced her to dance in the rain before." The hallucination's tone grows more distant as he recalls the memory. "We both got a fever the next day."

I'm about to go ahead and ignore the voice when it hits me. If this is an actual hallucination, then whatever it's saying is supposed to be what I'm thinking, right?

. . . So why is the hallucination giving me brand-new information?

"Um. Ma?" I interrupt her while she's raiding our medicine cabinet. "Any chance . . . did you ever dance in the rain?"

"How did you . . ." Ma gives me a surprised look, then shakes her head. "This is why I want you to learn from my past mistakes, Nika. My temperature hit thirty-nine degrees Celsius because of that."

What does it mean when my hallucination is speaking the truth? Does that mean I'm less or more delusional?!

Ma shoves vitamin C capsules in my hand while the hallucination says, "Did you know that vitamin C is Spanish?

"It's Spanish for *vitamin Yes.*" The hallucination hobbles over in laughter. "Get it? Because C sounds like sí?"

Fuuuuuuuuuuuuuck. I'm definitely turning more delusional.

"Annika." My body jolts when Ma calls my attention. "Are you even listening to me?"

"¡Sí! I mean, y-yes," I stammer, and tell Ma I'm going to go change.

I keep snapping the hair tie on my wrist and escape to my bedroom, ignoring the hallucination that keeps trailing behind. The panic in my chest continues growing while I stuff my books and notebooks in my backpack. I shove more things inside as I ignore the voices in my head that are suggesting that (A) I might be hallucinating, (B) I might be haunted by a demonic spirit, and most of all (C): What if this is actually my dad?

No, no, NO! *Shove that thought down, deep to the back of your head so it's buried for good. There's no way that Pa could come back . . . ever. You've been over this, your whole family has been over this. Why can't you get over this?!*

I resist the urge to spiral into a complete meltdown when I feel the hallucination silently watching my every move.

The hallucination only speaks when I grab my school uniform from the closet.

"You're really going to get sick if you don't change out of your wet clothes."

And that's the moment I lose it.

"Go away!" I yell, and throw my towel at the hallucination, which sails right through the Pa-shaped illusion and lands on the floor.

Then I hear him use Pa's nickname for me in his voice—and it feels like my heart stops beating.

"Superstar?" the hallucination says again after a beat. "Nika, how old are you now?"

This was what looking into Pa's eyes felt like. I'd always search for Pa in the audience during every show I was a part of. My dad was the reason I discovered that people could smile through their eyes. Every time I locked eyes with him, I always got the message that he sees me, that he's there for me. Getting that same look now makes my heart crack open at the possibility.

"My bunso," he says, his eyes glistening when he calls me his youngest child again. "Ang liit mo pa when I last saw you. Parang kailan lang . . ." The hallucination's gaze then flits up to the snowflakes on the ceiling. "I remember putting up these stickers. You asked me to play those songs from that Disney movie . . ."

"*Frozen*," I whisper.

"Your mother kept telling me not to enable you because seeing snow here is impossible. But I said—"

"That's why we dream bigger," we say in unison.

We lock eyes again and my heart feels like it's lodged in my throat. My backpack and all the books I stuffed inside fall off my bed and crash on the floor . . . and I don't care. Who cares about school, about my drenched pajamas, about my sister hogging the kitchen? Who cares when there's a chance that this could really be my dad?

. . . Could it really be him?

. . .

"Pa?"

9

IF I GOT A CHANCE TO SEE PA AGAIN, WHAT WOULD I DO?

The question has been in the back of my mind for years, but it was always a fantasy—something that was never *actually* going to come true.

So when the ghost of my father appears in my home, it makes sense that I would answer the current fantasy with another fantasy.

Ever since I was eight years old and Pa glued the snowflake stickers on my bedroom ceiling, he made a promise that he would take me to see actual snow one day. He passed away before we could make the trip, and right now could be our only chance.

"Shouldn't we discuss this with your mom?" Pa asks when I press the elevator button for the parking level.

God. If Ma was already disappointed about me skipping chemistry, what's she going to do when she finds out I've skipped to another country?

My mind pushes the thought away. There are bigger, more urgent priorities right now. Dealing with Ma could be future Nika's problem.

"I can tell her when we're about to board," I tell Pa, and press the B1 button again when the elevator takes forever.

"If we're flying somewhere to see snow, shouldn't you be packing more things?" He gestures toward the tote bag hanging by my side. "And what about flight tickets?"

Airports must let you buy tickets there, right? I mean, it's still a business. They wouldn't turn down a paying customer. Shit. How much is in my bank account? Am I a customer who can actually pay?! And did I check if my passport was really in my tote bag?

I consider going back to the condo to check when I remember how many minutes have already passed. No. I have absolutely no time to waste, to think, or breathe! Adding these all to my list of future Nika's problems.

The elevator reaches our floor and I rush inside.

"Where is it even snowing at this time of year?"

"Pa." I urge him when he's still hovering by the elevator, asking me a million questions.

"Superstar, I'm always game for a spontaneous trip, but we should think some things through. You can't ride a tiger without checking how tall it is first!"

My chest twists when I hear a classic Antonio Ilagan saying. While Ma is always hooked on superstitions, Pa loves giving advice that sounds like some ancient proverb.

I swallow the large lump in my throat when I say, "We might not have enough time."

Pa's face softens right there. It's something I've been scared to ask—how long does Pa have before he leaves? How long do I have before he's gone? When does future Nika's problem become losing Pa again?

He proceeds to float to the spot where I am and smiles. "We're off to see snow then."

PA'S BODY LEVITATES A FEW INCHES HIGHER WHEN HE SPOTS HIS OLD silver Toyota.

"You kept Martha!" Pa beams.

Ma did a deep cleanse of everything Pa-related when he passed, but Achi asked to keep his car, whom he affectionately dubbed Martha Toyota. Even though Martha's clock is broken and her air-conditioning only works when she feels like it, my sister has never considered changing cars.

Pa excitedly reaches for the car door, then his hand passes right through the handle.

He tries again and all he manages to grasp is air.

"Cool magic trick, 'no?" He laughs it off and turns to me. "Do you drive now, Superstar?"

Oh my god. He actually meant it as a serious question.

I already have my student permit, yet Achi and Ma still don't think I'm "ready" for the road. Like, how will I ever be ready if my family never lets me practice?

"Yeah, I can drive!" I hold up the car keys I sneaked out of the condo.

Although someone should've warned me that driving meant having to take on EDSA.

Just to be clear, I'm a good driver—above average even! Olivia Rodrigo could write a sequel to "drivers license" about how great my driving skills are. The only thing I haven't really mastered is driving on the highway.

My hands are still clutching the wheel as I watch cars, buses, trucks, and motorcycles flood EDSA from my vantage point of the Connecticut Street junction. I make a detour and park at the gas station on the side of the road. I've decided that I will merge once everything calms down . . . which I'm pretty sure will be any minute now.

Twenty minutes later, I'm still on the edge of my seat, waiting for the right moment.

Any minute now!

A plus side to my impressive patience is that I have some more time to catch up with Pa. And at first, Pa actually seems to take my questions seriously.

While he's pointing out all the buildings and billboards as if he didn't spend my entire childhood driving me on this same street, I ask, "Have you been a ghost this whole time?"

Pa faces me and I try not to stare too much at his translucent arm. "I'm not really sure. A lot feels . . . blurry." It seems like an eternity passes before his eyes smile back at me again. "I'm glad I'm here now, though."

"And did you really show up because . . . I didn't pagpag?"

Pa's mood turns more upbeat then. "Didn't I tell you that there's magic behind superstitions?"

Watching Ma made me think that superstitions are based on fear. If we sweep the floor at night, we'll be cursed with bad luck. If my pregnant cousin gives birth and takes a shower right after, she'll attract tons of health complications later on. I first heard about the pagpag superstition when my amah passed away when I was really little. When Ma told me that there was a chance that the spirits would follow us home after the wake, I stayed up late multiple nights, praying that the ghosts wouldn't find me. Pa was the one who made me less afraid.

He sat with me on my bed and whispered, "You know, I sometimes wish the pagpag superstition came true."

When I asked him why, he said, "So I'd get to see my best friend again."

Pa told me how he had to say goodbye to his best friend when he was in college. I remember Pa saying that if his best friend's spirit followed him home, he would catch his friend up on all that he missed. He'd tell his friend about his wedding, everything about me and Jackie. My favorite story was when Pa recounted how his best friend was the one who made him fall in love with music, who taught him how to play the piano. Maybe that's the origin story for why I don't find ghost stories so scary. I started imagining ghost encounters as Pa taking piano lessons from his best friend.

I try learning more about Pa's situation, but he starts becoming more and more evasive.

When I ask him if he knew he was coming back, Pa jokes, "You know who had a great comeback? Mariah Carey!"

"Where were you this whole time? Were you, like, roaming around, haunting people?"

"It's not good manners to haunt people, Superstar." Another joke and again, no elaboration.

I'm about to ask Pa how exactly he was able to come back when a car honks and swerves around us. "You might be blocking the entrance," Pa says, so I move the car over to another empty space by the fuel pumps.

"We need to merge onto EDSA to get to the airport," Pa reminds me.

"I know."

"Just making sure." He stares outside again when another car moves ahead.

"I'm waiting for the right moment," I assure him.

"You don't have to be so careful, Superstar. It's not like you can kill me twice."

I groan at his joke, then Pa coaches me to make small movements and inch Martha toward EDSA.

"Other cars aren't going to stop for you, so you need to assert yourself."

When I finally make my move, Pa cries out.

"Don't close your eyes! You might hit something!"

"I thought you said I couldn't kill you twice!" I say, barely keeping my eyes open.

"But you could kill yourself *once*!"

Pa tells me to keep going despite my knuckles turning white from gripping the wheel. When I manage not to get run over or hit by a bus, I realize . . . oh my god, I'm driving along EDSA!

There's the usual Monday traffic jam where all the cars including us are pretty much crawling down the highway, but still.

"I'm driving along EDSA!"

I feel like a dork for saying it out loud, but Pa proudly echoes, "You're driving along EDSA."

"Should we celebrate with some music?" His hand tries to push the car stereo knob and his face falls when his fingers slip through. I turn on the radio for him and he brightens when the familiar "doo-doo-doo" melody rings through the speakers.

"Is that really—"

"Uy!" Pa smiles and slaps his knee. "It's Mariah!"

Mariah Carey's voice fills the car and Pa immediately starts bobbing his head. He waits for me to sing along, but I tell him to go ahead. I give some excuse that I like focusing on the road when I'm driving.

I laugh when Pa trills his lips and makes blubbering noises. "Need to warm up my vocals." He massages his jaw and sings the phrase "Pa! Pa! Pa!" in different scales. By the time he's done warming up, the song's already in its final chorus. Pa jumps in and the flattest sounding note escapes his mouth when he tries belting with Mariah.

He beams when another Mariah song comes on the radio. "I feel like being a ghost improved my vocal range."

It's just like the million car rides I took as a kid. Being stuck in traffic while Pa in front remains unbothered since Mariah is playing on the stereo.

Whenever I fantasized about Pa coming back, I always wished he would show up in the big moments—graduation, when I become some CEO of a company, score a Tony, a Grammy (or both). I haven't thought about how much I miss him during the small moments too.

Pa stops humming along to "Fantasy" when he turns to me. "What's wrong?"

I wipe the tears rolling down my cheeks. "Just emotional about driving through EDSA."

"Well, it's a big deal, Superstar."

"Yeah," I agree. "It really is."

10

SOMETHING STRANGE HAPPENS WHEN WE REACH THE NAIA AIRPORT.

Back in the condo, even entering his car, it took a while for Pa to register that his current body passes right through solid things. I've noticed how he stops in front of doors for a moment before walking through them. I also see the frustration cross his face whenever he can't grip anything. We make our way toward the airport entrance and join the queue when Pa glances at the building's walls.

"Hey, Superstar," he whispers. "I have an idea on how we can get inside faster."

Pa moves from the line and floats straight to the entrance . . . and bumps his head.

After laughing it off, he tries again and knocks his head on the same spot.

For the third attempt, he backs up for some momentum, propels himself straight to the glass doors, and his body ricochets and falls on the sidewalk from the impact.

"No, no more." I leave the line and stop Pa when I catch him considering trying again.

He squints and inspects the building. "Are you sure this is the right airport? The building looks different."

"They made a new terminal for international flights," I explain. I try helping Pa, but he refuses when I reach for him. I don't really know what I was trying to do since my hands can't hold him anyway. When he gets up on his own, I suggest, "Why don't we try waiting for the doors to open like normal people?"

Pa tells me to go ahead and I fall in line with everyone queuing with their luggage carts and carry-on bags. By the time I enter through the sliding doors, Pa falls in step behind me and crashes again. People bump past me when I'm the only one in the crowd who sees my dad struggling to get up outside. It's like there's an invisible force field blocking the airport from the rest of the world.

"I'm okay. Being a ghost helps with all the back pain." Pa tries to smile it off, but I see the slight wince when he touches his head. If not for the powder complexion and the outfit that reminds me of Princess Leia's from the older *Star Wars* movie Kayla made me watch (the all-white robes one, not the metal bikini one), he could really pass as any other human. Well, any other invisible human.

I block his way when he heads toward the entrance. He insists he's fine, but I stand firm. "You're not doing that again." Ooh, look how the tables have turned. Usually, *I'm* the one my family needs to talk out of doing stupid things.

"It just takes some persistence. You can't give up on the sun when it's just about to rise."

"Well . . ." I rack my brain for some proverbial response that will stop Pa from hurting himself. "What if the sun has already set?"

Pa hesitates and frowns. "Superstar, that doesn't make any sense."

"Why don't we go somewhere else? There are lots of new things around Manila that you haven't seen yet."

"But what about snow?"

"We can do that later," I say, willing my brain not to worry about why Pa can't enter the airport. Again, future Nika's problem. Instead of wasting our time trying to break into an airport,

I should get moving and squeeze in every opportunity for bonding time with Pa. "There's this new museum I think you'll really like."

Yet, the pattern repeats everywhere we go. When I bring Pa to the recently opened art museum, his body can't cross the entrance. I take him to visit a record store in Legazpi Village and he can't even move his foot past the doors. At our third stop, he hesitates a bit more and waits until there's no one else around, but his body still bounces off the new Greenhills Mall. Why doesn't the universe want us to bond?!

I try to ignore the question that grows louder with every failure. If his ghost/spirit is losing his intangibility powers, does that mean his time is running out?

Despite the countless attempts, Pa still doesn't seem fazed when we return to the car.

"Where to next?"

Unlike all the places we've tried going to, his body manages to pass through Martha's car doors with no hitch. Maybe ghosts have more trouble with indoor places?

But Pa was perfectly fine when we were in the condo . . .

We both get distracted when my phone registers another phone call from Achi. "She's fine," I tell Pa when I grab my phone and press decline. "Achi's gotten a lot more chill since you last saw her."

did you seriously skip class again today????

DID YOU TAKE MY CAR

nika, i swear to god

you stole my car and now you're not answering my calls

IF YOU DON'T COME HOME IN AN HOUR, YOU'RE GOING TO BE IN SO MUCH TROUBLE. I MEAN IT.

That last message was sent fifty-eight minutes ago. When Pa

said that I could get "killed once," I wonder if he was foreshadowing death at the hands of my sister.

I type in the condo address on my maps and clip it back on the dashboard. "Let's drop by home first."

PA BRACES HIMSELF BEFORE ENTERING THE LOBBY DOORS, BUT HE'S able to float straightaway, kind of like the superhero Flash when he runs through brick walls.

Even in the lobby, Pa's arm is able to pass through the solid elevator doors back and forth.

"So does the intangibility thing just come and go?" I ask, stepping inside the elevator.

Pa pokes his head in after the doors close. "Hey, I can see right *through* this."

I groan.

We stop on the third floor and Auntie Baby pops up when the elevator doors open.

"Annika?" She stops short. "You're home early."

The fact that she's focused on my presence and not the reappearance of my late father clearly shows that she also doesn't see Pa. If the passing-through-walls thing has been inconsistent, the invisibility power has been holding up in every scenario.

"Uh. We have a half day," I explain when Auntie Baby's still waiting for an answer.

"Really? I'm meeting up with Grace and she didn't mention Kayla had a half day."

"Oh, *I* took a half day." I hold my stomach for emphasis. "Wasn't feeling well."

Like a light switch, Auntie Baby's face turns from suspicious to worried. "Is your stomach hurting?" She places the back of her hand on my forehead. "Any fever? Body pains? LBM?"

I slowly nod while Auntie Baby tells me she'll send over lugaw and reminds me to avoid dairy or greasy food.

After she starts sending me different WebMD articles on how to treat an upset stomach, my phone buzzes with multiple messages.

Ma: You have diarrhea? Since when??? –Beth

Kayla: Heard about the LBM from my mom! How're you?

Seph: feel better, ilagan! sending good thoughts to your stomach and toilet!

. . . How did Auntie Baby manage to spread information that quickly? Forget CNN and social media. I should be tuning in to Auntie Baby's gossip network for breaking news.

Pa floats closer to me and whispers, "Superstar. You know why my love for you is like LBM?"

Auntie Baby is busy on her phone, unaware of the impending dad joke.

"Because I can't hold it in," Pa says, chuckling.

I groan and hold my tongue.

"Uy, admit it. That joke was solid . . . unlike your diarrhea."

Pa's laughing so hard that I can't resist laughing along too. Auntie Baby then stares at me—as one naturally would if they saw a girl laughing by herself out of nowhere.

"Sorry." I hold my stomach again and gesture for Pa to keep it together. "Trying to laugh off the pain."

Auntie Baby then insists on accompanying me to my unit to make sure I'm all right. When I unlock the front door, I'm prepared to use Auntie Baby to buffer Achi's potential rage about borrowing Martha, but no one's home.

While Pa hovers closely behind us, Auntie Baby tucks me into bed and places my medicine kit on the table beside me.

She takes out the lotion, White Flower oil, baby powder, and starts rubbing the strange mix on my stomach.

"Feels better, right?" she asks. "When I was trying to get pregnant before, your Uncle Francis used to rub this on me, too, for good luck."

It feels like she's turning my stomach into papier-mâché.

Auntie Baby washes her hands, then tells me she'll get the leftover rice from her unit for the lugaw. "I'll be right back," she says when I insist that I'll be okay on my own.

When she leaves, I try wiping the gunk off my stomach, but all the creams mixed together somehow turned into a glue.

"Hey, my stomach is that color too," Pa says. Under my bedroom light, Pa's complexion doesn't appear as . . . translucent. If not for his feet floating inches above the floor, I think again how he could easily blend in as any other alive human being.

But he's not.

Then it sinks in how ridiculous it is that I'm spending the little time I have with Pa getting treated for fake diarrhea.

"You must miss a lot of things since you've been gone, Pa," I tell him, and grab my laptop. "Did you want to see a concert? There must be some band playing somewhere or someone doing Mariah Carey covers. Or karaoke? We can do karaoke!"

"Superstar." Pa then tells me to calm down. "There's nothing I miss more than you."

I blink away the lump in my throat and keep going with my research. "You didn't come back to just stay in my bedroom. We should make it more special."

"This bedroom is special," he argues.

"Pa."

"What? The bedroom where I saw my two daughters grow up is special," he says, and floats closer to the ceiling. "When I bought these snowflake stickers, I also found this instant snow powder at the toy store. I planned on surprising you with a whole bedroom covered in snow.

"But your mom was worried that you and Jackie would get allergies, so I promised to take you to see snow one day instead."

He floats back down and takes a deep breath. "I broke all the promises I made to you girls, haven't I?" Pa wipes his eyes, then gives an excuse that *his* allergies are stronger in the afterlife.

I reach to hold his hand, but my fingers just pass through his skin. I move my hand closer to the scar above his left eye, and I try brushing it but only feel the air through my fingers. After my sister told me the real story behind the scar, I'd often touch the spot on Pa's face and ask him if it hurt. I was never sure if he was telling the truth when he said no. Although, the thing that I was always sure of? Pa would've done anything for me. He still would.

My eyes then suddenly find the baby powder Auntie Baby left on the bedside table.

There's an explosion of powder on my bed when I shake the bottle all over my pillow and sheets.

"What are you . . ." Pa gawks at me when I sprinkle more on the floor, on the bookshelf, on the desk. I climb up on the bed and cover the tops of the ceiling fan with powder.

More concern floods Pa's face. "Are you feeling okay?"

"You promised to show me snow," I explain, climbing back down. When I turn on the switch for the fan, it starts spreading powder all over the room—coating almost every inch in white. If I didn't know any better, it really does look like snow falling from the sky.

"See, Pa?" I smile at him. "You kept your promise."

Pa laughs and spreads out his arms to bask in it all. He even sticks out his tongue, trying to catch the powder falling from the fan. "Who knew snow tasted like Johnson's baby powder?"

I laugh along with him while I start making snow angels with the powder blanketing the bedroom floor.

By the time I climb up on my bed again to refill the fan with more powder, I hear my bedroom door click open.

From the way Ma, Auntie Baby, and Achi are staring at me, you would think they're the ones who've seen a ghost.

11

ON SECOND THOUGHT, IT WAS A BRILLIANT MOVE TO USE DIARRHEA AS an excuse.

It might've literally saved my life.

While Achi was staring in horror at her clothes that were collateral damage from the powder, Auntie Baby said, "Nika must be so dehydrated. When I had a bad case of LBM from food poisoning, I started seeing things and acting woozy too!"

And since my sister is too polite to murder me in front of Auntie Baby, Achi just stood there in silent rage while Auntie Baby told me to rest and finish the rice porridge she made me. Ma even left one of her green jade bracelets on my bedside table for "better healing."

Although once Auntie Baby left, Achi convinced Ma to make me clean up this whole mess on my own.

I spend an hour trying to vacuum one tiny section of the room before focusing more on soaking in every moment with Pa. He asks me to catch him up on what's been happening with Achi and me. When I touch on Ma, I'm very careful to leave out any mention of Public Enemy Dentist No. 1. While I have way more stories to tell him, he insisted that I try to get some sleep once it was past midnight.

When I peek through one eye, Pa is still hovering by my couch in the dark. "Saw that," Pa says, catching me, and I close my eyes again. He laughs and the sound fills the room. "You used to do that when you were a baby too. Every time we put you down for a nap. One of your eyes would blink open once you thought we weren't watching."

"So I've been sleep deprived since I was born?"

"You were born talented too." Pa smiles. "Your mom and I signed you up for voice lessons after we heard you cry in perfect pitch."

Another thing I haven't mentioned to Pa—singing isn't a part of my life anymore.

When I was nine, a doctor told me I had to get my tonsils removed. I was getting tonsillitis multiple times a year growing up and the doctor said this could affect my breathing. I was terrified because I thought it meant I couldn't sing anymore. Right before the surgery, Pa came to my side and tapped the side of my wrist three times. "Superstar, do you know the secret of the universe?"

I shook my head and he explained, "When something bad happens to you, the universe actually owes you something good in return. So once you get through this operation, something really great is coming your way."

I'm not sure if I believed Pa at that moment, but a month later, I continued my voice lessons and got to hit notes my voice couldn't reach before. That summer, I was picked to play Ariel in my first-ever musical.

So I started seeing the world like this—that there was a delicate balance in how things worked out. If something bad happens to you, then the world owes you something good in return. Sounded fair, logical.

When Ma's take-out order got delivered to another house by accident years ago, she started baking more at home. When Achi missed out on being valedictorian by a point, she ended up getting awarded a merit scholarship to her dream university.

But then one day, my dad didn't pick me up from school.

And my sister told me he was gone.

I didn't hold my breath or wait for the universe to deliver

anything "good" after that. There was nothing that the universe could give me that would make up for losing my favorite person.

And then it hits me again—how fleeting this whole moment might be.

"Pa?"

My voice catches before I finally voice the question that's been in the back of my mind.

"Do you know how long you'll be here?"

Pa's face tightens before he smiles. "I just got here and you're getting rid of me already?" he teases, and floats closer so he's seated beside me on the bed. "Do you remember when we performed together at the office Christmas party?"

Whenever I asked her what happened to Pa, Ma kept changing the topic, saying that we can talk about it at a better time. The first time Ma brought us to the mall after Pa passed, I remember asking her again about that day.

Achi was the one who pivoted the conversation. She pulled me aside and whispered, "Let's try to make Ma happy today."

So I ride along with Pa on memory lane. "Didn't we perform the Jose Mari Chan song?"

Pa smiles and starts humming the Christmas carol.

I listen to Pa's stories, even while all the unanswered questions and the constant worry of him disappearing keeps nagging at me. I guess it's my way of listening to Achi and letting him be happy.

12

IF I END UP IN HELL, I'M PRETTY SURE THEY'D PUNISH ME BY HIRING people like my sister to wake me up.

"Why? Whyyyyyyyyyy?!" I groan and cling to my pillow when Achi tugs away my blanket again at the butt crack of dawn.

"After yesterday, did you seriously think I was going to trust you to make it to school on your own?"

The mention of yesterday suddenly snaps me awake.

Holy shit. Where's Pa?!

. . . Was that whole day with him a dream? But everything was so vivid, though . . . Is that what happens after years of sleep deprivation—dreams start feeling more real?

"And look at this!" Achi points at the part of the floor still coated in baby powder. "Do you expect someone to magically appear to clean this up?!"

Wait. If there's powder on the floor, then that must mean . . .

I spin around the bed, frantically looking for any signs of him.

There's nothing when I check my closet, under my bed, my desk. "What are you looking for?" Achi asks. "Your missing potential?"

I'm about to tell her to help me find Pa when I remember I'm the only one who can see him.

But maybe Pa's ghost went through some reverse metamorphosis overnight.

So I ask, "Did you see a butterfly this morning?"

"While I was watching the rainbows and unicorns?"

I say that I'm being serious and she cocks her head to the side. "You're really looking for a butterfly?"

"It's . . . for chemistry class."

"What do butterflies have to do with chemistry?"

"Weren't you the one who wants me to do well in school?!"

Achi grumbles while she checks the window blinds. "What does this insect look like?"

"A butterfly," I say, and double-check the closets again. "It kinda looks like . . ."

Once I open Achi's drawer, a hand suddenly reaches through the wall.

"Pa!" I exclaim when his body appears back in the room.

"The butterfly looks like Pa?" Achi gets up from checking under the beds.

"Sorry, I thought you'd still be asleep by the time I came back . . ."

Pa is trying to explain, but Achi's busy talking over him about some dumb school stuff.

"With or without the butterfly, you're going to clean this room and show up to class. I'm going to kill you if you don't graduate." Achi opens my closet and hurls my school uniform at me. "Be ready to go in five minutes."

Achi leaves the bedroom and I get to fully focus on today's itinerary with Pa.

I'm suggesting a day trip to Tagaytay when Pa asks, "Why did Jackie say you weren't going to graduate?"

"Just some attendance thing." I brush it off. "Ooh, you know, we could also go to La Union. I've never driven that far, but since I was able to handle EDSA—"

"You're going to school," he cuts me off.

"Pa, there's no way I'm going to leave you."

"Then we'll go to class together."

"Sure." I roll my eyes. "Everyone who comes back to life wants to go back to high school."

Pa agrees and takes my sarcasm way too seriously. "The best moments of my life happened in Saint Agnes. Bringing you and Jackie to your first day of school, all those fun parent-teacher conferences."

I'm trying to dissuade Pa when Achi opens the door again without knocking.

"Let's go!" she barks.

Pa follows her and looks at me over his shoulder. "You heard your sister. Let's go!"

MORNINGS AT SAINT AGNES ARE ALWAYS THE WORST KIND OF CHAOS. Before classes start and we can enter our classrooms, all the high school students swarm to find a space to sit in the gym that realistically only has space for half our population. By seven AM, you get lost in the sea of girls wearing the same plaid uniform.

Well, on this particular morning, it's a sea of girls in the Saint Agnes uniforms *and* a ghost father floating among them.

"We could be halfway to the beach by now," I say with my earphones plugged in. After getting weird glances from looking like I'm talking to myself, I start pretending I'm on a phone call whenever I speak to Pa.

Pa spreads out his arms across the crowded gym. "And miss out on all this fun?"

The girl seated next to Pa shouts out that she got her period and asks if anyone has an extra napkin. Pa instinctively ducks when surrounding students in the gym start tossing menstrual products to the girl in need.

"It's like when Batman turns on the Bat-Signal," he says in awe. "Your mom got her period during prom night, too, and five different girls offered to help."

For the past seventeen years, I never really heard much of my parents' love story. Pa used to joke that he was "hard to resist," and Ma seems like she's allergic to the past these days. My mind suddenly goes back to the prom pictures of my parents in their yearbook. "You never told me you and Ma started dating in high school."

"Didn't I?"

I shake my head. "You only said that she *stole your heart*."

"See?" Pa says, like *that* covered the whole story. "I told you."

"You left out all the details, Pa."

"It all feels so long ago now . . ." He takes a deep breath and chuckles. "But being here makes me remember. Hard to get talaga ang mama mo. Your grandparents were strict, so I had to court her for a long time. You can tell how much a fisherman wants a fish based on how far he's willing to swim."

I pause, trying to follow his proverb. ". . . So Ma was your fish?"

He nods. "My whole allowance, I spent it all buying the siopaos Beth would sell outside the school gate. I would buy her siopaos, then give them back to her as a gift," he reminisces, and smiles. "I even asked your ma to prom during our Battle of the Bands. Played our favorite Mariah song.

"I was so happy when she was allowed to go to prom." He takes a moment and gazes around the gym. "The dance was right here."

Pa's story gets interrupted when the Saint Agnes bell rings through the gym. Everyone rises to their feet and heads toward the classrooms. While I would rather stay here and catch up with Pa, he's already asking where we should go for our first class.

"This looks different," he says when I lead him to the other side of campus.

"It's the new senior high building," I explain. "I think they started construction right after Achi graduated."

As I merge with the rest of the class through the entrance, I somehow lose Pa in the crowd. When I look back, he's hovering and stuck outside. He attempts to walk in again and his body keeps bouncing back.

I quickly backpedal and pat the doorframe in case there's another way to get in. "You were able to enter the other buildings just fine."

"Maybe the new buildings have some secret ghost repellent."

Hold on. Is that it?

Pa is able to walk through walls and enter places like the condo, the Saint Agnes gym, and Martha Toyota. The spots he struggled with have been the new airport terminal, the new mall, the new Saint Agnes building—places he had never been to before.

The few students left around us start sprinting when the second morning bell rings.

"Superstar, you're going to be late."

"What about you?"

His eyes smile at me from the other side of the door. "I'll be fine," he insists. "I can roam around, rest back home. If you need me, you can leave a message at the *ghost* office." He chuckles. "Gets? It sounds like post office!"

My feet still don't budge no matter how many jokes Pa tells me. Nothing he says can distract me from the very real possibility that he might disappear when I leave him.

"Don't worry too much," Pa says, as if reading my mind. "Malay mo, Nika. I'll be staying longer than you think."

. . .

Did he say he was *staying*?

Could that happen?

Could Pa actually stay?

13

UPON FURTHER REFLECTION, I THINK SOME HIGHER BEING WAS guiding me in picking which classes to skip. God guided me to skip those other nine chemistry classes since he knew that attending the *tenth* would provide me with crucial information.

While Ms. Abad passes out worksheets for conducting our investigative project, she gives a refresher on the scientific method.

"Throughout history, the scientific method has helped the greatest minds answer life's biggest questions," she lectures. "Ever wondered why something is the way that it is? Why does something work a certain way?"

I look down at the worksheet on my desk.

BIG QUESTION:

Can I get my father's ghost to stay?

"Once you have your question, what else do you need?" Ms. Abad asks.

Dani's hand shoots up. "A hypothesis?"

"Yes! And to form your hypothesis, you must gather observations and data. What have you noticed that can inform your attempt in answering your big question?"

Under the *Observations* column, I start listing what's been happening with Pa.

1. He has trouble entering places he hasn't been before.
2. No one else sees or hears him.

3. His feet never touch the ground.
4. His skin is devoid of any color.

Ms. Abad sends us to research in the library, which is unfortunately also in the senior high building. Instead of panicking more about why Pa can't come in, I decide to be productive. I take Ms. Abad's assignment to heart and start researching like I've never researched before. But no matter how deep my dive through the internet goes, not one article or paper can tell me anything about what to do when your dead father shows up in your home. This includes me sorting through hundreds of blogs that recommend therapy and preach things like *Your dead loved one will always be a part of you.*

All of it is as useless as meditation.

I go through books and binders of scientific papers shelved at the high school library. Saint Agnes really needs to restock their resources on spirits and ghosts. The most relevant information I find is about some doctor who tried reviving dead cells in pigs.

By the time the bell rings, I've already run out of options. I've gotten so desperate that I've resorted to the Bible. They make such a big deal about Jesus's resurrection, but not one chapter, verse, or proverb explicitly states the logistics of how it happened. Considering how thick the book is, you'd think they'd have room for an instruction manual.

I'm skimming the New Testament when Kayla joins me in the library. She does a low whistle when she takes a seat at my table. "Wow, you look like shit."

She immediately apologizes after the (I'll admit) very accurate observation. Getting little sleep over the weekend plus reuniting with your dead dad's ghost really accentuates one's eye bags.

“Sorry, I went to orientation for Honesty Club and they require new members to be extra honest.”

That momentarily distracts me from the Bible. “We have an Honesty Club?”

Kayla shows me the button pinned to her uniform that says: *I serve hones-tea.* “I talked to Dani about which clubs needed more members and she said I’d be perfect for Honesty Club!”

I have a theory that all of Dani’s student council campaigning through the years has infected Kayla’s mind. Every time Dani gives her a compliment, Kayla’s face lights up like the sky has split open.

Right on cue, I see Ms. Class President doing her rounds and greeting everyone around the library. I’ve been in the same class with Dani since kindergarten, and her life’s mission has always been becoming student council president. We were asked to perform our favorite song during our third-grade Christmas party and Dani recited the Saint Agnes student handbook.

By the time we were freshmen, she volunteered to head the school tours for incoming high schoolers, brainwashing her future voters as soon as possible.

When our principal announced that the whole high school would be voting for which senior gets awarded the Gold Leadership Award at graduation, Dani immediately kickstarted yet another campaign.

Dani’s wearing her shiny student council president smile as she moves from table to table. “Don’t you think it’s impressive that Dani works this hard?” Kayla swoons again.

“She’s just doing all that so she gets the leadership award.”

Kayla shoots me a look and I point at her button with my pen. “Sorry, just serving *hones-tea.*”

Dani inches closer to our table and I bow my head down in

my arms in case she spots us. Every time Dani corners me, she goes on and on about ways I can "participate" more.

"Kayla! Nika!"

Ugh. Too late.

"Miss President," I deadpan with a slight bow.

Dani beams even more when she sees Kayla wearing the hones-tea button. "How did you like your first meeting? I'm so excited that we're only eight members away from our goal of ten members at Honesty Club!"

". . . So you have two members?" I clarify.

Her head bobs along. "Only eight away!"

Makes sense. You probably have to be a bit delusional to be a politician.

"Have fun," I mutter, going back to my Bible research. For some reason, Dani interprets this as *Please interrupt me and join our table.*

She pulls out the student handbook and puts it on top of my Bible—which I'm pretty sure is frowned upon in many religions. "I'm actually here for non-Honesty-Club-related business."

"Dani, whatever it is, I'm not joining."

"I'm just asking for your opinion." Dani flips through the handbook to a section bookmarked with a *prom* tab.

I gawk at the page. "There's really a whole chapter for prom?"

"As student council president . . . ," Dani starts, and I let out a groan. She always introduces herself as student council president whenever she's pitching something.

"In recent years, worldwide research has shown that teenagers have been exhibiting elevated levels of stress," Dani continues her spiel. "And one possible cause? Prom!"

There are probably a million researchers worldwide clamoring to dispute this claim.

"It's bad enough that we have to think of paying for dinner, getting a dress, but then we have to think about the stress of finding a date—at an all-girls school!" she declares. "So to make this a smooth transition for everyone, we, your friends at the Saint Agnes Student Council, have made it a mandate to encourage the smooth search for appropriate prom companions."

I wonder how long Dani can ramble on for without noticing I've completely zoned out. Each time she mentions prom, I think about another dreadful thing I'd rather do than show up on prom night. Eat the expired Buns by Beth pastries we usually throw out, sit through one of Achi's long rants about meditation, join Kayla for the next Honesty Club meeting.

Then Dani says, "That's why I appointed Nika as head of the committee."

Now, *that* got my attention.

Kayla and I burst out laughing. "Out of all the jokes you try inserting in your speeches, *this* is by far your funniest one," I say.

Dani keeps pushing the joke. "I really think you'd be an exemplary leader."

"*Exemplary leader?*" Kayla and I echo, then laugh even harder. "Ky, did I ever tell you it was my dream to be prom committee head?"

"I'm still processing the breaking news that you're an exemplary leader," Kayla teases back.

Dani beams at us. "Super love the enthusiasm!"

Our laughs die down and Dani is still very convincing . . . a little *too* convincing.

"You're not serious," I tell her.

"Why would I ask if I wasn't serious?" She reads out another bullet point in the handbook. "As student council president, the elected representative must encourage participation from *all* members of Saint Agnes."

"Then please discourage my participation," I say. "There are a dozen other girls who'd want to be prom committee head."

Dani chuckles. "I'm not making you head of the whole committee, Nika! That's a responsibility that needs years of experience. You're head of the PCS."

I stare blankly at Dani and she explains, "Prom-Companion Subcommittee. You're in charge of finding people dates.

"Consider it a feminist movement," Dani says.

One of my biggest icks about Dani: her new vocabulary. Ever since we covered social justice in class, Dani has been obsessed with inserting the terminology in every sentence.

When the juniors and seniors agreed to a tie during our volleyball intrams, Dani made a speech about how we "trumped classism." When the dance troupe members started calling one another sis, Dani called them out and said, "We shouldn't be cisgendering people."

Time and again, Dani proves she doesn't know what any of these "big words" actually mean.

"Forcing people into dates isn't a movement, Dani. If anything, it's moving *back* feminism," I state in bewildered horror.

"That's why I picked you. I know you'll be able to steer the committee in the right direction," she says with so much sincerity, as if we're joining forces to solve global warming.

I'm not buying it.

"What's the real reason, Dani?"

I stare her down and block her from reciting another passage from the student handbook. She turns to Kayla for help, but Kayla only pats her hones-tea button in response.

"Fine," Dani says, dropping the act. "During our meetings with the parents' association, Auntie Baby keeps asking me to get you involved."

I blink at her. "You were gonna give me a prom comm position . . . because of Auntie Baby?"

"The alumni also get a big say on the leadership awards."

"Well, well, well," I say, twirling my fingers. "As student council president, I thought you'd know better than to give in to nepotism."

Dani stiffens. "I never give favoritism to my nephews."

I'm about to explain that nepotism isn't just limited to nephews, but I decide to use my energy elsewhere.

"Not interested," I tell Dani firmly, annoyed at how long this conversation has gone on for.

"You lose a lot of things when you shut people out, Nika," Dani says as she gets up from our table and hands me a flyer with text that looks like it was typed in 90-size font: 39 DAYS UNTIL PROM!

After emphasizing to Dani that I'm very comfortable with losing things, she finally gets the hint and I can finally return to my research.

Except Kayla keeps watching me.

Then she carefully asks, "Everything okay?"

"Yeah," I say, folding the ridiculous prom countdown flyer and highlighting another Bible verse that mentions spirits.

"It's just . . . you're reading."

"I know how to read."

"But you're reading the Bible," Kayla says. "That makes a best friend worry."

My heart always feels a little fuller whenever Kayla calls me her best friend. I mean, she's definitely *my* best friend, but I always wonder how I qualify as hers.

In grade school, Kayla was once given an award for compassion. Like, our teachers felt the need to award her for being a good person. When we had a fifth-grade viewing of *The Lion*

King, Kayla stepped out in tears because her heart was breaking over the animated lions.

Can you blame me for questioning why someone that nice gets me for a best friend?

I've never even talked to Kayla about what happened to Pa. As the daughter of Auntie Grace, one of the founding members of the Marie-tres, I'm pretty sure she's already heard plenty of stories. Still, during Father's Day last year, I remember Kayla bought me Potato Corner fries out of nowhere. She never explained and I never asked why.

Talking to Dani made me lose so many brain cells, but she might be onto something about me shutting people out.

So I ask my best friend, "You believe in things you can't see, right?"

"Nika, that's the literal definition of faith."

That's when the words spill out of me. I tell her everything from not following Ma's pagpag rule to seeing Pa in the bathroom and him being invisible to everyone else. I ramble on about all my theories, every random fact I picked up online, even about the scientist who experimented on dead pigs. Panicking over how I have absolutely no idea how much time I have left with Pa.

As I'm verbalizing all these thoughts that have been whirling around in my head, everything suddenly sounds . . . ridiculous. Absurd, preposterous, like some batshit headline you'd see in a Facebook post that gets spread by aunties and uncles. What am I doing telling this to another person?

And Kayla is patient enough to listen through my whole speech! By the time I'm done, her gaze is still fixed on me and I'm half expecting her to report me to the clinic.

Then a smile crawls across her lips. "This is what happened in Kathryn Bernardo's hit horror movie, *Pagpag: Nine Lives*."

14

I'M WATCHING A MODERN-DAY MIRACLE HAPPEN BEFORE MY VERY EYES. For the first time in her seventeen years of living, Kayla Tan decides to break curfew. Under her parents' strict orders, she's always supposed to go straight home after school.

When the milk tea stand at our canteen malfunctioned one day and everyone who stayed after school got free drinks, Kayla still went straight home. Even when a Taylor Swift impersonator had an impromptu performance at Saint Agnes, Kayla skipped because it was scheduled after dismissal.

And plot twist, her parents were surprisingly cool with it. When Kayla called her mom, Auntie Grace gave her permission to go home later than usual when Kayla said she was bringing me to Bible study (not taking credit, but I *did* come up with the alibi). My rebel best friend didn't even crack when we asked my sister for her ID so I could leave school with Kayla.

Since the Swifties Who Crochet club took over the library for their weekly "stitch meeting," Kayla and I sneaked into Achi's office again to do more research. Correction: *I'm* doing research. Kayla's been binge-watching the *Pagpag* movie again.

"So the ghost appears because the group broke all the superstitions they were supposed to do at the wake . . ." Kayla keeps dictating the *Pagpag* movie plot as she replays the same scenes over and over again on the office projector.

She then fast-forwards to where the movie shows the ghost's backstory. "And the reason the ghost shows up is because his wife made a deal with the devil—that her husband could come back to life if his ghost murdered nine people . . ."

The room goes silent and I look up to see that Kayla paused the movie. Concern floods Kayla's face when she looks over her shoulder. "Niks?"

"Yeah?" I say, while still trying to decipher another article about the dead pigs that were brought back to life.

"Is there . . . would you . . ." She pauses and lowers her voice. "Did you do a . . . deal too?"

I stop and scan her face. "Are you asking me if I'm capable of murder?"

"I mean, I think you're capable of anything."

Only Kayla Tan can make a murder accusation sound like a compliment.

"As much as I love the idea of murder—"

"Murdering nine people," Kayla clarifies.

"Murdering nine people," I repeat. "I don't think we'll find the answers behind my dad's reappearance from some ghost movie."

"Should we try another movie then?"

I tell her to stop scrolling through Netflix and check out my progress. She gets up from the couch and takes the other desk chair. "See?" I say, gesturing toward Achi's computer and my extensive notes. "Scientific research."

Kayla's forehead scrunches as she reads the back of the prom countdown flyer that Dani shoved in our faces. At least she provided me with extra paper for my notes. "Why are you writing about pig organs?"

"There are scientists from Yale who were able to revive these pigs that had been dead for an hour."

"How?"

I read the note I had underlined. "With a nutrient-rich fluid."

"Very specific," Kayla says sarcastically. "Maybe we can pump your dad's ghost with Gatorade." She purses her lips and skims more of my notes. “These theories sound way too scientific.”

“And you think your murder theory is better?”

“Than reviving a ghost with Gatorade?” she says. “Um, yeah!”

Kayla then asks me to repeat more details of when Pa first showed up, what his ghost exactly looked like, if he mentioned anything about a timeline.

I double-check again to make sure that Kayla’s actually being serious. Kayla has always rode along whenever I’d rant about Dr. Derrick, Dani, how white chocolate doesn’t deserve to be called chocolate—but this whole stuff about Pa and his ghost?

“You really believe what I told you?” I ask. “The whole thing about my dad coming back as a ghost?”

She staggers back with my question. “Is he . . . with us?” Kayla suddenly ducks and raises her arms to the side. “Did I accidentally hit him? How long has he been here?!”

I move her arms down and tell her he isn’t here. “Why do you believe me?”

“Why wouldn’t I?”

“Because the story sounds crazy,” I tell her. “I wouldn’t believe it if you told me.”

Kayla sighs and swivels my chair so I face her. “How long have we been best friends?”

“Probably since our moms’ first sonogram,” I joke.

“Yeah, and you never talk about your dad. Not since . . . well, since what happened,” she says. “So if you’re telling me that his ghost came back, I believe you.”

Then she adds, “Best friends.”

My heart squeezes at that. “So does that mean you’ll defend me . . . even if I murder nine people?”

Kayla rolls her eyes. "My parents wouldn't approve."

"Auntie Grace *loves* me," I remind her. "Didn't she extend your curfew because we're together?"

"Yeah, but she'll never let me leave church if she finds out I'm friends with a murderer," Kayla says, and I laugh. When I click open a new window on my sister's computer, I suddenly notice a shortcut that's labeled *Secret*.

. . . My sister can't label a folder in her computer *Secret* and expect me to *not* open it.

Oh my god.

My sister's such a hypocrite!!!

Achi kept gloating about how responsible she was, how Ma entrusted her with Ma's red notebook while all this time, my sister scanned *everything*.

"What's that?" Kayla asks.

"My sister's betrayal."

She categorized all of Ma's superstitions into different tabs—*New Year, health, love, death*. Achi even highlighted and added notes in the margins for Ma's superstitions for taking exams.

Beside *Wear red undergarments to attract good luck!*, my achi wrote, *2011 medicine boards topnotcher allegedly wore red briefs and ate a red empanada*. She didn't even type it. It's in her signature scratchy handwriting!

There's even physical proof that Achi made copies of Ma's notebook behind her back! I take several screenshots for insurance. The next time Achi tries to throw out my pancit canton stash, I'll have *leverage*.

"Wait," Kayla says when I'm about to email myself all the evidence. "There was a paragraph there about death superstitions."

"These are just random superstitions that Ma writes down. They never make any sense—"

Kayla then takes the mouse and scrolls through the page. She keeps gasping the more she takes in. "This aligns with everything you've been telling me about your dad."

Pagpag superstition: Don't go home immediately after a wake or risk spirits following you home.

"Well, Pa's ghost showed up a day after I didn't pagpag, and technically it wasn't his wake . . ."

"*Butterfly superstition.*" Kayla reads another entry. "*Butterflies are a sign of a dead loved one making their presence felt.*"

Before I can argue, Kayla says, "True or false. Didn't you say that a butterfly appeared right before you saw your dad? And isn't that a sign of a loved one making their presence felt?"

"You know, it's hard to do true or false when you give two statements at the same time."

She chooses to ignore my very valid point.

Kayla scrolls through more entries and then clicks on a tab labeled *Forty-day prayer.*

Many Filipinos believe that the souls of the dead wander the Earth forty days after their death. To help them pass on, the family does a forty-day prayer.

She faces me and jabs her finger at the screen. "Before you point out all the ways this isn't logical . . ."

"I wasn't going to," I say—even though I was definitely going to.

"Consider this for a moment," Kayla urges. "You've been doing all this research on dead pigs to figure out how long your dad's ghost is staying. What if the answer is in Auntie Beth's superstitions?"

"Again, the cells of the pig were revived after being dead for an hour," I point out. "It's groundbreaking scientific research!"

Kayla rudely closes the tab when I show her more of the pigs. She sighs and says, "When your dad shows up as a ghost,

I don't think that has anything to do with science, Niks. It becomes a matter of faith."

Despite my gut telling me that the pig research has more scientific value, I try to think like how Ma would. What if the answers *are* all in Ma's superstitions?

Achi and Ma had a fight about Pa's fortieth day years ago. Ma wanted to host a big prayer service for Pa, but Achi thought it was better to do something more private. In the end, we all had to put on our everything's-fine-with-the-Ilagan-family faces while going through another round of people telling us they were sorry for our loss.

I keep staring at the number forty on the screen. "What if . . . the forty-day thing doesn't only apply to recently dead souls?" I consider. "What if . . . *all* souls only get to wander the Earth for forty days . . . then maybe we start counting from when Pa's ghost first appeared . . ."

"Which was a day ago, right?" Kayla confirms.

"Right . . ." I flip over the flyer I've been writing on and read the headline: 39 DAYS UNTIL PROM! If this forty-day superstition is correct, then Pa's ghost has until prom night.

And then Kayla tells me, "Time to believe in things you don't see."

15

PA IS HOVERING BY THE WAITING AREA OF OUR CONDOMINIUM LOBBY, as if he's a visitor who needs to be buzzed in instead of a . . . ghost.

"Is he *here*?" Kayla asks while I'm processing that Pa didn't go away. Her hand quickly goes to the cross on her necklace and she turns on her phone's flashlight.

I shield my eyes when the light hits my eyes. "What're you doing?"

"Waving smoke around is supposed to drive off evil spirits."

Pa stands to the side while Kayla looks like she's one of those airport marshals guiding a giant plane on the runway. "I didn't bring incense, but maybe my phone light can work," she explains.

"Hey!" she says when I swipe the phone and turn off the light.

"My dad isn't an evil spirit."

"This is what happens in many horror movies," Kayla says. "Ghosts appear looking like your friend, your dad, then they turn out to be a headless priest or a vampire-like baby."

I tell Kayla she's being ridiculous and leave out the fact that I had the same exact thought yesterday.

"And I would've never qualified to be a priest," Pa says, chiming in.

I spend the next ten minutes assuring Kayla that Pa's ghost isn't headless, vampire-like, and doesn't resemble the White Lady of Balete Drive (even though I have no idea what *she'd* look like and have no interest in finding out, thank you very much).

Kayla inches closer to me. "So how do I greet him to show I come in peace?"

"Curtsy?" I say with a shrug.

I meant it as a joke, but Kayla goes on to do a full-body curtsy about ten feet from where Pa is actually floating.

I spin Kayla around and direct her to where Pa is located. Kayla does another bow. "Nice to meet you, Ghost Dad."

Pa smiles. "I can't believe this is little Kayla Tan. She was just here before," he says, pointing to his waist.

"She wanted to call you Demonyo Antonio, which I vetoed." Kayla also suggested Ghost Daddy, which I vetoed harder. "What time did you get back?" I ask Pa.

He glances at the clock atop the elevator. "Around noon?"

"You've just been waiting here?"

"I went up to the unit," he says. "Then your Auntie Baby visited and I thought they wanted privacy since Marie-tres night was always your mom's girls' night."

"What's he saying?" Kayla whispers.

"Something about a girls' night . . ." I pause and realize the date. Tuesdays are always Ma's mahjong night at Auntie Baby's.

"What time do our moms finish mahjong?" I check with Kayla.

She shrugs. "I'm always asleep before my mom gets home." Then it dawns on her. "How are we going to ask Auntie Beth's advice about the forty days?"

"What forty days?" Pa turns to me.

"We have this theory that your ghost only has forty days to wander the Earth."

Then Kayla follows up with another question. "What does Ghost Dad think of the theory?"

And Pa asks, "Why are you making up theories about me?"

Okay, just because I can *see* ghosts doesn't mean I've agreed to be the interpreter. "One question at a time," I say, urging my best friend and Dad to chill.

The elevator pings at the lobby, and while both sides keep giving me more things to say to the other person, I focus on the situation at hand.

"My mom thinks I brought you to Bible study!" Kayla protests when I push the button for Auntie Baby's floor and tell her we're going to crash their mahjong session.

"Well, if Auntie Grace asks, you can say I *did* read the Bible today," I say in my defense.

"That's not how Bible study works!"

While Kayla freaks out about my lack of biblical understanding, Pa is questioning Ma's superstitions.

"How did you find out about the forty days?"

"Ma told us that your soul would go up to heaven on your fortieth day." I fix my eyes on the elevator floor when the hot feeling rises in my throat again. On Pa's last fortieth day, I remember Ma sobbing so much when all the visitors left. It was the most I had ever seen my mom cry. She sat in front of Pa's picture and murmured how she wasn't ready to say goodbye.

Stop it! Why are you bringing back those memories when your dad is here?

I shake all those thoughts away and smile at Pa. "I know it's a reach, but what if the forty days applies to your ghost too?"

The elevator doors open and I lead Kayla and Pa toward Unit 3H.

"Superstar, I don't think we need to bring your mom into this—"

Pa gets cut off when Seph opens the door.

"Is my mom here?" I ask him.

Instead of answering my question, he leans his arm on the doorframe, blocking the unit's entrance. "Sorry." He raises his shoulders and places his hand above my head. "Must be this tall to enter."

Pa hovers and inspects Seph without him noticing. "Is this Baby's son?"

Unfortunately.

When I try looking over his right shoulder, he adjusts his stance to the right. I go to the left and he moves to obstruct my view.

My patience runs very thin when he blocks me from the door again. "Where'd you get your reflexes?" he asks, looking like he's actually enjoying wasting my time.

I'm about to slam my body against him and enter the unit through brute force when Kayla says, "Nika's going through an emergency."

That wipes the smile off his face and he looks at me like he's actually concerned. "Wait. What's wrong?"

"You," I say through my teeth. "You're pissing me off."

"Niks, I'm not sure this is the best way to ask for his help with Ghost Daddy."

. . .

I wasn't really sure if I'd tell Seph anything about Pa, but I guess this is how we're doing it.

"Ghost Daddy?" Seph's eyes bounce between me and Kayla. "Is that the title of some Taylor Swift song?"

We all startle when we hear a loud thud from the 3H unit.

Before any of us have time to react, Pa's already peeking through the wall. "Your mom's inside with Baby, Grace, and Jackie," he reports back.

"What's Achi doing here?"

Seph spins around. "*Who* are you talking to?"

Pa peeks again. "They're fixing a mannequin that fell down."

I'm about to ask why they'd need a mannequin for mahjong when Pa says, ". . . Beth has a wedding dress on."

Excuse me?

Seph must see how furious I am because he doesn't even try to block me when I tell him to move. When I enter the 3H unit, the couch and Moseph shrine are pushed to the side to make room for a clothing rack of dresses. Auntie Grace and Achi crowd around Ma, holding up different styles of wedding gowns.

"Nika?" Ma starts when she sees me. My whole body tenses at the sight of her in a wedding dress. "What are you doing here?" she asks.

As I'm struggling to find words, I hear Kayla squeak from behind me. "We came from Bible study!"

Ma's wearing a veil and a beaded off-the-shoulder gown that hugs her figure. She takes steps toward me, and the dress glides along with her every move. My mom has never looked more beautiful.

"Wow," I hear Pa breathe out, as if the wind got knocked out of him—if ghosts had wind in them, at least.

My brain's still short-circuiting when Ma stammers, "W-we didn't want to bother you, so I asked Baby if we could try on wedding gowns here. I know how busy you are with school and classes . . ."

Achi can't even look me in the eye when I turn to her. I'm not dumb, and my family doesn't need to sugarcoat things for me. We all know why Ma didn't want me around for this. Who in their right mind would include the daughter who bails on the engagement, hates the fiancé, and yells at her mom?

My feelings about the wedding aside, I'm tired of being the person who makes my mom's life harder. No, I want to be the reason something good happens to her for once.

"I want to help," I hear myself say.

Auntie Baby doesn't notice the painful tension wafting among the Ilagan family members. "See, I told you Nika would want to be here," Auntie Baby says, scolding Ma. "You know, Seph really inherited his father's sense of style. Sobrang porma din ni Francis. Look how great Seph, Kayla, and Nika carry themselves. Their generation knows fashion!"

No one points out the irony that we're all wearing our wrinkled school uniforms.

Auntie Baby orders Ma to face the full-length mirror in their sala. "I'm sure Nika would agree with me about the fit."

Ma tries pulling down the lining and glances at me through the mirror's reflection. She then carefully asks, "What do you think, Niks? Is it too tight?"

"No," I hear Pa answer for me.

But Ma doesn't hear him, so she's still studying my face, waiting for an answer.

"You look . . ."

Like a bride. Ma looks like a bride.

My throat catches when I try uttering the words. I scrunch my hair tie between my fingers, willing all my real thoughts to stay secret. Just say that Ma looks good, that the dress fits well—hell, even complimenting how good her calves look is better than standing in silence. *You can handle holding things in and being supportive for Ma right now.*

Yet the very thought of her marrying someone else, of our family moving on and everything changing . . . all of that makes me want to crawl out of my skin.

Shut it down, Nika. Shut your emotions down!

"Nika?" Achi prompts, and I can feel my eyes start to well up. This whole room with veils and dresses is all too loud and overwhelming.

"Sorry," I tell my family, and give some lame excuse that my stomach was hurting before bolting right out of there.

16

THE STOMACH IS REALLY AN AMAZING GIFT TO HUMANKIND.

If you ever need an excuse or an alibi, just say that you have stomach problems. Highly recommend!

People actually leave me alone when I say my stomach is feeling weird. When Ma came by the bathroom to check on me, I said my stomach was feeling funny. She then gave me space, and that's the proper thing to do when someone hints that they have diarrhea. On the other hand, my sister, who's apparently unfamiliar with common courtesy, kept hammering on the door. I turned on the shower and blasted music until I heard her footsteps finally walk away from the bathroom.

Using the funny stomach excuse also worked wonderfully with Kayla. Instead of asking me how I'm handling seeing Ma in a wedding gown, she's messaging me with links on how to diagnose my stomach issues. Annoyingly, Seph has been trying to check up on me too.

He sends me a video on how Apple will create a teleportation device worth $29 million.

Seph: if you forgive me, i'll donate to your teleportation fund

I don't reply and ignore all his messages.

You'd think that my body would be at its limit from being upset at Dr. Derrick, Achi, and Ma—but it turns out I still have space in my heart to stay pissed at Seph too.

Thankfully, it seems like I have the bathroom all to myself—my safe corner of the world where I can pretend everything's okay in peaceful ignorant bliss.

And then I see a pale detached hand pass through the door and wave at me.

"Can I come in?" I hear Pa's voice from outside.

The hand holds out a thumbs-up and seconds later, a thumbs-down.

I wipe my eyes with one of the hand towels before I mutter, "Come in." Pa's body proceeds to pass through the bathroom door and slides next to my position sitting against the foot of the tub.

"How're you doing, Superstar?"

"*Great*," I lie, and blow my nose.

"I always found listening to the best heartbreak song of all time cathartic too."

Pa sways and hums along when Mariah continues playing through the bathroom speakers. When it loops back to "We Belong Together," Pa mimics playing the piano riff in the beginning. I can't help but laugh when he joins in the final chorus, his voice croaking when he attempts once again to belt it out with Mariah. I remember that this is how he used to cheer me up too. He would play music (often songs by singers with operatic vocal talents) and try to reach the notes until his vocal cords sounded like they were going to give out. He only stopped singing once he saw me laughing.

He's out of breath by the time the song finishes.

"You would think ghosts wouldn't really need oxygen," he jokes.

". . . How do you do that?" I ask him.

"Lots of vocal training, those breathing exercises I used to teach you—"

"Not the singing," I cut him off, and consider how to word my question. "You saw Ma in the wedding dress. You must know that she's . . . she's . . ."

"Engaged."

I scan Pa's face and his expression remains the same. Calm as ever.

"And that doesn't bother you?"

He pauses.

"You're not mad? Hurt? Jealous?!"

Pa leans back and takes a deep breath. "I guess when you get older, Superstar, emotions don't overwhelm you as much anymore. You learn to manage your feelings better. That's what helps you deal with the hard things that life brings you."

I still have no idea how he does it. How am I supposed to manage my emotions when my insides feel like a ticking time bomb? I mean, I'm even confused about how my sister handles *her* feelings. How can Achi be so mature and completely happy about Ma and Dr. Derrick?

Maybe that's the point of growing up. Does getting older mean you're not supposed to feel things anymore?

So I try to shove every emotion back down, not let things get to me when I ask another question.

"Is my theory true?" I ask, and Pa turns to me. "That you only have forty days here?"

Pa smiles at me then. "Nika, let's just enjoy the time we have."

"But it's true?"

That's the only moment his expression breaks; the smile falls from his eyes. "I didn't want you to worry," Pa says. "I was trying to protect you from knowing . . ."

"I'd rather know," I assure him.

A beat passes before Pa finally nods. "You're right."

"Okay," I say, steadying my voice.

"So that means you only have thirty-nine days left?"

He turns to me and puts two thumbs up. "And we're going to make the most of those thirty-nine days, right?"

My throat feels hot when this sinks in. *Listen to Pa's advice. Manage your feelings, don't let emotions overwhelm you.*

"You're sure you can't stay longer?"

Pa moves to pat my wrist even if I can't feel his touch. "We have to accept the things we can't change, Superstar."

I force a smile when Pa resumes singing along to my play-list. See what happens when I stay calm? Pa actually takes me seriously and gives me direct answers. So I focus on being in the moment and forgetting that Ma's marrying someone else.

And that I only have thirty-nine days before I have to say bye to Pa again.

17

IT TURNS OUT, I'M A NATURAL AT MANAGING MY EMOTIONS.

I woke up this morning pissed at a lot of people. My sister climbed to the top of my list after she rudely woke me up by ripping the blanket off me again.

How this would usually play out in the past: I'll yell at her for grabbing my blanket, she'll yell back that I'm just pissed at her for hiding Ma's dress fittings from me, I'll yell again because now I'm doubly pissed, and so on and so forth.

This morning, though, I chose peace.

Scratch that. I chose *maturity*.

As I was lying on my bed, still adjusting from being blanket-less against my will, I stood up and greeted Achi, "Morning." No yelling, no insults, no anger. Even Pa was speechless from my perfect display of control.

Achi, on the other hand, moved on to being straight-up disruptive. As I was minding my business and getting things ready for school, she opened every single drawer and cabinet in the bedroom. The worst part? She didn't close any of them!

"I think she's trying to get your attention," Pa told me.

But she won't get it. I was resolved with this whole new level of unbothered maturity.

After she was done with all the drawers, she moved on to opening and closing the door repeatedly. My patience started to run out around the twentieth time. Instead of snapping at Achi and asking if she planned to stop being annoying anytime soon, I said, "Thanks for giving me a ride to school again."

I can tell my gratitude threw her off the whole morning.

It was so satisfying that even when Pa told me he'd meet me after school, I didn't linger on the fact he has thirty-eight days left. I waited until I was *in* class before I spiraled.

When we reviewed our investigative project pitches during chemistry, I kept staring at the big question on my worksheet.

Can I get my father's ghost to stay?

My throat starts to constrict when I see everyone else in class listening to Ms. Abad like our investigative project is some life-or-death situation. So many of my classmates, kids all over the world, get 365 days a year with their dad, and I'm supposed to settle for forty days? I know Pa said that line about accepting things we can't change, but what if I don't want to accept this?

Speaking of things that are hard to accept, we're forced to stay a few minutes after class because Dani has to deliver yet another prom announcement.

"Saint Agnes Class of 2015 set the record for most attendees to their prom," Dani declares from the front of the room. "As your class president, I'm determined that we become the new record breakers, the trailblazers. Remember that all the proceeds from prom go to our scholarship fund. Let's not crumble to the Class of 2015. Let's not be victims of classism!"

Dani's very passionate delivery actually gets a few people in class to nod along to her call against "classism." The worst of them all is Kayla, who even claps for this mess.

"It's for a good cause," Kayla protests when I shoot her a side-eye.

Dani flashes a prom teaser video in front of the room that ends in a countdown with a bigger font than the flyer: 38 DAYS UNTIL PROM. The countdown even has fireworks and Barbie animations on the side cheering.

Great. It's like Barbie is cheering for my dad's impending second death.

Even when the dismissal bell finally rings, I still can't get rid of Dani. I try taking the most complicated route out and I still hear the heels of her loafers pattering behind me. She continues to hound me the whole way to the exit gate.

"Nika?" she asks when she catches up to my pace. "Were you in front of me this whole time?"

This type of acting is how stalkers get away with their crimes.

My indifference makes her drop the BS. "You know, there are many perks to heading the Prom-Companion Subcommittee," Dani mentions.

"Is there a bigger perk than *not* joining the committee?"

"You can organize pre-prom events with the boys' schools," Dani offers, continuing her pitch. "Don't you want to be the first one to flirt with potential prom dates?"

I've decided that this suggestion doesn't warrant a response.

"It's why I told Auntie Baby you would help plan a soiree at her place."

"You did *what*?"

The only thing cringier than prom is the concept of a soiree. Leading up to prom every year, students at Saint Agnes organize these weird modern-day mating rituals. Since all-boys schools and all-girls schools have limited interaction, some decide to organize meetups where one class from the all-girls school hangs out with one class from the all-boys school.

"During our last prom comm meeting, Auntie Baby suggested that we have a soiree with Seph's class, and since you two are neighbors, we thought you could cohost!"

"No."

"Auntie Baby even said that your parents met through a soiree."

"No," I say again.

"And that you and Seph are really close."

Is there a way that I can shut Dani up and still succeed in managing my emotions?

As I'm about to turn down Dani for the tenth time today, my sister unexpectedly comes to my rescue.

"Ms. Ilagan!" Dani gets distracted and runs over when she spots Achi. My sister quickly wears her resting constipated face once she hears Dani's voice. It's my sister's expression whenever she has to deal with difficult customers at the bakery.

"Did you get to review my recent student council proposal?" Dani asks. "The action plan about ensuring appropriate behavior during club events? We want to make sure we *all* practice appropriation."

Achi sighs and tilts her head at Dani (way more politely than when she does it with me). "Yes, I got your twenty emails. Have you signed up for that social justice workshop that I recommended?"

After Achi and I take turns trying to shake off Dani, Achi swipes us both out and we're finally leaving Saint Agnes school grounds.

I'm still making sure that Dani isn't following us when Achi hands me a paper bag. "In case you're hungry."

It's one of her fancy bento lunch boxes packed with noodles.

Hold up.

"Did you make me pancit canton?" I gape at my sister.

"They're special Japanese noodles."

I open the box and eat some using the chopsticks placed inside. The chilimansi flavor already wafts through my nose before I take a bite. "Definitely pancit canton," I say through more bites.

"Again, special. Japanese. Noodles." Achi continues insisting on the lie.

"Wow." I smile and look up at her. "You must feel *really* guilty about lying to me."

She rolls her eyes. "I didn't lie to you."

"You didn't tell me about Ma trying on wedding dresses," I point out. "That's hiding the truth. Definition of lying."

"That's not the same as lying."

"Still felt like a lie," I say, grumbling. I hate how my voice sounds like a little kid's.

And I hate how my sister is now looking at me like I'm a little kid too.

"Sorry na, okay?"

I ignore her and focus on my special Japanese noodles.

She tries again. "Do you wanna talk about it?"

My heart twists at Achi's offer. I never considered confiding in her about Pa . . . yet maybe, she would know what to do?

Achi then switches to lecture mode. "You can't blame Ma for wanting to keep the dress fitting a secret. Look how you acted during the ting hun, at the memorial. You even insulted Uncle Derrick's barista skills."

And just like that, all hope empties out of my chest.

"I was giving *Dr.* Derrick constructive criticism."

"Well, give nicer criticism," she says. "He took time off from his clinic to help out again today."

"What? He's there again?!"

Great. Just what I need, watching Dr. Derrick and his sluggish coffee-making insert himself in Ma's business.

When we round the corner of Buns by Beth's street, I stop when I see a pale, ghostly white figure hovering by the storefront.

"Nika? Jackie?"

Every time Pa sees my sister, I can tell he's bracing himself, hoping for the chance that Achi sees him too.

Then Achi walks straight past Pa, oblivious to his presence, and opens the door.

I want to ask if he's okay when Achi says, "Why are you just standing there?"

"I'll . . . finish my Japanese noodles first," I tell Achi, and lift the lunch box for emphasis. "Don't want to set a bad example for customers and bring in outside food."

Achi looks at me skeptically before leaving me (and Pa) alone.

I hold my phone to my ear in case Achi watches me. "How did you know this was Ma's bakery?" I ask Pa.

"Beth has a bakery?"

"Yeah, this is Ma's store."

His eyes light up when he scans the place. "Buns by Beth." Pa's body levitates even higher when he reads the store sign. He reaches out his hand through the window display.

"Wait," I say, in case Ma's bakery has some force field ghost repellent too.

But his arm goes straight through.

"Did the force field disappear because it's your old warehouse?"

I try explaining how Ma converted the place, but Pa keeps butting in with comments about how there are so many customers, how the space looks so impressive. He doesn't seem interested in figuring out the mechanics of when he's tangible or not.

Pa's hand traces Ma's name on the sign. "You think I can go in?"

"We can try?"

I step inside and leave the door open for Pa to float through.

Pa braces himself and carefully moves toward the entrance.

I keep one eye closed since I hate seeing Pa get rejected by spaces. Then he makes his way in—no falling, no ricocheting. He immediately starts marveling at the pastry displays, the newspaper articles about the store that are framed on the walls, the customers lined up at the register. "Always knew she could dream bigger," he says under his breath.

Through it all, he asks me millions of questions.

"How did your mom start?

"She did this all on her own?

"What's her bestseller? It's her siopao, 'no?"

I try answering while inserting some bragging on the side. "The bakery is always featured in lists of pastry shops you need to try in Manila," I tell him. "Her siopaos would be sold in every supermarket if Ma didn't keep turning them down."

He keeps asking me questions when I realize something. Pa didn't know that Ma has a bakery.

"How did you get here?" I ask him.

Pa stretches and wiggles his arms. "I floated," he jokes.

"You didn't know this store was Ma's," I say. "And I never told you the address or wrote it down anywhere in my room . . ."

"Superstar, I was married to your mother. That bond doesn't go away," he explains. "Even in the afterlife, I can sense her presence anywhere—"

Pa suddenly stops talking when Dr. Derrick steps out of the kitchen carrying an armload of coffee mugs. "Annika!" He startles and my heart lurches when a mug falls to the floor. I kneel down to clean up the shards when he waves me away. "Ah, let me take care of it. The full moon makes us all a little clumsy."

Once Dr. Derrick goes to the back to throw out the shattered mug, Pa says, "He's really into the moon, 'no?"

"The moon is his best friend," I deadpan.

"Kaya pala he has a moon bumper sticker. You would think that a dentist would rely more on science—"

"Right?" Thank god *someone* in my family is finally calling "Dr." Derrick out. "Achi told him I had trouble sleeping once, and he said I should pay attention to the 'lunar cycle.'"

Pa scoffs and I feel extremely vindicated.

I'm about to continue my rant when another realization dawns on me.

"When did you see his bumper sticker?"

"What?"

"Dr. Derrick's car," I repeat. "How did you know he has a bumper sticker?"

Pa takes a moment before answering. "Saw it outside."

"But he always parks his car by his clinic."

"That's what I meant," he says. "I saw it at the clinic."

"How do you know where his clinic is? Ma was always the one who dropped me off for my dentist appointments."

Pa crosses his arms. "Superstar, what's with the interrogation?"

. . .

Wait a minute.

"Were you *stalking* Dr. Derrick?!"

He opens his mouth but struggles to form a response. If Pa's cheeks had color, they'd totally be flushing right now.

"Oh my god. You're jealous!"

"I am *not* jealous," he says, still frantic from all the jealousy. "It's my responsibility as your father to background check anyone who spends time with my family. I have the right to have questions about his obsession with the moon and why he insists on a purple tie."

"Sobrang selos mo, Pa," I tease him.

"I'm not."

"Then why're you so defensive?"

His mouth twists. "You're enjoying this way too much."

I really am. I mean, if I was a ghost and my wife got engaged to someone else, I'd stalk him too! It's refreshing to have someone in my family act like how *I* would for a change.

Dr. Derrick then emerges from the kitchen with Ma this time. Pa levitates a little bit higher when Ma gives Dr. Derrick instructions at the counter. It's like when Kayla's Pomeranian straightens her posture before she pees to mark her territory.

Ma notices me and gestures toward my phone. "Who's that?"

I raise the phone closer to my ear and tell her I'm on a call with Kayla.

When Ma's focus switches back to the dentist, I look at Pa, who's hovering even higher, practically close to the ceiling. "Want me to tell Ma that you're taller than Dr. Derrick?"

He floats back down and lies again. "I'm not jealous."

"I can also show him old pictures so he can see that you have better style."

He shakes his head, but his eyes hint at a shadow of a smile. "No need to state the obvious, Superstar."

I'm about to assure Pa that I'd pick him a million times over Dr. Derrick when I hear someone call my surname.

"Ilagan?"

Seph enters the bakery, his face breaking into a smile and nose scrunch when he sees me.

I have the impulse to say hi when I remember that I'm still pissed at him.

I point to the phone next to my ear when Seph keeps trying to talk to me. *Busy,* I mouth, and turn away from him.

"Seph? What're you doing here?" Ma beams and runs around the counter as if a celebrity was visiting the bakery. Even my mother is always so weirdly protective over him. "Are you hungry? Want some merienda? I'll make you one of our special pies."

"Thanks, Auntie. I'm here to pick up an order—" Seph gets drowned out by Ma offering him more food.

Then Pa asks me out of nowhere, "Nililigawan ka ba niya?"

"*No!*" I say so loudly that people shopping by the pastry displays shoot glances at me.

I lower my voice and hiss, "He's not courting me."

"Sure ka?" He hovers closer, his gaze bouncing between me and Seph. "You're seeing him a lot."

"I see you a lot and you're not courting me."

He crosses his arms and smirks. "Why so defensive?"

"Wait lang. *I'm* the one teasing you—"

"What?" I spin around when I feel someone tapping my shoulder.

It's Seph holding out a Buns by Beth package. His lips quirk up when I face him, but his expression seems less . . . cocky. Like, he's nervous for some reason? I peer at the box he's holding. Maybe he's trying to return a box of expired siopaos.

Yet Ma continues to rave about Seph behind him. "He ordered some siopaos to get sent to our place, but I told him he didn't have to go through the hassle. Give them while we're all here!"

I stare at the ten-piece siopao box. "You ordered this for us?"

He offers the box again with a tentative smile. "Chaperone's treat."

"Uy." I hear Pa tease. "I did that, too, when I was courting your mom."

It takes all my willpower to not answer back, *Seph is not courting me!*

Also, no offense to my mother, but if I were being courted, I would want something nicer than a box of siopaos.

Then I hear Ma order me to take the box. "Kawawa naman si

Seph. He put all that effort into giving a gift and you made him hold that box for so long."

"It barely weighs a pound," I tell Ma. "Also, he bought siopaos that *you* made to give back to you. You made more of an effort with his gift."

Ma then starts lecturing me about having better manners.

"You know, I used to love it when your dad would buy siopaos from me. I never had a day with zero sales because your dad always bought me a box!"

She keeps going on about the proper protocol when accepting gifts, but my mind barely registers anything past her first sentence.

. . . Did Ma just bring up Pa?

I don't even remember the last time Ma casually brought up a memory of my dad.

Meanwhile, my father is still fixated on Seph's siopaos. "If you're not going to accept your sweetheart's gift, I'll take it," he teases.

My cheeks immediately flush at Pa's "sweetheart" comment. When I whisper to Pa to cut it out, he keeps teasing me to accept Seph's siopaos and reaches for the box. But instead of his hand slipping through like it does with all solids, his fingers actually . . . make contact. I turn to Pa and notice how his body is less pale. It's like his body is slowly filling in with more and more color. The white robes he's been wearing morph and cling closer to his body so he starts looking like he's wearing a white suit. It reminds me of when I got hooked to an IV in the hospital and saw the fluids course through the tubes. Instead of the chalk-white complexion, Pa's hands are almost the same shade as mine.

No one else in the bakery notices that my ghost father looks like he's been brought back to life.

18

"DO YOU SEE HIM NOW?" I ASK KAYLA AFTER I PASS PA A SLICE OF UBE cake.

From my bed, Kayla squints at where Pa's floating, then shakes her head again. "Sorry. Nothing."

I sigh and cross out the ube cake bullet point from our list.

Ever since Pa regained the ability to hold things and his complexion turned back to pre-ghost normal, I've been rewinding the moment at the bakery, listing down the events that led up to Pa's transformation. Using the trusty scientific method, I'm trying to rule out all possibilities.

My first hypothesis: If I give Pa more siopaos, then he will turn visible.

After showing him dozens of siopaos with different fillings and flavors, I used my deduction skills and moved on to other items in the Buns by Beth menu. We've tried pies, cakes, some more siopaos to be safe. No matter what dessert or pastry I hand to Pa, he's still invisible.

Kayla pokes the pastry when I pass Pa a croissant. "Ma would tell Father Melvin she witnessed a miracle if she saw floating bread."

She still can't see Pa, so she's been fixated on how the pastries look like they're flying when I give them to Pa's ghost. I tell Kayla to focus on the task at hand, and she says, "I don't need to see Uncle Ton to know he's there. I believe you."

"Seeing is believing, Ky." I then ask her again, "How about now?

"Are you sure you don't see him?" I ask Kayla again.

Pa waves his arms in the air while Kayla rubs her eyes and concentrates. "What am I supposed to be looking for?"

I get distracted when Pa does a warrior pose. For the last few attempts, Pa's been playing around and doing different yoga poses when I offer him the pastries.

Pa then lies horizontally and starts wiggling his whole body. "Look o, this is called the worm!"

"You seriously don't see anything?" I check with Kayla.

"Is he doing something new?"

I groan. Why isn't the scientific method working???

Pa stands upright and says, "Maybe we shouldn't read too much into this."

"No, I'm sure that had to mean something. Your body was still white before Seph gave me that siopao box."

Kayla's eyes widen. "I didn't know Uncle Ton was white."

"Not *white* white. Like, ghost white."

"Like White Lady white?" Kayla asks, her eyes growing even bigger.

I sigh and distract her by asking about her fruit basket again.

When I messaged Kayla that Ma's siopaos might've turned Pa's ghost more human, she arrived at the condo with the fanciest-looking fruit basket. It's wrapped so elaborately that there are even ribbon bows on some of the apples.

"Do you wanna try the bananas, grapes, mangoes?" Kayla twists the basket so we get a view of every angle.

"Where did you even get the basket?"

"My parents were supposed to use this for the offertory at Sunday Mass."

Stealing a fruit basket from God doesn't bode well for our mission to bargain for Pa's soul.

I try handing Pa a banana and ask Kayla if she sees Pa this time.

"She's not going to see anything," Pa answers on Kayla's behalf.

Oblivious to Pa, Kayla rummages around her fruit basket. "Do you think a mango would work better?"

Then Pa asks, "Superstar, why do you want her to see me so badly?"

I dig through the basket with Kayla, sorting out the fruit, and ignore the rising feeling in my throat. My eyes are already welling up when I think about answering Pa's question. Because if others can see him, then that means Pa is here for real. Then maybe the universe would agree with me that he doesn't have to go away.

Pa floats to the space in front of me so he meets my eye. "I'm here. Only thing that's changed is that I have more blush on my cheeks," he points out. "And that I can say that I'm more good-looking than the other spirits now . . ."

He continues to joke and not take any of this seriously. He can downplay this and do all the yoga poses he wants, but I'm sure that incident at Buns by Beth meant something. My gut tells me that it's the way he can stay past his forty days.

"I'll get more siopaos," I say, and tell Kayla to keep watching in case she suddenly sees Pa. My mind starts to calm down a bit once I leave the bedroom. Maybe if I get a break from Pa's yoga poses and Kayla's fruit basket, I can think more clearly.

Then I hear a voice that wakes my brain right up again.

"Annika!" Auntie Baby startles when she sees me. "Were you hiding out in your bedroom by yourself? Didn't your mom tell you about Auntie Grace's second cousin's ex-boyfriend's niece who got robbed because she was listening to music in her bedroom?"

My head's already throbbing from trying to follow Auntie Grace's family tree. When Ma and Achi are busy at work, Ma sometimes asks Auntie Baby to come over and check in on me. I then usually have to spend hours listening to the drama happening in the alumni association.

I force a smile and make a fuss over checking the time on my watch. "Kayla actually came over and we're doing homework—"

"*We* have a lot of work to do!" She doesn't take no for an answer and tells me to sit with her at the dining table. "I have a million questions about the soiree we're hosting. How many of your classmates are coming? How many pizzas should we order?"

"I'm pretty sure Dani—"

Auntie Baby cuts me off and takes out a thick book from her bag. She holds a finger to her lips when she flips open her Saint Agnes yearbook. "Don't tell your mom that I picked up her copy. She keeps saying that high school is so long ago, but our past is our greatest teacher. The key to being a great event planner is to analyze the mistakes of past events."

She turns the pages to the soiree photo spread. "You see how the boys and girls were so separated in our soiree before?" She points to a picture where the guys crowded the left side of the room and the girls were on the right. "You and Seph should figure out how to make people mingle this weekend."

Out of all the things that I can possibly worry about, making my classmates "mingle" at a soiree comes in dead last.

"Did you and Seph discuss the soiree? Your mom made kwento that he went out of his way to give you a gift pa."

All the adults in my life are making his siopao gift *way* too big of a deal.

She bumps my shoulder then. "Giving baked goods to each other, planning a soiree," she says with a smile. "It's like you're re-creating your parents' love story."

I'm about to refute every word of Auntie Baby's statement when the photo of my parents at the soiree catches my eye. Then I remember how right before Pa's skin color changed, Ma commented how Pa used to buy her siopaos back in high school.

Ma usually stiffens or goes scarily quiet whenever I reminisce about Pa. Achi told me to stop bringing up stories long ago when I mentioned one of Pa's Christmas parties and Ma ended up pulling an all-nighter at the bakery. It's why I started keeping memories of Pa to myself. If my family didn't want to talk about him, I'd go through old photos of Pa on my own. I'd stare at the snowflakes on my bedroom ceiling, shut my eyes, and try to remember what Pa's voice sounded like. Think about all the times his eyes smiled at me when he called me "Superstar."

. . . Is that why I'm the only one who can see him?

I'm the only one in my family who makes the effort to keep memories of Pa alive. Does that give me the power to see his ghost?

Maybe it's not that seeing is believing . . . Maybe it's that *remembering* is seeing.

That's when everything comes together. The answer isn't in the siopaos, it's in the memories!

"Auntie," I interrupt her while she's dropping hints about what color suits me best for a prom dress. "Can you tell me more about my parents' love story?"

19

WHY DID MY PARENTS *HAVE* TO MEET AT A SOIREE?

They could've met in a more pleasant setting, like prison or . . . hell.

I would rather slam my head against the wall a concussion-worthy number of times if that meant I could be anywhere else tonight. It's bad enough that I'm at a soiree, but the fact that I got dragged into cohosting one?

Lord, take me now.

After debriefing my "memories" theory with Kayla and telling her my parents' love story, she insisted that we needed to go to the soiree. "This is even more powerful than any fruit basket, Nika," she urged. "This is your parents' meet-cute."

A big part of me was hoping that Dani would turn me down and say I was too late in RSVPing for the soiree. Unfortunately, she was *thrilled*. When I subtly asked for the soiree details, she quickly added me to her soiree-planning spreadsheet. My email inbox is now full of notifications of Dani tagging me to check on this, follow up on that.

Another hassle of this whole experience is convincing everyone in my life that I'm interested in this thing. When Auntie Baby mentioned that I was cohosting the soiree, she had to keep repeating the line to my family.

"Annika *wanted* to host?" Ma asked for the billionth time.

And Achi followed up with, "She wanted to hang out with boys?"

"Yes." I smiled through my teeth. "Yay, boys."

On the bright side, I didn't need to worry about how I'd get my parents to be in the same soiree. Ma wanted to witness me "cohosting" with her own two eyes and volunteered to take care of the food. There are more pastries in this soiree than in our Christmas noche buena spread.

This all leads me here—getting stuck in Seph's living room and taking orders from Dani all night.

Dani assigned Seph and me to be in charge of welcoming guests and handing out stickers to use for name tags. While Seph King, pro-flirter, is busy mingling with all my classmates, Kayla and I are using Dani's stickers to name different furniture.

I place a sticker on the snack table and write, *Steve.*

Pa listens closely while Kayla and I discuss what name suits the couch. "Aren't you supposed to be making friends at a soiree?"

I gesture to the snack table. "Haven't you met Steve?"

The whole room gets interrupted when Dani calls for everyone to pay attention. She stands in the center of the room and makes sure to wave at each person before speaking. "As class president, I'm all about unity and camaraderie. It's so nice to see the sister and brother schools—Saint Agnes and Saint Francis—come together."

When Dani asked if I wanted to deliver a welcoming speech as the cohost, it took me a while to process that she wasn't joking. I insisted that she should have the honor as our one and only class president.

"Before we start the games and mingling, we wanted to open the night with a soiree success story," Dani says, and waves for Julia and Sean to take the floor.

Julia then goes on with her story on how she and Sean first met at a soiree at the start of the school year. On that fateful night, the two of them locked eyes from across the room and spent the whole evening talking about their shared love of

K-pop and horoscopes. In her words, "He's the Cancer that my Pisces has been looking for."

It reminds me of Dr. Derrick's love story with the moon.

Julia ends her whole speech with a pitch about how a soiree is a great way to find a prom date, or maybe something more *wink* *wink*.

My take: Things like soirees only benefit those like Julia, the ones already highly likely to get over-the-top promposals. Someone who's awkward with guys isn't going to magically turn into a boy whisperer if you stick them in a roomful of guys. It's an excuse for those who are already pros at flirting to keep flirting, and leaves those who are awkward to stay awkward.

Hence Kayla and me, awkward non–boy whisperers, standing by Steve the table next to my ghost father. Seph keeps trying to make eye contact with me all night, but I refuse to engage. I'm still pissed at him for hiding Ma's wedding dress fitting from me.

"Can you please tell me what's in the backpack?" I ask Kayla again. The only reason why Kayla was allowed to go to a soiree was because both Auntie Baby and Ma were here. Still, Auntie Grace gave Kayla the condition that she could only go if she promised to do homework right after. Based on the giant backpack Kayla arrived with, it's like she brought all her school supplies with her.

"Since we wanted to remember your parents' love story, I thought this would help . . ." Kayla unzips her bag and reveals a shoebox stuffed inside. She lifts the lid and it's filled to the brim with folded pieces of paper.

"I thought getting some love notes would help kickstart Auntie Beth's memory," Kayla says. "True or false. This type of romantic gesture always works in the movies. Think *The Notebook, To All the Boys I've Loved Before . . .*"

I unfold one of the papers and Pa reads the note. "*Dear Beth, My love for you is like my body . . . undying.*"

Pa's face almost goes pale again after looking at more notes.

My personal favorite: *Dear Beth, Ten years have passed and you haven't aged a day. Dying didn't make me age too.*

"I don't think your mom would find these romantic," Pa says, stating the obvious.

I mean, of course. These love notes look like letters written by a serial killer, but that doesn't change the fact that Kayla put in a ridiculous amount of effort.

"Maybe this could be plan B?" I offer.

Kayla doesn't look discouraged and pulls out a stack of paper hearts from her backpack's other pocket. "I also made these to get your parents in the mood . . . ," she says, then her face lights up. "What if I stick these on the walls? Maybe that'll remind Auntie Beth of Uncle Ton."

Before Pa or I can chime in, Kayla's already on the hunt for masking tape.

My attention gets diverted when Ma emerges from the kitchen. "Anyone like banana-cue?" She waves a deep-fried banana skewered on a stick. "Don't be shy to ask for more!"

Other mothers might protect their daughters from hanging out with strange boys; my mother, on the other hand, bribes them with food.

Okay, time to rekindle my parents' romance. I maneuvered this perfectly. When Dani told me the date for the soiree, I called Dr. Derrick's office and inquired about his schedule. I made sure Dr. Derrick was unavailable tonight so Ma could pour undivided attention into reminiscing about Pa.

"Work your magic," I whisper to Pa.

He looks at me, perplexed. "What magic?"

"It's a soiree. Isn't this where you and Ma first met?"

My hand sweeps across the room while a group of guys act out a sword fight with barbecue sticks.

"Should I tell your mom that my love for her is like my undying body?"

After hearing my parents' high school love story from Auntie Baby, I was so excited to share my memories theory with Pa—that maybe helping Ma remember her love for Pa could be key to making him less "ghostly." But Pa didn't even give it a chance. He still keeps insisting that him no longer being translucent is no big deal.

Pa falls silent when I don't laugh at his joke.

"So what do you want me to do? Flirt with your mom?"

I smile up at him. "You'll really do it?"

"If it means a lot to you, Superstar. Of course I will." He then hesitates when he spots Ma retreat to the kitchen. "How do I flirt with your mother when she can't see me?"

Hmm. This is the part I didn't think through.

"Try floating around her," I suggest. "You said you guys have some sixth marriage sense, right? Maybe Ma will somehow feel your presence."

After more persisting, Pa finally relents and drifts toward Ma, who's rearranging the dishes on the snack table. He keeps going around Ma in circles, like he's a bird circling his prey instead of a man courting his wife. Maybe my father would have better romantic chances at a zoo.

"Hey, cohost buddy."

I jump when Seph appears behind me out of nowhere. "You still mad?" he asks.

"Nope."

"At least you're talking to me now. That's progress."

I almost give in when I see his nose scrunch again.

"Why are you even at a soiree?" I ask him. "Aren't Saint Agnes moms already begging you to take their daughters to prom?"

"I'm here for emotional support while my friends mingle. A lot of guys in my class aren't as pogi," he says, and I groan.

"Some come to me for advice on flirting," he adds, and I groan even louder.

I'm saved from hearing more about Seph's "flirting" when Dani starts recruiting people for a Never Have I Ever game.

Seph nudges me. "Do you need any help talking to anyone here?"

"From *you*?" I ask.

"Yeah, you know Sean?" He points to Sean of power couple Julia-and-Sean fame. "He asked for my advice when he got paired with Julia for a soiree game before. Now they're going to prom together. Lots of guys got inspired to talk to their crush after seeing how they connected."

And that's when I realize the crucial detail of my parents' meet-cute—the ice game!

My head is buzzing with new possibilities, and Seph is still bugging me about talking to random boys. "If I help you secure a prom date, would that make it up to you?" Seph asks.

"Focus on getting your own date, Moseph."

"Hey, Dani!" I leave Seph and rush toward Ms. Class President while she's asking people to form a circle. "Don't people always do Never Have I Ever at every single party? Have you ever heard of the ice game?"

Once I pitch the game rules to Dani, she's already ordering me to find ice cubes. "I really love how this event is maximizing your potential," she adds.

I bypass my parents and Kayla, who is sticking hearts on the wall, on the way to the freezer. Pa is still hovering aimlessly around Ma.

It's not working, Pa mouths at me, and I flash him a thumbs-up to keep trying. Although, Ma thinks I'm signaling at her so she answers me with her own thumbs-up. "You're having fun, Nika?"

"Super."

Watch me have more fun when I pull off getting your husband back.

This could really be my parents' breakthrough. Pa didn't change colors because he and Ma were flirting. That all happened because Ma saw Seph give me siopaos, which made her remember Pa.

Once Ma sees all these high schoolers awkwardly holding hands with ice cubes, she'll then remember the moment when she awkwardly held hands with Pa. All the memories will rush in, Pa stays for good, Dr. Derrick disappears—a win-win for everyone!

While I station myself at the kitchen counter where I have an optimal view of my parents, Dani marches toward me.

"Hey, Nika, are you seeing anyone?"

My heart stops for a second.

Is Dani trying to signal to me that she can see Pa's ghost too?

"Like, are you and Seph a thing?" she clarifies, and my heart quickly resumes its regular activity.

Never mind. She's asking me about unimportant stuff.

"Did Auntie Baby put you up to this?"

"I just noticed some vibes," she says, and pauses. "Will I get on Auntie Baby's good side if I bring you and Seph together?"

After I tell Dani that my love life will have no merit on her leadership award standing, she waves for a random boy to come over. For some unknown reason, the boy actually follows.

"Why is he walking toward me?" I whisper, trying not to panic as he inches nearer.

"Hans Ang. I overheard him call you cute and his sister used to work in the production crew of some musical you were in."

Before any of this information registers, Dani forces an ice cube in my hand, and the boy is suddenly standing in front of me. "Nika, Hans; Hans, Nika," Dani introduces us. "Enjoy the game!"

My mind is racing for ways to escape when Hans engulfs the ice on my hand with his hand. My eyes scan the rest of the room and everyone else is paired up and "mingling" over ice cubes.

Who in their right mind invented this stupid game?!?!

I try catching Kayla's attention, but Dani got to her first, probably forcing her into holding hands with another strange boy. Meanwhile, Pa is too focused on circling around Ma and enjoying the privilege of being invisible.

After the world's longest stretch of silence, Hans speaks. "Your name is Nika, right?"

"Yes."

"Is it short for anything?"

"Annika."

"Cool."

Another long pause.

God. Why is my heart beating so fast? I'm in the middle of resurrecting a ghost. Talking to a boy shouldn't make me this stressed.

I clear my throat. "And you're Hans? Is that short for anything?"

"Just Hans."

"It'd be funny if your last name were Some."

"Oh, my last name is Ang."

"Right," I say, grateful that the ice is masking the sweat dripping down my palms. "But if it were Some, your name would be Hans Some. Gets?"

"Ahhhh, gets."

Dani then reminds us that we're not supposed to switch partners until the ice cube we're holding fully melts. I suddenly wish I paid more attention in chemistry class. Maybe I missed a lecture where Ms. Abad shared ways on how to increase your body heat.

"You might know my sister . . . ," Hans then mentions. "She used to volunteer for the production crew at all the Trumpets shows. Trixie?"

"Trixie Ang!" I say, excited that we finally reached a topic I can talk about.

"Is she still doing prod work? She was the reason the *High School Musical* set was so good. Trixie has such an eye for detail and she really knows how to light a stage too."

I go on and tell Hans about my first Trumpets musical and how Trixie went above and beyond to make sure my wig looked real for my *Little Mermaid* role.

"Your sister is super talented!" I say. "The only time that the theater acoustics sounded good was when Trixie was handling production. I've always liked your sister. Really, really liked her."

Hans blinks. "Sorry, she's uh . . . taken."

"Oh! No, no, I don't mean I like Trixie in *that* way. I'm not one of *those* girls who like other girls in *that* way."

"Um. My sister is one of those girls who like other girls *that* way."

My face grows hot when I sense the bite in his tone.

"Love that for Trixie! L-love that for other girls too! I love that they can all love one another. We need more love. That could be a great surname too. Hans Love."

While I'm burying myself into an increasingly deeper grave, Hans looks over his shoulder. "I think it's time for us to switch partners."

I glance at the ice in our hands. "I don't think it's melted yet . . ."

Hans nevertheless moves on and leaves me with a half-melted ice cube. To be honest, I don't blame him. It's for the best.

Before anyone else notices that I've been abandoned, Seph swoops in and joins me as my ice game partner.

"Nice to meet you." He reaches out his hand. "I'm Seph Love."

I bite my lip, hating the part of my brain that found that remotely funny.

Dani's timer goes off and she tells people to switch partners while handing out a new batch of ice cubes. She lingers and gives me a knowing look when she passes by Seph and me. I return her look by sticking out my tongue.

The second round of the ice game commences and everyone starts holding hands again. This time, I make sure that my hand is lifted and slightly hovering over Seph's hand and the ice cube. I truly don't get the point of this game. Imagine thinking sparks would fly with someone all over a block of ice.

"Go on with the jokes," I tell Seph. "All the hirit. I can take it."

"Telling a guy his last name could be Love isn't so bad."

"He thought that I was hitting on his sister and then realized I'm actually homophobic."

Seph blinks.

"So . . . you're saying people go to you for flirting advice too?"

I can tell he's holding in a smile. "You're proud of that joke, 'no?"

"Made you laugh," he points out.

I scowl in defiance.

"What made you nervous anyway? Did Hans say anything weird?"

"Dani said he called me cute."

"Oh." His face twists when he realizes I have nothing to add. ". . . How dare he?"

Seph laughs when I elbow him.

"And for your information, I wasn't nervous."

He cocks his head. "So you usually hit on guys through their sister?"

"Moseph, I'm going through a lot right now and talking to guys is the least of my concerns."

His mouth then bunches to the side. "And where does staying mad at me rank in these concerns?"

"Still top priority."

The smile on his face fades and I'm surprised he doesn't reply with a comeback. If I didn't know any better, I would think that Moseph actually looks . . . affected.

"I thought Auntie Beth wanted to surprise you with her wedding dress," he explains. "I didn't know you were going to be hurt—"

"I don't want to talk about it."

"I'm really sorry, Ilagan," he says, ignoring what I *just* said.

I groan. "We're still talking about this?"

"Yeah, I'm still sorry."

Seph finally drops the subject after I stop responding. But just when we settle into semi-comfortable silence, he asks, "Are you still mad at me?"

I want to say no, but from the way he's pouting, it's like turning down a puppy.

"You really can't stand people not liking you, huh?"

He shakes his head.

"There are many benefits to you forgiving me."

I laugh. "Yeah, like what?"

"I can help you with Hans!"

When I shut him down, Seph asks, "Any other guy you're interested in?" He gestures to the Saint Francis class president. "Can vouch for Gio. He's smart and fun."

"Oh, dumb and boring guys are more my type."

He shakes his head, laughing. "Come on. Maybe by the end of this soiree, you'll be able to talk to guys *you* find cute."

"I have no problem talking to you."

The words come out of my mouth without me thinking. I blame the ice. Freezing my hand is messing with the part of my brain in charge of impulse control.

"Don't," I warn Seph in case he gets the wrong idea. Judging from his expression, though, I'm already too late.

"You think I'm cute?" he asks, his cocky grin on full display.

"Nope."

This only makes his smile grow even bigger. "Can't believe Nika Ilagan thinks I'm cute."

"Hey, you know, I think it's time for us to switch partners . . ."

My face flushes when I notice the ice cube Seph's holding has fully melted, and my hand has been resting on his. This is actual skin-to-skin contact. Like, I-can-feel-the-calluses-on-his-fingers type of intimate contact. I know I'm holding Seph's hand, but does this mean that we're actually *holding hands*?!

I stop spiraling when the flash on Auntie Baby's camera almost blinds me and Seph. Our hands immediately spring apart.

"Ay!" Auntie Baby covers her phone's camera lens as if that would hide the fact that she's been recording. "Beth, you didn't tell me the flash was on!"

Great, just what we needed. Enabling Auntie Baby's delusions of pairing her son and me together even more.

But all thoughts related to Auntie Baby's matchmaking go out the window as soon as I notice Ma right beside her. It's her expression when she goes to her scary quiet place again.

"Ma, are you okay?" I reach for her when I see her eyes welling up.

She pats her cheeks and waves me off. "Ah, it's nothing," she says. "Seeing you and Moseph just brings back memories."

Ma leaves the room and I trail her, unsure of what's happening. Pa appears beside me and I whisper-ask him what happened.

"Your mom was just watching you hold hands with Baby's son."

"What? We weren't . . ." I avert my face from him when my cheeks flare up again. *God, Nika, focus! There are way more important things going on than the stupid ice game with Moseph.*

Was this plan too much? Maybe we pushed Ma too far?

I check in on her again. "Ma, are you okay?"

"Go, keep enjoying the games," she says. "I'll just freshen up in the banyo."

Pa's floating in front of the bathroom door when Ma sidesteps around him. "Sorry, excuse me," she says, swerving before she enters.

. . .

Did Ma just swerve around Pa?

Swerving means she must see him, right?!?! One does not swerve for anyone—especially not for invisible people!

"Pa, do you think—"

I stop when I notice his feet, which are now firmly planted on the floor. I frantically check my legs and if everyone else in the soiree noticed anything. People would have some kind of reaction if the world's gravity system suddenly changed, right? My phone would probably be blowing up with breaking news about gravity from my aunties. No, it doesn't look like the world changed . . . Only Pa's ghost did. For the first time since his ghost appeared, Pa isn't floating.

20

"UM. PA?"

"Just a few more minutes, Superstar," he says, squeezing his arms around me.

Ever since Pa could hold physical objects again, he's been hugging me nonstop. I didn't want to sleep last night because I had this fear that I wouldn't get to hug Pa anymore in the morning. Thankfully, the sun rose and Pa's hugs still stayed. I just wish I were better at multitasking since it gets tricky when I need my hands for other things too.

Since Pa still doesn't let go, I use my hip to bump the elevator button for the basement floor. I don't remember the last time I visited our condo's storage area. It must've been around the same time I gave up piano.

His eyes and his same dorky smile light up his face when he sees his old keyboard.

"You kept it?" he asks.

"Thought you'd want to try playing again."

Pa's old keyboard takes up most of the storage space with Ma's boxes stacked around it. Achi was the one who suggested moving things to storage. She gave some excuse about how clutter was bad feng shui, but we both know she was doing it for Ma's benefit. Ma cried every time she saw something in the condo that reminded her of Pa.

He takes a seat on the bench and pats the space next to him. "How about a jam session?"

Pa and I always played the piano together—I would be on

the right playing the high notes and he would be on the left playing the low notes.

"I wanna hear your solo first," I say. He hesitates but doesn't try to convince me to join him. I wonder if Pa already sensed that I don't play anymore. Maybe a gifted piano player could detect when a person abandons the instrument.

He shuts his eyes as he runs his fingers along the keys. "It's like gaining my superpowers again."

"Technically, your invisibility is wearing off, so it's more like you're *losing* your superpowers."

Pa responds by stretching his arms and cracking his knuckles. "Ready to be amazed?" He rolls his shoulders, takes a deep breath, then plays the most exaggerated rendition of "Chopsticks."

I laugh when Pa restarts punching the same keys and singing made-up lyrics to the "Chopsticks" notes.

"This is how I proposed to your mother."

I turn to Pa to make sure he's serious. "By playing 'Chopsticks'?"

"Your mother said yes," he reminds me.

"But you could've at least picked a more romantic song."

Pa chuckles and sighs. "We were so young then, but I already knew I wanted to marry Beth," he shares. "She was worried that we weren't ready, that we were so far from reaching our dreams.

"Then I played her a song." His fingers start a softer, quieter melody. "That's the way I got your mom to relax—by playing her favorite music. We would be sitting next to each other by the piano like this, and she'd tell me about her dreams of owning her own bakery," he says with a smile. "I told her that after we got married, I'd help her put up bakeries around the country.

"I told her that no matter what happened to us, I'd make the dreams of my family come true. Protect her from the things she worries about."

The piano falls silent after he breathes out that last line.

"Sorry I didn't get to do that for you, Superstar," he says, his eyes lingering on the keys. "Wish I could tell your sister that too." His head is bowed, his shoulders drop lower like there's another force weighing on his back.

"Pa, you don't have to—"

But he cuts me off, swiftly changing the subject. I almost tell him that my head feels dizzy every time he takes a detour in our conversations.

"Did you save what I kept inside the bench?" Pa motions for me to stand and props open the lid. He takes out a binder tucked below piles of sheet music and songbooks.

He smiles when he peeks inside. "They're still here."

It's a stack of envelopes, cards, and papers tied together by a rubber band. Pa tells me to check the first one on top and it's a birthday card that has yellow and pink stamps covering every inch of the page. I remember working on a joint birthday card for Pa with Achi and arguing with her that she hogged all the space with her yellow stamps (so I naturally retaliated with my pink stamps).

"Are these all from us?" I ask, scanning the stack.

"Kept everything you girls gave me."

He literally did. There's a paper butterfly folded inside that I made for Pa when I had an "origami" phase.

"You made me promise to keep this in case the butterfly would come to life."

Another memorable fight in the ongoing Nika vs Jackie saga: my sister freaking out when I folded her quiz papers into hearts. She got even more pissed when I said I'd fold her a bigger heart so she wouldn't get mad at me all the time.

"I still have the vision board your sister made in high school."

Oh god. How can I forget about Achi's *vision board*. She took that assignment so seriously that it hijacked our whole bedroom. Everywhere I turned, there were magazine cutouts, colored paper, photo albums. And the few times I would complain about the mess, Achi would always say that I was disrupting her "vision."

Despite multiple previous attempts, this is the first time I'm actually seeing what's inside this famous vision board notebook.

It opens to a pop-up map where you can drag a cutout Jackie in a plane to different parts of the globe. No wonder my sister was salutatorian. She was so extra with every single assignment.

When I grow up, I want to travel to every continent and learn more about how other people in other cultures live their lives. My dream is to get a PhD and see the world.

"Did your achi get to go to Australia yet?" Pa asks. "She told me that would be her first stop."

My sister has never mentioned anything about traveling. Her college friends invited her to go to Boracay after their graduation and she stayed behind because "*What will I learn if I go to the beach?*"

It's why it didn't make sense when I saw her suddenly apply to schools in freaking Florida.

"Maybe Achi's dreams changed when she got older," I tell Pa.

I keep exploring more sections of her notebook when Pa tells me to go to the last page.

Maybe my sister figured out how to add a 3D installation of Florida.

Wait. Why am I in the notebook?

On one of the last few spreads, there's a collage of pictures from my childhood performances. She decorated the area around the collage with stars and music notes too. My sister even saved the ticket stubs to my shows and laminated them so the print hasn't faded one bit.

At the bottom, Achi wrote: *My little sister is my favorite person to watch perform. She's probably going to be a superstar someday.*

I try to wipe my eyes on my sleeve, but Pa already notices. His thumb brushes my cheek when a tear slides down my face. "I thought she hated it when you called me Superstar."

"Why?" he asks. "She called you Superstar first."

But didn't my sister find my singing annoying? During our car rides to school growing up, Achi always said that no one asked to hear me sing when Pa and I had jam sessions.

While I'm still getting choked up on Achi's vision, Pa asks if I can do him a favor.

"I was thinking about writing letters to Beth and Jackie. Would you leave my notes with them?" he asks. "There are things I want to tell them before . . . I go."

It's like the blood in my body goes cold at the thought.

"Maybe you don't have to go."

He's already shaking his head. "Those aren't the rules."

Every time I try reasoning with him, pointing out that we've been breaking all his "rules," he still doesn't budge. If Pa can walk on the ground, if his hands can play the piano, then surely it's a sign that he's coming alive—that he can stay here longer than the forty days.

When he asks me again if I can deliver his letters, an idea dawns on me.

"What if you can talk to Ma and Achi?" I ask.

I keep talking before he has time to argue. "Ma almost saw you during the soiree! If we continue re-creating your memories from high school, maybe Ma can see you for real.

"What if Achi could see you too? Pa, maybe this is your chance to get to talk to them again, do a proper goodbye."

For the first time, Pa doesn't change the subject. He actually looks like he's considering what I said when I see the slight glimmer in his eyes. He takes a deep breath and asks, "So what memory do we do next?"

I go over my ideas, asking for more details from Pa's high school memories. Every time he shows any doubt, I remind him about the possibility of Achi and Ma seeing him.

I don't mention that I'm still holding on to the hope that this is the way Pa could stay for good.

21

THE NEXT DAY, I VISIT THE GUIDANCE COUNSELOR'S OFFICE SO I CAN request my sister's permission to re-create another part of our parents' love story. If the soiree was able to make Pa solid, maybe joining Battle of the Bands would finally make my family see him. Re-creating the moment Pa asked Ma to prom must rank pretty high in memories that would trigger a ghost's resurrection.

Even though Saint Francis is the one hosting the Battle of the Bands event, Saint Agnes has some weird rule where we have to secure admin permission before participating in other schools' programs. My sister had to sign five permission slips for Julia last year since she got invited to the proms of five different all-boys schools.

Achi narrows her eyes at me when I take the seat across from her desk. "Are you trying to get out of chemistry again?"

"No."

"You're in trouble with Ma again?"

"No."

Well, not currently. I think.

I take out the permission slip from my bag and place it on Achi's desk. "Do you mind reviewing this for me?

"Thanks," I add when Achi picks up the paper.

Suspicion still clouds her face. "You've been acting so weird."

It's because I've forgotten how to act around my sister.

Whenever I want to make a joke or snap back at her when she tells me I'm doing something wrong again, I just keep thinking, *My sister thinks I'm a star*. This morning, she accused me of eating the star-apple fruit she left in the fridge and my brain thought Achi was calling me "star apple."

How am I supposed to get mad at her when she has *that* hanging over me?!

"Since when did you have a band?" Achi asks after reading my permission slip.

"Trying something new."

Do you still think I'm a star?

Achi frowns at the print. "Your band name is *The Band*?"

"It's *very* new." So since I know that Achi secretly thinks I sparkle onstage, I've been very confident that she'd automatically sign off on my band proposal.

It's my fault that I forgot that my sister is still my sister.

"I can't approve of a band that only has one person," she protests.

"It's not just one person," I say. "Kayla is with me."

"Kayla plays an instrument?"

"Yes . . . her voice."

Achi tilts her head, throwing me her resting constipated face. "Saint Francis also has guidelines that require all participating bands to have at least one Saint Francis student."

"Yeah, Seph is playing guitar." I peek at the form, bullshitting out of my pants. "I must've forgotten to write that there."

Achi sighs and puts down the form. "Nika, these interschool activities aren't meant for you to flirt."

"I'm not signing up to flirt," I argue, feeling my face go hot at the baseless accusation. "Also, you literally sign off on my classmates so they can flirt at prom! My request is for a celebration of *music*."

She answers me with a scoff. "I heard what happened at the soiree."

I stop short. Could Achi possibly be talking about Pa? Does she secretly see his ghost too?

Then she says, "Heard your classmates talking about you and Seph."

Again, big fan of chismis—probably my favorite form of entertainment. However, gossip is always better when *I'm* not the topic of conversation. Are people seriously talking about the ice game between me and Seph? Are they talking about it over at Saint Francis too? I get that we go to Catholic schools, but surely, there must be more scandalous things happening.

"Ma was so happy that you were actually participating in something for once. What am I going to tell her if she finds out you were making out with Auntie Baby's son in their living room?"

Excuse me?

"What?! All we did was play the ice game."

Achi pauses. "You were making out with ice?"

"No!" I say, and have to explain yet again the mechanics of this ridiculous ice game.

Her mouth's pinched when she inspects my face. "So . . . you and Seph aren't MOMOL buddies?"

"I don't even know what that means."

"Your other classmates use that term," Achi says in defense, and her cheeks go pink. "They say it's like friends with benefits. The benefits being making out—"

"No." I shut her down before she explains further. "We're not buddies, no friends with benefits. Absolutely no benefits to our friendship.

"You need to get better at gossiping," I tell Achi.

She scoffs at this and goes back to reading my slip. Thankfully, clearing the air makes my sister more cooperative about my Battle of the Bands inquiry.

After she asks more logistical questions, she suddenly says, “If there is something going on with Seph, you can . . . talk to me about it.”

“Achi, for the last time, we didn’t make out in Auntie Baby’s living room.”

“No, not that,” she says, and corrects herself. “I mean, also that. But maybe not yet. You’re so young and there are more appropriate places than our aunties’ homes—”

“Are you okay?” I ask when her words stop making sense.

Achi sighs. “I’m your sister, so we’re supposed to share things.”

“We don’t share.”

“We share!” she insists.

“Okay.” I fold my arms. “Have *you* had any MOMOL buddies lately?”

Her cheeks flush even harder at that. “Again, you’re too young.”

“Cool. Maybe when I’m thirty, we can try sharing then.”

Achi weighs my words and leans back on her desk chair. After a beat, she slides her phone toward me.

“Oh my god. Are you letting me read your messages?”

“Sira.” Achi rolls her eyes and makes sure I don’t scroll past the email on the screen.

“Remember that psychology program in Florida that I applied to for fun?”

“Yeah?” I focus my gaze on her phone, hoping Achi doesn’t hear how fast my heart starts beating from reading the University of Florida offer letter.

“They answered back today that they had a slot open,” Achi says like it’s nothing. “Funny, right?”

I catch the huge *Congratulations* on the letter, the part where they rave about how Jackie Ilagan was one of this year’s most impressive applicants, the section about getting offered funding and a scholarship. My eyes then search my sister's. "But you're not going . . . ?"

"No, Nika." She breathes out and takes back her phone. "This is me sharing. You can tell me what's going on with you. Even the small things."

"You sure you don't want to share anything about your love life?"

Achi groans and signs my slip. "Don't make me regret this."

When I stand and make my way out of the guidance office, I catch Achi still scrolling through the letter on her phone. It's suddenly so obvious that her applying to this program was never a joke.

I wasn't telling the truth with Pa earlier. I don't think my sister grew out of the dreams in her vision board.

22

SETTING FOOT INSIDE AN ALL-BOYS SCHOOL FEELS LIKE GETTING transported to a different planet. Like, how can there be classrooms, cafeterias, libraries—but with *just* boys??? How do they make sure that the place does not spontaneously combust at any moment?

The last time I was here, it was when Auntie Baby invited our family for Moseph's grade school graduation. I still vividly remember sweating my face off since the auditorium had no air-conditioning. Imagine having a school just for boys and skimping on the air-conditioning. That's basically creating a hot spot for body odor.

Thankfully, it's not so stuffy inside the auditorium this time around. Or maybe my senses haven't woken up yet since it's early morning.

"Doo-doo-doo, dow." Kayla attempts to sing the ad-libs of "Always Be My Baby" once again. I still have no idea how she manages to hit four different keys with each "doo" syllable, and how every one of those keys are off pitch.

Pa scribbles his feedback on the whiteboard in the room. Since he can hold things now, we discovered that he's able to communicate with Kayla through writing. When I ask Kayla what she sees, she says it's like watching the marker floating and moving on its own.

Kayla reads Pa's writing on the board. *You forget your breathing when you're nervous.*

"See?" Kayla then tries to shoo me away again. "Can you stay somewhere else?"

"I've been sitting here quietly!"

And it's true! I've been keeping my thoughts about Kayla's atrocious singing to myself . . . mostly.

"You're making me forget my breathing!" she protests.

I turn to Pa for backup, but he doesn't come to my defense. "Maybe more space can help Kayla with her process, Superstar."

Apparently, the only person who doesn't give Kayla stage fright is my invisible father. So I put up my hands, give Kayla some space for her "process," and retreat to the backstage area. Unlike the soiree plan, Pa has been fully focused and committed to making this Battle of the Bands memory happen. And when we do pull this off, make Ma and Achi see Pa again, that will solve everything! Ma will forget about Dr. Derrick and Achi will forget about Florida. Win-win for my family and lose-lose for the dentist and Florida.

After I built the imaginary band, I thought that Seph would be the harder one to convince. Plot twist: Kayla's situation was the real logistical nightmare. Since Kayla has Honesty Club meetings and church commitments going on after school, her only free time to rehearse is *before* class starts. I actually offered that we wing it and do the Battle of the Bands on the spot, but Kayla insisted on practicing.

"Your mom's not going to remember your dad's performance if we don't make this special," she said.

And I know I should be grateful that Kayla's going so far as to learn how to sing for this plan, but her calling this a "performance" makes *me* forget how to breathe. Because what if I'm not capable of performing anymore? What if I end up choking like last time?

I make sure the area is vacant and I'm alone when I sit in front of the abandoned keyboard behind the stage. During the past few mornings, I've been telling Kayla I need to catch up on homework and that I already practice a lot at home.

At least I'm better than Seph. I'm not so self-absorbed to say that "I don't need to practice."

In line with Moseph's King brand of humility, Seph responded to my band invite by bragging that he's the reigning Saint Francis champion of the soloist category: "I wouldn't mind winning the band category too."

In any other situation, I'd take a statement like this from Seph as an opportunity to challenge and humble him. His cockiness is how I ended up winning the better role in *The Little Mermaid*.

Then I saw how simple playing the guitar was for Seph.

He skimmed the sheet music for Ma's favorite song and played it in one go, like he hardly gave it a second thought. Seph didn't seem to care at all that Kayla and I were watching him with his guitar. Playing in front of people doesn't come easily for me anymore.

My palms slam on the keys when I see someone's silhouette peeking from the curtains.

"Why'd you stop?" Seph says when he emerges from the shadows.

I try to look unfazed even though my heart's still racing. "Did Auntie Baby never teach you manners?"

Seph ignores that and slides next to me on the bench. "I haven't heard you play since we were rehearsing the 'Soaring' song."

When I shoot him a confused look, he starts playing the opening riff to "Breaking Free."

I laugh. "How are you so bad at remembering song titles?"

"Never stopped me from remembering the lyrics." He taps his temple and continues playing. "We're soaring, flying . . ."

Seph pauses singing and turns to me.

"There's not a star in heaven that we can't reach," I recite, completely monotone.

His shoulder bumps me. "See? Your pitch got even better."

I roll my eyes while Seph tells me to take over.

"No."

"Come on. Please," he keeps urging. "That bit I heard was so good."

For the record, I'm mortified and incredibly pissed that Seph spied on me playing. But still. Part of me wants to know.

"You thought I was good?" I ask.

His eyes crinkle when he smiles up at me. "I'll let you know if you play again."

"Never mind." I groan and unfold the cloth cover back on top of the keyboard.

"Why don't you perform anymore?" he asks.

"Never liked it."

"Bullshit," Seph calls me out. "You loved it."

I shrug. "I don't think theater was ever for me. And I've been busy."

"With what?"

My head turns in his direction. "For your information, I have a very packed academic schedule."

I take my laptop out of my bag and place it on top of the keyboard controls to prove my point. "I was working on a big paper before you interrupted."

"Looks like you're making great progress," he comments, sounding weirdly amused.

When I look back, I see my computer opened to my working document of nicknames I have for Dr. Derrick. The doc is labeled *An Ode to a Pervy Dentist.*

"It's a . . . creative assignment."

"Here." He swivels the laptop toward him and starts typing.

Beneath my entry *Derrick the Human Root Canal,* Seph writes, *Derrick the Oral Overlord.*

I quickly type, *um. EW????*

Seph smirks.

It super sounds like a bad guy in a movie.

I type: *Yeah. A porn movie*

Just continuing your ode to the pervy dentist.

We keep taking turns writing, and the document gets filled with more and more possible nicknames for Dr. Derrick, his suggestions more X-rated than mine.

Did you hear? Seph glances at me before he types, *Gab Pangilinan is going to be a guest mentor in this summer's workshop.*

"Are you serious?!" I ask him out loud.

Gab Pangilinan was the first theater actress I ever saw in person. During the summer of my very first Trumpets workshop, we took a field trip to watch a production of the musical *Mula sa Buwan*. Our teacher told us that the lead actress, Gab, used to attend the Trumpets summer workshops, too, and that blew my mind. My whole world shook at the idea that someone from where I was could end up onstage, singing and performing in theaters full of that many people.

"Did they confirm she's mentoring? How often is she going to be there? Is she actually teaching?" My whole chest starts humming when I start remembering watching *Mula sa Buwan* live, the moments I listened to the soundtrack on repeat and imagined that I was the one singing, the times I actually got to perform onstage and felt the most delirious, soul-invigorating joy when I got lost in a character or a story.

Anywhere else, I'm a regular old drop in the ocean. But when I stepped on that stage? I felt like a tidal wave ripping through all that surrounded me.

I have a million more questions but stop when I notice Seph smirking at me. "I thought you said theater wasn't for you?"

He's right. That life isn't for me. I don't get to be the tidal wave. I'm the person who gets knocked over and nearly drowns from trying to catch up with the current.

"It's not," I say firmly, going back to focusing on my laptop and shutting down all urges to ask more about Gab Pangilinan.

Then I see Seph type another question. *Why did you quit Trumpets?*

I frown at the screen. *Next question.*

Sorry. Not allowed. He pushes the computer toward me and shrugs when I side-eye him.

Brings back bad memories, I answer.

What do you mean?

Long story. My hands pause before adding, *Haha I'm sure me performing reminds you of bad memories too.*

His brow furrows at my joke and he takes the conversation off the screen. "What do you mean?"

"When I didn't show up for opening night," I remind him. "Bad Luck Ilagan, right?"

Seph's face only grows more confused. When I explain to him what I overheard the last time I visited the Trumpets studio almost five years ago, his gaze suddenly softens.

"You heard that?"

I shrug so he thinks it's no big deal.

Seph frowns and shakes his head. "I was so mad when Kevin kept saying we shouldn't say your name since it's bad luck. Direk Myka switched the basketballs to these softball props because I kept 'accidentally' almost hitting Kevin in our next shows—"

"Wait. That wasn't you?"

"Oh, you heard about the time I hit Kevin in the head? He was fine. The basketball barely touched him."

"No," I say. "I meant saying my name was bad luck . . . I thought you started it."

His face tightens then. "You thought I'd do something like that?"

"Isn't that why you started calling me Ilagan?"

"Yeah, cuz I was fed up with Kevin's stupid joke!" he cries out. "You know, I think the people at Trumpets believe you're our lucky charm now. I always mention your name during our pre-show circles and no actor has forgotten any of their lines since."

Seph's cheeks are flushed and he looks so flustered, but I keep thinking how this might rank in the top five sweetest things anyone has ever done for me. It would've even made it to top three if not for the revelation about my sister thinking I'm a star.

Then he goes on a huge rant about how I could ever accuse him of starting a joke like that. His hair looks like he's been electrocuted since he's been combing his hair with his hands so much from the stress. "Why would you ever think I'd say you were bad luck?"

"I—I thought you were upset that I didn't make it to our show." My chest tenses when I go back to opening night.

That's the moment Seph looks me in the eye. "Ilagan, you were going through a lot that summer."

The mention of Pa almost escapes my mouth, but this whole conversation already feels way too personal.

Silence hovers around us until Seph starts typing on my laptop again. I've been so focused on our conversation that I haven't noticed how close our hands have drifted to each other. I get distracted from noticing the color of Seph's eyelashes when he pivots my computer screen to my line of sight.

Does performing remind you of my cute face, though?

Ugh. I knew he'd never let me live that down.

Don't remind me of more *bad memories.*

The familiar nose scrunch pops up when he reads the screen. He takes longer to type out his response and I start noticing more little things about Seph. How he always smiles with his whole face, how his cologne smells like a blend of vanilla and fresh laundry, how I don't hate the feeling of having his hand so close to mine.

He finally spins the computer back and my breath hitches when I feel his pinkie graze the side of my finger.

Then I read:

FYI. You don't remind me of bad memories, Ilagan. Everything's good when I think of you.

. . .

What the fuck does that mean?!

My whole face feels like it's burning while the screen's cursor keeps blinking, begging for me to reply. This isn't how Seph and I talk. When I tell a joke, he's supposed to tease me and joke back! What does it mean when he says he *thinks* of me?

. . . What does it mean when I've been thinking of him too?

Our eyes don't meet, yet I feel our fingers intertwine, making the whole world somersault inside my chest. We're not stuck in some stupid soiree game; there's no melting ice cube housed between our palms. Seph and I are holding hands. It's a fact that's getting harder and harder to dispute the longer we stay like this.

"Nika!"

My hand immediately pulls back and Seph catches my laptop from falling off the piano when Kayla's footsteps thunder through the backstage. "I think I figured out how to sing on key!"

I stand up so quickly that my knees click. "Did you hear that, Seph? Kayla sang on key!"

"G-great!" Seph agrees, echoing my enthusiasm. Electrocuted hair making a comeback. "On-key singing! My favorite kind."

We both scutter out of that area, and I stow away my computer, cleaning up all evidence of what just happened.

23

EVEN THOUGH NON-SAINT FRANCIS STUDENTS CAN ATTEND EVENTS like Battle of the Bands, the place is still like a modern-day parting of the Red Sea. Groups of girls hang on one side while all the guys stay on the other—the perfect endorsement for same-sex education.

When Kayla and I entered the auditorium, we recognized a few Saint Agnes girls among the crowd. The patron couple of Saint Agnes and Saint Francis, Julia and Sean, were already mingling before the program started (while dressed in matching couple T-shirts).

"Who are you here for?" Julia asked when she saw me.

"For the music!" I answer, and then she and Sean give me this knowing look. As if the only reason I'd be at the Saint Francis Battle of the Bands event is for some boy!

There should be a way to broadcast my intentions for attending an event. For example, people need to be aware that I'm here for the noble cause of reuniting my parents and bringing back my dead father—not that I care what people at school think. Who cares if my classmates think that Seph is my MOMOL buddy? Joke's on them since Seph and I have never made out! He even acts like us holding hands had never happened! Not one message, call, DM, nothing!

And I haven't given him any thought either. Every time I check my phone, my eyes don't even search for Seph's name in my notifications. I already know he's not going to be there.

Thank goodness I'm a chill person who's always unbothered.

And I have way bigger things to think about, noble causes,

in fact! My eyes keep searching the audience for any signs of Ma and Achi—the reserved seats under my name are still empty.

"Moseph's competition is . . . interesting," Pa says after Liam, another soloist contestant, goes on.

This is the second guy who's attempted to sing a BINI song. Before the band rounds, we have the unfortunate honor of sitting through all the Saint Francis soloists. To be fair, this guy might have done our nation's girl group justice if he wasn't doing such aggressive screams and choreography. He had to restart the song after his voice cracked and he knocked over the microphone stand from a failed backflip.

Maybe this is the real curse that manifested after breaking Ma's superstitions.

"Can't believe this is how you asked Ma to prom."

The girls in the front duck for cover when Liam braces himself and announces he's going to end the performance by crowd surfing. Thankfully, the host intervenes before there are any casualties.

"She found it romantic that I serenaded her," Pa points out.

I cringe thinking about getting sung to in front of the whole of Saint Agnes *and* Saint Francis. "At least you picked something better than 'Chopsticks' . . ."

The host onstage is going down his list of sponsors to thank for tonight's event when Pa asks me the most random question. "Are you thinking of asking anyone to prom?"

"Not really the serenading type, Pa."

"There are other ways of asking," he says. "The boy earlier seemed to appreciate cartwheels."

Pa keeps suggesting more ways I can ask guys out, so I say, "I'm not going to prom."

The smile in my dad's eyes slightly dims. "But you always wanted to."

Back when Achi was going to her prom, I remember asking Ma if I could dress up and go with her too. It wasn't that I found prom appealing—I just always wanted to go wherever Achi went. Pa found me sulking in my bedroom when I wasn't allowed to go.

He promised me he would take me once it was time for my prom.

"Not really . . . ," I say, clearing my throat. ". . . I was only gonna go if you were taking me."

Pa motions for me to give him another hug and I play it cool even though my whole heart hums every time I'm in his arms. Another soloist goes on to perform a Bruno Mars cover when I hear Pa whisper, "It's a good thing I'm going to be here then."

I smile up at him. It's the first time he's talking about something in the future. Maybe we're aligned in thinking we can find a way to make him stay . . .

"But I wouldn't mind if you wanted to take Baby's son too."

My body recoils at the suggestion. "You like him, right?" he asks.

"What?"

"Moseph." Pa declares his name like it's a fact.

"*No.*" I hear my voice crack like Liam's so I tone it down. Lower, more unbothered. "No," I regroup and say casually. "Your head must've gotten dizzy when you turned solid, Pa."

"The heart speaks a different song when it's in fancy," he says, reciting another one of his confusing proverbs.

"My heart doesn't speak songs and nothing about me is fancy," I protest. "Plus, I don't know Seph that well," I say even more casually. "He's just our neighbor, an acquaintance, a neighborly acquaintance, you can say."

"Aren't you friends?"

"Well, yes," I say, and feel compelled to add, "but we're definitely not buddies."

His forehead creases. "There's a difference between friends and buddies?"

Yes, apparently some people attach the word MOMOL to buddies. And to be clear, Seph and I are definitely not *that*.

After the host has to cut off the Bruno Mars soloist from extending his set, the program segues to thank all the sponsors for Battle of the Bands once again. This time, the host says he wants to switch things up. "Sound booth, can you give me a beat?" he yells out, and proceeds to . . . rap about all the event sponsors.

"BDO, BDO, we find ways with BDO. Even those with BO wanna bank with B-D-O!"

The whole first row looks perplexed as the host raps some more bars, continuing to try to rhyme the name of a bank and body odor. They should've given more air time to the Bruno Mars songs instead.

My ears are cringing from listening to more rapping about bodily smells when I hear Pa's question. "How does he handle it?" Pa asks. "Not having his dad around?"

"Moseph?" I confirm, and he nods.

"He has a dad. Uncle Francis."

Pa considers this, then says, "Maybe things are better now."

After all that buildup, he proceeds to drop the subject and focuses back on the host's sponsor rapping. Uncle Francis isn't always around, but that's because his job requires him to go on work trips abroad. And even if he's stationed in Amsterdam, Auntie Baby always talks about him.

So I ask, "What were things like before?"

"It's not my story to tell, Nika. And spreading chismis isn't healthy for people your age."

Doesn't Pa know that people *thrive* on chismis? It's why Ma and her friends have such healthy skin.

I still nudge Pa about it again.

"I thought you and Moseph aren't friends?" he teases.

"Yes, but my father taught me that I should be concerned about all people, even my acquaintances."

There's a hint of a smile in Pa's eyes when he says, "You must have a good dad then."

"He's all right. Not the most *lively* one," I joke, and Pa lets out a small chuckle.

After there's a commotion backstage with committee members signaling to cut out the rapping, the host spits out one last bar about Nestlé being "the corporate world's Beyoncé" before getting back on track and announcing that it's time for the final soloist contestant. "Are you all ready for our reigning Saint Francis soloist champion?" Most of the cheers that erupt are from Auntie Baby and the blow horn she brought with her.

"Ladies and gentlemen, to the stage . . . Seph King!"

Pa keeps shooting me looks while I clap for Seph's entrance. "Pa," I remind him. "Neighborly acquaintances."

"All right." He crosses his arms over his chest, still glancing at me.

"Also, why are you encouraging this? If people my age shouldn't chismis, then we shouldn't be dealing with dating and those feelings too."

Pa's smiling when he shakes his head. "Superstar, you feel the *most* at your age."

I scoff under my breath. Pa should notice how much progress I've made with controlling my feelings. I basically have none at this point!

The applause gets louder when Seph speaks into the mic. "Good evening, Saint Francis!" he yells, and I hear Auntie Baby's screams from where we are. "It's an honor to play for you once again. My name is Seph King, and I'll be performing Moira Dela Torre's cover of 'Torete.'"

My body goes still when I hear the song title.

Seph starts plucking his guitar and Pa asks me, "Did you tell him?"

"Years ago . . ." But Seph couldn't have remembered. We were just kids at our first theater workshop when I told Seph that Pa played this song during one of my very first piano lessons. That hearing Pa play "Torete" is what made me first fall in love with the instrument.

While Seph strums the opening notes, I can feel my fingers following along, tracing the notes as if I were playing the piano along with him. Then the guitar quiets, and Seph holds on to the mic. "Sandali na lang . . . ," he sings softly.

After the initial start, his voice grows fuller as he swings his guitar to his front and starts playing. Seph's eyes then shut when he hits the high notes, and I remember how I always thought that Seph sings like how other people pray. There was a time when he never opened his eyes when he sang or even listened to music. I asked him about it once and he said that he didn't want the outside world bothering him.

My chest buzzes watching him pour his whole being into building the tension to the booming chorus. Another thing that I'll never admit to Seph's face: I can see why people get crushes on him after watching him perform. I think he likes picking love songs because he sells them so convincingly. Hearing him sing the lyrics with such pleading and conviction . . . it's really hard not to buy that he means every single word.

Once he gets more of the crowd's attention, and the music builds to the chorus, I see that familiar glint in his eyes. Seph and I always had that in common—we really love showing off.

"Your mom liked this song too," I hear Pa say beside me.

Everyone finds this song romantic. I did, too, when Pa first played it, but years later, when I actually *read* the lyrics? I discovered it was incredibly depressing.

"Torete" is basically a song where this girl sings about how she's head over heels for someone to the point that she says lines like, *I hope the sky will reach your smile.* But wait, there's more. She then goes on to say that she wouldn't even force the person to like her back, then proceeds to repeat over and over again that she'll still be crazy over them until the song fades into silence.

We never even hear the other person's side. We don't know if they'd answer back with *I hope the stars meet your dimples* or whatever lyric singers find romantic. In summary, it's a drawn-out, one-sided love tragedy with a good melody.

If I'm supposed to be "feeling the most" right now, I don't want any business with these "Torete"-type feelings. No thank you. Why would I want to be in that situation—liking someone so desperately that I wouldn't care whether they liked me back?

That sounds awful.

By the time Seph hits the outro, he asks the audience to flash their phone lights and sway to the beat. My eyes scan all the people swaying and singing along, then I feel a tug in my heart when I find Ma's face.

She's sitting with Achi in the reserved section for friends and family, and my mind travels back to five years ago.

That night, the last time I was supposed to perform in

our Trumpets show, I overheard Achi in Ma's bedroom. I hid behind the door and peeked at Achi consoling Ma. In the middle of Ma's sobbing, I caught what Ma kept repeating.

"I'm scared that she'll remind me of Ton."

The sound of Ma crying kept ringing in my ear later in the bathroom when I was gasping for air.

I've already seen what happens when someone feels too much.

They get hurt.

24

IT'S LIKE EVERYTHING ELSE IN THE AUDITORIUM DISAPPEARS.

The host announces onstage that it's our band's turn, and all I can think is: *My mom is watching.*

The feedback screeches through the room when Kayla holds on to the mic—and my mom is watching.

Seph plugs his guitar into the amp, the screen behind the stage shows live footage of him and Kayla onstage—still, my mom is watching.

My feet are glued to the floor when Seph and Kayla glance at me, lost at why I'm still stuck on the side of the stage and haven't joined them. "Nika," I hear Pa whisper. "Are you all right?"

The last time I froze this badly, I never even made it to the theater.

My hand goes to my chest, my pulse is ringing in my ears, my breaths keep getting heavier.

You're Bad Luck Ilagan. No one can count on you. Why would they when you make everyone's life harder?

Then Pa calls out to me again. He extends his hand and the throbbing in my brain slowly settles. I don't know if it's the work of some higher power or the fact that Kayla starts harmonizing in questionable keys, but I find the will to make my feet move to the front.

Then I'm there.

Sitting at the piano bench onstage.

With Ma watching.

Seph plays the opening notes, Kayla enters with the ad-libs, and this is supposed to be my cue. It's like everything tightens, from my throat all the way to the tips of my fingers. The music keeps happening around me, and I sit there, doing absolutely nothing.

"Hey, hey." Pa takes a seat beside me in front of the piano, blocking my view of the crowd. "Don't mind them. It's just the two of us."

"I'm s-sorry." My voice cracks at the thought of me falling apart in front of my dad.

Then my insides steady when I feel his grip on my wrist, right above my hair tie.

"I used to get so nervous before performing too, Superstar."

My eyes widen at the implausible idea that Pa ever felt nervous.

"You know my trick?" he asks. "Other musicians, they get so distracted by looking at everything. But me? I only focus on the people I want to see."

I hear Seph restart the song in the background and Pa's hands fall on the piano, playing the opening notes for me. When I slowly join him and my fingers start to find the keys, he lets go bit by bit until suddenly, I'm taking over. As we reach the song's bridge, I feel Pa bobbing his head and smiling right next to me. I laugh when he even starts clapping along to one of the cheesiest songs in the world. For a moment, I close my eyes, not wanting the outside world to ruin whatever's happening.

My heart feels like it's lodged in my throat when we get nearer to the final chorus. Seph sings the lyrics about being part of someone indefinitely and how time can't erase something so strong between two people.

I hope Pa knows this is what I've been wanting to tell him for the past five years.

Pa reaches for me during the song's last few lines and I

brush the scar above his left eye. He leans closer and the mic catches Pa's voice when he sings to me that I'll always be his baby.

It's only later on that I find out that my sister heard his voice too.

25

I DON'T CONSIDER MYSELF A SORE LOSER. IT'S NOT SORE LOSING WHEN we were *robbed* from winning.

The Battle of the Bands judges wanted audience participation? Check. The whole auditorium was singing along during every chorus of our set.

Stage presence? Check. Did they not see how breezy and dreamy Kayla's doo-doo-doos were?! I bet *they* couldn't learn how to sing in tune if they were given a week.

It factor? We had a literal ghost join us onstage. We had an it factor from a different dimension!

The judges not only deprived us of an award, they also had the audacity to rationalize why we didn't *deserve* an award. When they declared the band after us as the winner, one judge added, "We actually had a hard time picking between Mercury Retrograde and The Band. But since The Band had to redo their song, it was obvious who our champion tonight should be."

He wagged his finger in our direction before saying, "Lesson for all you kids: Life doesn't give you any redos."

If Mariah Carey had to clear her throat and redo the beginning of a song before delivering an otherworldly vocal performance, would these judges also rob her in broad daylight?!

"Didn't you say we could just 'wing' the performance?" Kayla asks after she dragged us back to this forsaken auditorium.

"I'm not upset," I tell her again.

"Then why are you stabbing the mango?"

She glances at the spoon I'm holding with a death grip. I

smile and let go, showing Kayla that I'm calmly enjoying the fruit basket she brought for our "celebration."

But really. Why are we even celebrating right now?! Last night, Kayla sent a message that we should meet at the Saint Francis auditorium before class since it's our last school day before Christmas break and we should celebrate a "great performance." She also brought another one of her parents' fruit baskets with her for us to all share. I was going to reply that I wasn't in the mood or some BS excuse about catching up on all the work before Christmas break when I saw Seph's message.

sounds good. see you guys then!

Keep in mind: This is the first time he's messaged me since we held hands. Actually, no. I've decided that I remembered that moment incorrectly. Seph and I never held hands! We barely make eye contact as it is. Honestly, the next time I run into him in the condo elevator, I can't promise that I'd recognize him.

And as I'm trying to relax and enjoy a mango while we're seated on the stage, Kayla whispers to me.

"Is this because of your dad?"

The mango skin breaks when I jab it too hard with my spoon. "It's not!" I snap. Was I disappointed that my family still couldn't see my dad after the performance? When Achi and Ma woke up this morning without any mention of Pa's spirit? Of course I was. But the key to success is pushing through disappointment. I also expected the performance to have *some* effect on Ma, yet she was on the phone with Dr. Derrick all night talking about scheduling some appointment, most likely something wedding-related.

When Pa told me that he wanted to stay home today to look through more of the photos and letters that were stashed in his piano bench, I was completely calm. I'm definitely not panicking that it's mid-December, which means we only have mere weeks until his forty days are up.

Then Seph asks, "Is that a book behind the bananas?"

Kayla is peeling one of the oranges when she says, "Dani must've left it there."

"Dani? Like Danielle Bautista?"

Kayla nods.

"Like class president, future dictator Dani?"

She looks up from the orange in her hands to swoop in as Dani's defense. "She's actually a big supporter of democracy."

I choose to leave the discussion about Dani's politics for another day. "Why would her book be in one of your parents' offertory baskets?"

"Oh, I didn't get the basket from my parents," she explains. "The fruits are from Dani."

Seph and I exchange looks then, and I momentarily forget that I'm supposed to be ignoring him. I must not be the only one who thinks sending a fruit basket sounds like flirting. Didn't Ma's whole thing with Dr. Derrick start because she got so turned on when he gave her a care package? In a Venn diagram of romantic gestures, I'm pretty sure care packages and fruit baskets go in the same circle.

I should know if there's something going on with Kayla and Dani, right? I mean, Kayla's my best friend and I'm always *very* aware of Dani's presence.

"Dani gave you a basket?" Seph clarifies.

"Yeah," Kayla says like it's no big deal. "There's an open forum at our Honesty Club meetings so she knows how nervous I was about singing," Kayla shares, her face starting to drip with kilig. "I think I mentioned once how it'd be so nice to be given a fruit basket, and I guess she remembered. The fruit basket is to congratulate our band."

I thought Kayla only reserved this giddy look on her face for Kathryn Bernardo. She looks like she has a whole banana stuck in her cheeks from how hard she's smiling.

Momentarily pausing my silent treatment toward Seph, I tell him to pass the book in the basket. It's a copy of *To All the Boys I've Loved Before*—a movie that Kayla has been obsessed with since the dawn of time. When I turn to the page that's flagged, I notice the writing on the bookmark.

Orange you glad you joined Honesty Club? I am. Always thought you were one in a melon :)

Below some fruit doodles, there's a question written in the same handwriting.

Wanna go to prom together?

Oh. My. God.

"Kayla!" I exclaim, and she almost drops her orange. "You got a promposal!"

"What! Where?" Kayla scans the auditorium instead of the book I'm holding.

I show her the bookmark so it's loud and clear. "Dani asked you to prom!"

And it's like I can almost hear the fireworks going off in Kayla's head. Her voice is so quiet when she asks, "Are you sure it's Dani?"

My hand turns over to the back of the bookmark that's labeled *Property of Danielle Bautista, Saint Agnes Student Council President.*

Then the banana-size smile envelops Kayla's whole face. "Can't believe that Dani is a banger for me."

"A bang what?" Seph asks, and I tell him it's an inside joke.

Kayla keeps gazing at the bookmark, but I catch how her shoulders start to slump. "I can't believe I missed the promposal."

"But you have *prom* to look forward to," Seph interjects.

Her shoulders slump even farther.

"My parents are never going to let me go," she says, her hands fiddling with the orange peels. "And I don't know how Saint Agnes feels about two girls going together too . . ."

Right. This is the same school where Sister Marissa freaked out when one of our classmates dared to show up with a pixie cut. The next day, our school handbook had a new rule that students should have hairstyles that displayed "proper feminine expression"—whatever that means.

"We can figure something out," I insist.

"The admin said that students are allowed to go in groups, and if I go with you, three people already make up a group," I suggest. "Dani memorizes the school handbook inside and out, so she, of all people, would know how to get away with things. And as for your parents, just say that Dani's in choir. She goes to Mass all the time too."

I'm brainstorming more ideas when Kayla says, "You said you would rather get braces again than go to prom."

"I was exaggerating—"

"And you hate Dani."

"I don't hate Dani," I defend myself. "There are just people in this world that I'd prefer to take in small doses. Dani happens to be one of them."

"You also said you would beatbox while wearing a bikini before setting foot inside prom."

"Kayla." I quickly cut her off and ignore the smirk that materialized on Seph's face when Kayla mentioned the bikini idea. "Ignore what I said before."

"It's just . . ." She pauses and her eyes mist over. "You would really go to prom with me?"

"I'm not the one who gave you the fruit basket," I remind her.

I then feel the need to add, "True or false. Best friends, right?"

"True." That gets me her biggest smile yet.

"Oh my god." Kayla suddenly sits up. "I need to answer Dani."

"Saying yes in person is better," Seph says.

"Why don't you tell her in class?" I suggest.

Kayla suddenly gets shy. "We're actually meeting after this.

"Dani and I sometimes catch up before school, whenever we don't have band practice," she admits.

Seph does a low whistle. "You've been having busy mornings."

"Do you think I should prompose to her back?" she asks Seph. "I could sing to her, or maybe you can sing to her?"

"Moseph doesn't have to sing," I answer before he plans on doing another Ed Sheeran cover. People really need to know that there are other romantic gestures besides serenading.

Kayla's face is still emanating stress. Her expression is the same one she had when her mom once told her the only movie she'll ever need to watch is the documentary she showed us about the Bible.

But then she listens when Seph says, "All you need is to say yes.

"She clearly likes you enough to ask you, and she seems like she gets you too." He gestures toward the fruit basket, apparently Kayla's love language.

Kayla processes this while eating the last of her orange slices. She wipes her hands on her skirt and stands with conviction. "I'm going to say yes."

Seph and I both whoop, but Kayla hesitates. "Should I bring her a fruit basket too?"

"Go, go!" I push her before any doubt creeps back in again. "No serenading, no fruit baskets, just go say yes already."

It takes another dozen back-and-forths before Kayla finally takes off—which leaves me and Seph alone in the auditorium.

Okay, now I can finally resume ignoring him. Once we finish packing our things, Moseph King will go back to being the boy who happens to live in the same building. Nothing more.

Although his constant watching isn't helping. At all.

Every move I make around the stage, I can feel Seph's eyes following me. Plus, he keeps opening and closing his mouth, never saying anything. Even if I was planning on ignoring anything that comes out of his mouth regardless, it's still so *frustrating*.

My patience reaches its limit when I feel him watching me pick up trash.

"Can you stop?"

"What?" he asks, as if *I'm* the one acting weird.

"Quit staring."

Seph makes a face at me. "Feel mo naman." He brushes it off while sneaking yet another glance.

I groan and resume keeping him out of my sight *and* mind.

Then he says, "I thought about calling you yesterday."

Hearing this makes my heart thump in my chest, and I tell myself to quit it. This boy isn't worth all that. Holding hands with Seph never happened, remember?

Still, I ask, "Yeah? What about?"

"How we deserved a prize over Mercury Retrograde."

"Right? *Right?*" Him bringing it up gets me going. "Did you see how their singer was mumbling through the lyrics?"

"No one in the audience was singing along during their set!"

"And they performed a Beatles song," I say. "If you can't get people to sing along with you during a Beatles song, then that's a *you* problem."

The sides of his eyes crinkle when he grins. "You were this worked up over not getting the solo to *The Little Mermaid* too."

"'Part of Your World' is *Ariel's* song," I state the fact yet again. "It doesn't make sense that Direk Myka gave it to the other mermaids just because the parents wanted to see their kids sing."

"So you enjoyed performing again, huh?"

Seph smiles with his whole face, and honestly, it's getting annoying. Like, people aren't supposed to look cute when they're super smiley! Having his eyes crinkle and his nose scrunched up that much must give him premature wrinkles.

"Did you hear that whoever won BOB would perform at the Saint Agnes prom?" Seph then asks.

I scoff. "Glad that's not us then."

The dread sets in when I remember my promise to Kayla. "How long do you think I have to stay? If I leave prom after five minutes, would Kayla notice?"

"Is this before or after your bikini beatboxing performance?"

He's still laughing when I kick the back of his leg.

"It won't be that bad." His foot bumps the side of mine. "Come on. You should at least get some of the food."

"Fine," I relent. "Ten minutes then."

We're interrupted when my alarm for school goes off. As I'm grabbing my backpack, I hear Seph ask, "Want me to go with you?

"You said that the school would allow Kayla and Dani to go together if they were in a group," he adds. "Maybe it'd be more convincing if you were four people."

I pause, still processing his words.

"Are you asking me to *my* prom?"

"No," he says immediately. "I mean, I'm just offering . . . In case you wanted someone else there while Kayla and Dani have their moment."

"I don't mind being on my own," I tell him.

"I know."

"And you can't ask someone to *their* prom," I argue. "That's not how it works."

"That's why I'm just offering."

He blinks; I blink. Seph stands in the empty auditorium in silence; I stand in the empty auditorium in silence.

. . . Does this mean Seph is a banger for me too?

Nope. No way. Here we go jumping to conclusions again. Seph is just probably looking for an excuse to get into the Saint Agnes prom and flirt with my classmates.

"You're offering, not asking," I clarify.

"Clearly."

I fold my arms over my chest, covering whatever noise my heart is making again. "I'm still not staying beyond ten minutes."

Seph's mouth curves into a grin. "We can even leave after five."

26

I'M TRYING TO FIGURE OUT WHAT I DID TO UPSET MY SISTER THIS TIME around.

Did I forget to put her clothes in the laundry?

Did Ms. Abad tell her I was napping during chemistry?

Did she hear more gossip about Seph and me being MOMOL buddies?

All options could be a possibility at this point. After dismissal, Achi always tells me to meet her by the school's exit gate so she can swipe me out. She's already pissed whenever I'm late and make her wait (even if I always have very valid reasons!). But even when we have a shouting match or don't speak to each other for weeks, she's always on time during dismissal. Until today.

No message, no call, no advance notice.

I check the clock affixed atop the guard's post at the gate. At this point, she's over an hour late.

This is one moment when having a ghost father who could spy on people would be very useful. Since he stayed home to go through some things, we decided to meet back at the condo. Now that he has solid hands, I should probably give back Pa's phone so I can at least reach him when we're apart. Unless he's like my sister, who already has a phone but can't be bothered to check it.

hello?????? I message her again.

Nothing.

pls reply so i know you're alive

Oh god.

What if something happened to Achi? She's usually all alone in her office, clueless to the world with her headphones on. What if she's in danger, called Ma, but Dr. Derrick is the one who picked up, and now he's currently moving in his sloth-like pace while my sister is in danger?!

"Achi, Achi!" I barge through her guidance office and find my sister . . .

. . . at her desk.

She slides down her headphones. "Nika, doors exist for people to knock on them."

My head turns from the door to my sister. She seems to be relatively fine. The office doesn't look like it was the site of a guidance counselor hostage situation.

"Did you not check the time?"

Achi jolts from her seat when she glances at her phone. "How is it five already?" she mumbles while clearing the papers on her desk.

"You're the best, Nika. Thanks for being so patient, Shobe. Sorry for making you wait," I say, motioning my hands like a conductor when I receive zero apologies.

Achi scoffs. "Please. It wasn't even that long."

"You once assigned me to write a reflection paper on 'being considerate' after I was late by two minutes," I remind her, and she brushes that off. *Shocker.*

My attention then drifts to the headphones still plugged into the computer monitor. "What were you busy with anyway?"

"The days before Christmas break are like hell week for faculty," she says, rolling up her charger. "They shouldn't call it a holiday with the amount of work they pile on us, plus all the wedding suppliers seem to have forgotten how to answer their phones, so I'm stuck with a million more things to do."

Achi being Achi, she requested that all of Ma's wedding

planning go through her. She's the one coordinating with the venue, the food, the supplier who agreed to Dr. Derrick's bizarre request of handing out travel-size toothbrushes as wedding giveaways.

But if I know more details about the wedding, maybe I can figure out more ways to stop it.

I make my move when she's distracted. The moment my achi isn't looking, I rush behind her desk and see . . .

Pa on her computer screen. My whole body goes still when the details sink in. The video title, the outfit Pa used to wear every Sunday, the faces in the crowd that I now recognize from watching this video a million times.

The screen is paused on the same video I always watch—Pa playing the Mariah Carey song on the mall's piano.

Is my sister the reason why the video keeps getting so many views?

Achi then freaks out when she sees me using her computer. "So do you just not understand the concept of boundaries?"

She grabs the mouse and quickly exits the page showing the video. My mouth's struggling to voice all my questions when I watch her close countless tabs of the University of Florida website, the professors at the Counseling Psychology program, multiple Google searches on Florida (even one article about a Florida alligator that chased a golf cart).

I always thought that Achi was immune to strong emotions, that she was genetically built to be less affected . . . but maybe she feels them all too. Achi's still pissed off by the time she logs off her browser. "I knew, I *knew* you always go through my things, but you don't even have any boundaries in my workplace," she grumbles, and stuffs files into her binder. "My favorite leggings, Nika? I've never seen them since you 'borrowed' them."

"I'll give back your leggings before you move to Florida."

And it's like my sister stops breathing.

"You wouldn't be looking up the school so much if it was a joke," I say, gesturing at the computer that had a hundred different open tabs on Florida. "You obviously want to go."

Her voice is barely a whisper when I hear her say, "I can't."

My heart wants to leap out of my chest. *Just agree with her! She said she can't go so don't let her go!* But then I keep remembering her scratchy writing on her vision board notebook. *My dream is to get a PhD and see the world.*

"I was just exaggerating about the alligator stuff," I tell Achi, ignoring the part of me that's begging my mouth to shut up. "Their stamina on land is actually really bad, so if you manage to outrun them the first few minutes, you could probably survive."

She sighs. "I'm not worried about the alligators."

"Is it the money?" I guess. "Because I remember your offer letter mentioned some fellowship and that they're giving you funding."

My sister logs off her computer. "Niks, I'm not leaving you and Ma. End of story, okay?" She reaches for her handbag and takes out her gigantic shades to wear in this office with very dim lighting. As she smooths out the crumpled pages in her binder, I don't point out that I can hear her sniffling.

Usually, this would be my signal to back off, give my sister space. It's against our unspoken rules for me to prolong the conversation.

"I watch that video of Pa a lot too."

Her body freezes when I speak.

"It's the only one I can find where he sings."

Then she says, "He could play the piano in front of anyone, but he got weirdly shy about singing."

"That's because he picks the hardest songs in the world."

"His love, Mariah," she says, laughing. She looks at me then. "I wish he got to watch you last night. He'd be really proud of you."

My heart squeezes at that, so naturally, I tell a joke. "But I really just joined Battle of the Bands to flirt . . ."

But apparently, Achi's very determined to make me cry.

"You don't sing anymore, Niks."

I shrug, pretending like it's no big deal that she noticed.

"You used to sing everywhere. Every single car ride, in the mornings I'd hear you from the shower. I remember you singing when I went with you for your first day of kindergarten. It felt so quiet when you stopped." She sighs and shakes her head. "It was hard for me sometimes since music was your thing with Pa . . . but I should've done something when you quit Trumpets . . ."

"Ach, that wasn't your job."

"But I'm your big sister." Achi's voice trembles. "I'm supposed to look out for you."

A beat passes, then I hear Achi say, "You're my only shobe."

Her words are making me tear up while she's fixated on her damn binder. I wrap my arms around her, but she recoils from my grasp.

"I think you're a star too," I tell her.

"Ew?" she says, squirming and acting like she doesn't feel the same way.

"Can you stand still so I can hug you?"

"This is disgusting," she mutters.

"Agree." I try again.

While I convince her to stay still long enough for an awkward embrace, I jump at the sight of a giant mouth under her desk.

"Did you behead someone?!"

I steer clear when Achi grabs the box with what looks like giant dentures inside. "It's a teeth cake," she says.

"A *what*?"

"Uncle Derrick's sister makes cakes." She lets out a heavy sigh. "She made this for the wedding. Apparently, it's a special dental theme for her brother."

Even if I wasn't trying to stop this wedding from happening, I still think this cake should be banned from any celebration. It is offensive to everything Ma stands for—as a baker, and generally, as a person with eyesight!

Dr. Derrick's sister could've at least made this a cute little cartoon cake. Who would want to eat dessert that actually looks like someone's gums?!

"This is the third cake she's baked," Achi adds. "The others had icing that looked like tooth decay."

Putting that image far out of my head. "Did Ma see them too?"

"Yeah, I've been helping her think of ways to let Uncle Derrick's sister down gently."

I turn the cake around so its head isn't staring directly at me.

"I've also been meaning to ask you about song choices," Achi mentions. "I started a playlist with songs that Ma might like, but I think we need more upbeat stuff. I only remembered how much Ma loved 'Always Be My Baby' when your band sang it."

"Did you know that's how Pa asked Ma to prom?"

Achi laughs. "You know, for a moment, I thought I even heard Pa's voice while you were up there," she says so casually as if her words didn't just change *everything*.

My whole body's already buzzing when I'm trying to figure out if I heard my sister correctly.

"I listened back to Pa singing in the video, and it's fascinating how the mind works!" Achi says. "Some studies actually say that one in ten people will experience hearing voices at some point in their life."

My hand shushes Achi before she goes further into psych mode. "Did you just say you *heard* Pa?"

"I didn't technically hear Pa, Nika. It was an auditory hallucination."

If my sister can hear Pa's voice, too, does that mean . . .

Oh my god. Our plan is still working.

"Achi, something happened during Pa's death anniversary."

She doesn't comment the whole time I recap the last few weeks. She doesn't say anything when I tell her about Pa appearing at our condo, re-creating our parents' high school love story, even when I tell her he was up onstage with me during the Battle of the Bands performance.

By the time I'm done, all she does is take out her phone.

"Ach?"

She's typing.

"Did you hear me?"

She's dialing.

"Do you know someone who's had experience with spirits?"

"Hi, Doktora," she says once the other line picks up. "So sorry to bother you, but I wanted to inquire if my sister and I can drop by to inquire about counseling?"

What? Counseling?! We need to figure out our ghost father situation, not counseling!

"Oh great, yes. We can pass by the clinic now. Thanks so much for squeezing us in."

"We don't need to be squeezed in!" I hiss at her, but my sister already has a death grip on my hand. She adjusts the sunglasses on her face before dragging the both of us to some counselor's clinic.

27

PLEASE LIST ANY POSSIBLE REASONS FOR UNDERLYING DISTRESS.

I write below in all caps, *MY SISTER*.

If there was more space on the form, I would've expounded on how she's holding me hostage at this clinic. Even after waiting for an hour (for the record: That means my sister has wasted two hours of my time today), Achi insists that we stay put so we can interrupt a therapist's very busy schedule. Dr. Broso was apparently Achi's advisor when she was in college so we're disrupting the schedule of a therapist *and* professor.

When the receptionist handed me a clipboard with a health evaluation form to fill out, my sister lingered at her desk to bug her about Dr. Broso's availability—and she still hasn't left the obviously busy receptionist alone. It's a miracle my sister can see anything with her sunglasses that cover half her face.

Once the receptionist has had enough of her, Achi returns to her seat next to me in the waiting area and tells me I'm next in the queue. My eyes stay glued to the clipboard on my lap—because *I've* had enough of her too.

My sister annoyingly doesn't get the hint.

"What's on your mind?" she asks.

"That I really want pancit canton right now."

Achi scowls. "Nika, we're next to a diabetes center. Do you know how many people get treatment there from eating the stuff they put in instant noodles?"

I place the clipboard in front of my face, blocking my sister from my sight and mind.

She still doesn't shut up. "Hallucinations can happen when the brain is having trouble processing loss."

"I'm not hallucinating," I say through my teeth.

"There was one time I thought I saw Pa at the bakery, and it turned out to be Father Melvin."

"Father Melvin isn't Pa's ghost!"

Achi drops her voice, explaining things to me like I'm a kid. "Dr. Broso is the absolute best at grief counseling," she explains. "When I was in college, she taught me all about helping kids and teenagers adjust while navigating through loss."

I drop the clipboard and face Achi. "Did you ever talk to her?"

"In college? All the time. I did my thesis with her."

"No, like, did *you* go to her for grief counseling?"

She frowns. "Why would I need counseling?"

"Because you need adjusting."

"I'm very well adjusted." Her voice is soaked with denial.

"You still have your shades on because you don't want people to know you've been crying."

She pushes the glasses up her nose. "It's not my fault I get bad allergies, Nika."

"Allergies to what? *Light?*" I throw up my hands. "Do they even allow people scared of therapy to get PhDs?"

Achi and I keep bickering until the door of Dr. Broso's office clicks open. The clipboard on my lap clangs to the floor when I look up and see Ma walk out the door. "What are you doing here?" all three of us say at the same time.

Ma's eyes bounce between the two of us. "Oh . . . you know . . . ," she stammers, and clutches her bag. "Just making some deliveries. Buns by Beth is really popular in this building."

Dr. Broso's clinic shares the building with only one other office—the diabetes care center.

"You're serving pastries to diabetics?"

My leg buckles when Achi kicks the back of my knee. I shoot her a side-eye. *It was a valid question!*

"Nika and I were just dropping by Dr. Broso's clinic."

I'm about to add that I'm here against my will when Achi says, "The faculty head at Saint Agnes wanted me to provide a letter of rec before they consider me for a promotion."

Promotion? But what happened to Florida?

Ma shakes her head at this. "You'd think that we're not a family of Saint Agnes alumni. They're lucky they have a summa cum laude graduate for their counselor. Your qualifications are enough of a recommendation!"

While Ma gets distracted probing more about Achi's "promotion," I soon get what she's trying to do. I can also tell that my sister is still wondering why in the world Ma is here too—but then again, aren't these the rules of our family? Downplay things, keep conversations positive, hide what you feel. Do everything that we can to minimize Ma's worries.

Just like Achi said, if Ma sees we're okay, then she'll be okay.

I leave the clipboard with the receptionist when we head out of the clinic, my sister forgetting all about my supposed appointment. Ma says that Dr. Derrick dropped her off, so Achi offers to drive and the three of us slide into my sister's car. From the back, I see Ma's leg jiggling and get a closer look at her face in the rearview mirror.

Her eyes are swollen too.

The next question I have for my sister: What happens when I can already tell that Ma's *not* okay?

28

SOME PEOPLE LOOK FORWARD TO MIDNIGHT ON CHRISTMAS EVE TO open gifts, but for the Ilagan family? It has always been about the food.

The moment school let out, Achi had me working nonstop. I spent the first day of Christmas break going around the Buns by Beth store and checking which pastries we can take home. The next day, she dragged me on a grocery run. And the next day, she assigned me to be her "sous chef" in the kitchen—or more accurately, her kitchen minion.

While all this is happening, Ma and Achi are acting like we didn't just run into each other at a therapist's office. In fact, it's like my sister has forgotten that whole day existed. Every time I try to bring up Dr. Broso, Florida, or even fish about her hearing Pa's voice, she barks at me with some new Christmas errand.

I'm actually relieved by the time we head off for Christmas Eve Mass. At least my sister stops ordering me around when she's listening to a priest.

Ma usually has to drag me to attend Sunday Mass, but I always look forward to the holiday service. With the Christmas lights illuminating the building's facade, the star lanterns hanging above the altar up front, and the choir singing all the carols, there's a different kind of . . . coziness in church this time of the year. Walking inside is close to the feeling I get from one of Pa's hugs. The Mass is completely packed, but we manage to snag the last empty pew in the back. Whenever someone tries taking Pa's seat, I block them and say I'm saving it for someone.

"Nika, you should've let him sit there," Ma says when I shoo away another man who tries sitting in Pa's place without asking.

"I'm saving the seat," I repeat myself.

Achi narrows her eyes. "For who?"

"The Holy Spirit," I deadpan.

Pa chuckles when the rest of the family groans at my joke. Technically, my father *is* a holy spirit.

Then Pa points to the front. "Isn't that Kayla?"

I follow his gaze and see Kayla, Auntie Grace, and Uncle Walter seated on the other side of the church. Then I notice the family right beside them.

!!! I quickly message Kayla. Dani met your parents????

Kayla replies after the first reading. Ma invited her to sit with us when Dani introduced herself as student council president

Of course she did.

Pa nudges me when I'm in the middle of texting. "Hey, no phones during Mass.

"You won't be able to learn from Father Melvin's homily," he adds.

Weird. I never really thought of Pa as super religious. Ma was the one who enforced weekly Mass for our family, and I assumed he went along with the routine for her. There were even moments growing up when I'd catch Pa dozing off during the Mass readings.

The priest continues his homily and I notice Pa leaning forward in his seat, wearing the same expression of full concentration he used to have when he'd analyze piano pieces. I've been half listening, but I catch the priest say stuff about how we're never alone even when we feel like we've lost our way.

I open my mouth to tell Pa something when I feel Achi's eyes on me too. So instead I type on the Notes app on my phone.

do you believe in god more when you're a ghost?

His eyes smile when he reads the question. "Ghosts need to find their way too."

We stand when it's time for the Lord's Prayer and Pa clasps his hand around mine. While the rest of the church begins to sing "Our Father . . . ," Pa leans closer. "It's hard not to believe a god exists when I get to spend my favorite holiday again with my family."

I feel Pa squeeze my hand and I try to ignore the heat rising in my throat when I imagine what next Christmas will look like. The thought still lingers in my head when I line up for Communion and go back to the pew and kneel next to my sister.

Attending Catholic school means I already have go-to requests when I talk to God.

Dear God, can you help me get the lead in our next musical? Dear God, can you find a way to cancel tomorrow's exam? Dear God, can you talk to Ma so she forgets about Dr. Derrick?

But I only have one request for this Christmas. I bow my head closer to my clasped hands and repeat my question over and over in my head to make sure my prayer reaches heaven.

Dear God, can you let Pa stay?

The choir ends the service with Christmas hymns and Pa looks like he's having the best time out of everyone in the building. But his rocking to "Joy to the World" gets cut off when Achi says we have to rush back home to finish our noche buena prep.

Every single year, Ma and Achi make enough food to feed an entire barangay—which, I guess, is the goal. We usually spend Christmas Eve delivering pastries to Auntie Baby, Auntie Grace, people at the bakery, the staff at the condo, and Pa's former coworkers from the warehouse business.

"Are these for the Christmas party?" Pa asks when I help Achi arrange the spread of kakanin on our kitchen table.

I check that Ma and Achi are busy in the kitchen before I tell Pa that there's no Christmas party this year. Our place used to be so full with friends and family every Christmas Eve. I don't have the heart to tell Pa that we haven't thrown a party since he passed.

"Bibingka, Nika! We need more bibingka!" Achi yells out to me while I'm still trying to pack the pichi-pichi and the other rice cakes together.

Ma then enters the kitchen and tells us we can pack one less pastry box. "Just got off the phone with Baby. She said Francis can't make it for Christmas."

She tells Achi something about how Uncle Francis's flight from Amsterdam got canceled, but I just keep thinking about Seph . . . and how much it sucks to spend Christmas without your dad.

"So Moseph is spending Christmas alone?

"I mean, with Auntie Baby?" I add when Pa shoots me a look. "*Auntie Baby* is spending Christmas alone?"

"Well, like you said, Nika, she'll be with Moseph," Ma answers, and goes right back to checking whatever's heating up in the oven.

Then I blurt out, "What if we invite them over?"

My family's suddenly staring at me as if I proposed to cancel Christmas.

"We have lots of food," I point out. "And we used to host all those Christmas parties before too."

My sister's eyes widen. "*You* want to throw a party?"

"It's Christmas!" I say, putting on the biggest smile I've ever worn. "Isn't it supposed to be a party?"

Ma presses the back of her palm to my forehead. "Are you feeling okay?"

I nod and convince her that my temperature is completely

normal. "Auntie Grace might be game too. Kayla said they're just at home."

". . . I can call Grace," Ma says carefully.

Ma's eyes bounce from me to my sister.

"Great!" I clasp my hands together. "So that's Auntie Baby's and Auntie Grace's families. Anyone else?"

Ma and Achi exchange looks, probably trying to figure out why in the world the most antisocial member in the family would want to throw a very last-minute Christmas party. The more I try to seem cheery, the more my family looks like they *fear* me.

Once I finally sell them on the idea, Pa teases, "Sweet mo naman kay Seph."

"I convinced them to have a party for you," I whisper to Pa when the rest of my family is out of earshot.

I'm making sure Pa gets a great Christmas, that Auntie Baby isn't alone, and that all of Ma's baking efforts get maximized. It's merely a coincidence that Seph happens to be Auntie Baby's son. And this is me showing great levels of empathy. I know what it's like to miss your dad during the holidays, so I'm just putting myself in Seph's shoes. Truth be told, I'm actually getting the short end of the stick considering I have to go through noche buena with a nagging toothache. But still, I'm going to eat Ma's desserts because I don't want to hurt her feelings.

This is me acting out of concern for other people.

Ha! Who says I'm not learning a lot from church?

29

FROM PICHI-PICHI AND BIBINGKA TO MA'S SUMAN AND PUTO bumbong, our dining table has every form of delicious rice cake you can imagine. Ma whipped up something extra special too: the Buns by Beth buko pie with a crust that's somehow extra tender and filling that's extra creamy. As for my contribution, I also prepared my specialty: scrambled eggs with the perfect runny texture.

When Auntie Baby arrived with a cooler of wine bottles in one hand and her portable karaoke machine in the other, she immediately ordered us to turn down Jose Mari Chan on our speakers so she could sing her own rendition of his songs. She decorated our Christmas tree with garlands of sampaguita before setting up her magic mic in our living room. There are very few things in this world that Auntie Baby loves more than karaoke.

And every single time, she proves that Seph's singing abilities don't come from her side of the family.

While both Kayla and Auntie Baby struggle to find pitch, the difference with Auntie Baby is that she *believes* she's a terrific singer. And not just karaoke terrific—one time, we watched a clip of Lea Salonga performing on Broadway, and Auntie Baby commented that she and Lea sounded alike.

She said this as seriously and matter-of-factly as someone would declare that the world is round. In Auntie Baby's mind, I truly suspect that she believes that her singing is as good as a Tony Award–winning vocalist's.

In theory, I should be annoyed that Auntie Baby's stalling

everyone from eating so we can sit through another performance of Christmas carols. She's already on her second glass of wine when she begins her third repeat of "Christmas in Our Hearts."

Yet Auntie Baby butchering a Christmas classic just seems so in line with the holidays.

On the other side of the room, Achi and Kayla are competing with each other to see who can build the longest line with things in their pockets.

"Yun o!" Kayla raises her fists after she slowly positions her necklace at the end of her line. She then mimes answering a phone with her hand. "Ms. Ilagan, I'm getting a call from the guidance office. The rest of the faculty wants to congratulate me on my win."

Achi keeps a straight face while she watches Kayla gloat. "Hold the phone," she says, and takes out five pens from her pants pockets. She places them at the tip of her line very slowly and deliberately, staring Kayla down while her line gets longer and longer.

Once she's done, Achi holds her hand to her ear and copies Kayla's phone gesture. "Yes?" she answers her imaginary hand phone. "Is this the Saint Agnes faculty? You're saying I won by a landslide?" She gasps and glances at Kayla. "And that I'm this year's Christmas champion?"

It's the dorkiest display of trash-talking I've ever seen. No one even addresses how weird it is that my sister has an unending supply of pens on hand. But I decide to keep some comments to myself. To be honest, it does feel kind of nice to have so many people here. I don't know, maybe there's something about the holidays that makes everyone's quirks more endearing than annoying.

Everyone just seems so happy—especially my dad.

More than once, I've caught him smiling and taking the whole scene in while watching Ma or Achi.

"You should try to see if Achi can hear you," I whisper to Pa while I stand next to him by the food spread. "Follow her around and say stuff in her ear."

Pa bristles at the suggestion. "Wouldn't that scare your sister?"

I shrug off his concern. "Fear is very effective in convincing people," I argue. "Ooh, you can tell her things like I've always been your favorite daughter."

"That's new information," he says, then chuckles when I pretend to be offended.

Then Pa suggests, "Why don't we take a break from our plan for tonight?"

"Pa, we're getting really close to your fortieth day."

"But it's Christmas Eve." He checks if anyone's watching before taking a sampaguita garland from the Christmas tree and slipping it around my neck. "We shouldn't be haunting people during Christmas.

"Plus, you shouldn't worry about me," Pa adds. "I think someone else is distracting you tonight."

Before I can argue, my phone lights up with another notification.

Seph has been to our unit a hundred times before. Having him here on Christmas Eve is nothing special. We've barely spoken to each other since he and his mom arrived, but every so often, I'd catch him flashing a little smile from across the room.

When Auntie Baby finally takes a break from her nonstop karaoke and makes her way to the buffet, it's the first time Seph and I are almost at an arm's length from each other. "Tsiah lo, tsiah lo." Auntie Baby urges me to eat while her son keeps glancing at me, smiling like an idiot.

Auntie Baby stops when she reaches my dish. "People make scrambled eggs for noche buena?"

"Ma, that's the best dish," Seph immediately answers. I bite back a smile when he makes it a point to fill almost half his plate with eggs.

As soon as he accompanies his mom back to her karaoke station, my phone lights up with a message.

Even him messaging me through the night isn't a big deal. Seph and I have been messaging so often lately that tonight barely registers on my radar.

Me wanting to check my phone is merely a side effect of my natural curiosity.

Great eggs!

I look up at Seph and he flashes me a thumbs-up.

Sipsip, I type back.

:) Merry Christmas Ilagan

I roll my eyes and type, it's still two hours till midnight

"Is Moseph having a good time?"

I startle when Pa's looking over my shoulder and quickly cover my phone.

"For your information, I've been researching strategies on your ghost situation."

"Ah, ganun pala." Pa nods, that smug look still not going away. "Research seems to make you happy."

"Very," I deadpan, and excuse myself to check on who rang the doorbell. When Pa has his back turned, I take another peek at my phone.

wanted to make sure i was the first one to greet you :)

I stuff my phone in my pocket, covering my mouth to hide the smile on my face.

Pa is reading too much into this. I'm a naturally smiley person who's just in an extra good mood because of all the holiday spirit.

Although, my mood immediately switches once I open the door and see Dr. Derrick in his striped purple tie.

30

SOMETHING I'M GRATEFUL FOR THIS CHRISTMAS: THE FACT THAT WINE makes Auntie Baby more talkative. While we're gathered around the dining table for our noche buena meal, Auntie Baby has taken control over the whole conversation. Works for me. It means I don't have to participate in any small talk with Dr. Derrick.

I can't believe he had the nerve to show up here on Christmas Eve. Doesn't he know Christmas is supposed to be a *family* thing? Pa's smiling and making jokes beside me, but I can tell he's upset too.

"I used to find it so romantic, all those Hollywood movies where couples share a kiss under the mistletoe," Auntie Baby says, taking another sip from her glass.

"Baby convinced me to cut class once to visit different florists so we could find mistletoe," Ma chimes in.

"Did you know that there's a new breed of mistletoe that's been growing in Cebu?"

"Maybe that's why Cebuanos are very romantic," Auntie Grace says.

Auntie Baby ponders this before going back to her story. "But when we were in school, I couldn't find any mistletoe anywhere, and one florist felt so bad that he gave me these garlands of sampaguitas for free. How was I going to get a kiss with a sampaguita?"

"That's why your Auntie Baby decorates her Christmas tree with sampaguitas," Pa whispers, lending his own commentary.

I hear Seph groan. "Ma, do we have to listen to this story every year?"

Auntie Baby reaches over and pinches Seph's cheek. "Christmas is more magical when you're kissed." She pats his cheek before saying that he'll understand more when he's older.

"And I was so excited that year because that was my first holiday with an actual jowa!" Auntie Baby beams, then turns to Seph. "But your dad is such a gentleman that even when we had gone out on dates, I could tell he was careful about kissing me. And I wasn't going to bring it up! As a proper lady, you're not supposed to initiate."

I catch Dr. Derrick sneaking a glance at Ma at the mention of kissing. *Disgusting.* Aren't people with medical degrees supposed to know how to read a room?! "So I hung all the sampaguitas up on the window in his car, giving him the signal like I was a Hollywood girl waiting to be kissed," Auntie Baby shares.

"And then Dad started sneezing," Seph mutters.

Auntie Baby then reenacts the dialogue of the whole moment.

"Baby," she imitates Uncle Francis with a voice that sounds like Cookie Monster's. "I'm allergic to all these flowers! We have to remove them from the car."

And Auntie Baby protests, "No, they're supposed to be romantic!"

"How are my allergies romantic?!"

Enter Auntie Baby's dramatic pause, which Ma takes as her cue to ask, "What did you say next?"

Auntie Baby ends her story with the line, "Because the flowers are supposed to be our mistletoe."

Long story short: Uncle Francis gets the hint, they make out in the car, Auntie Baby declares the story of her first kiss as a Christmas miracle for years to come.

When I sneak a glance at Seph, he's scowling and ripping the bibingka on his plate into smaller and smaller pieces. I guess hearing about his parents making out puts him in a mood.

"Don't worry," Auntie Baby says, pinching Seph's cheek again. "Your father said he'd try to make it to graduation."

"Of course he did," Seph says, his voice dripping with sarcasm.

Auntie Grace clears her throat. "It's frustrating how few tickets they allot for these graduations. How many tickets do they give for family at Saint Francis?"

"I think you can request for four," Seph says.

"At least that's one more." Auntie Grace sighs and turns to Kayla. "How are we going to bring your grandparents when your school only provides three tickets?"

Ma looks at me then. "They gave out graduation tickets already?"

My eyes dart to Kayla for help.

"They just announced it," I lie, keeping my voice steady.

"Didn't your teacher hand them out at the beginning of the school year?" Auntie Grace asks.

Shit.

"Ow!" Auntie Grace grimaces. "Kayla, why are you kicking me under the table?"

Kayla shakes her head and mouths *Sorry* at me.

Then Auntie Baby says, "Three tickets should work out for your situation, Beth."

. . .

It was a quick moment, but I noticed it. I saw how Ma and my sister sneaked a glance at Dr. Derrick.

No.

No freaking way is Auntie Baby implying that Dr. Derrick is attending my graduation.

"I'm not inviting *him*," I make it clear.

"Niks," Achi says, warning me to reel it in.

Dr. Derrick has the audacity to insert himself into the conversation. "Baby probably meant you can invite another family member to your graduation, Annika," he says. "I'm sure you have a cousin, another aunt—"

"Yeah, my *dad*."

My whole body tenses when the words slip out of my mouth. I look up and see the familiar concern flood Ma's and Achi's eyes again. He's right here! If they only knew how he's been here with us for the past few weeks, they'd know that he can't possibly be gone.

I'm about to tell my family the truth when I hear Pa say that he doesn't need the ticket.

"You don't need to waste your ticket on me, Superstar," he says, giving me a sad smile. "My days will be up by then."

From that moment, it's like my brain stops processing. All the noises around me get muffled. I vaguely hear when my aunties try to give me comforting words about Pa, when Ma attempts to offer me more food, or when Achi says something about handing out gifts. Their voices get drowned out by the panic hammering in my head.

Will Pa really be gone by graduation? How many of the forty days do I have left? "Excuse me." I push my chair away from the table and get away from there.

31

I KEEP TELLING PA I'M FINE WHEN HE FOLLOWS ME. "SUPERSTAR, LET'S talk," he tells me again.

"Pa, I'm *fine*. Just wanted to get some air." I plaster a smile on my face to prove the point.

"Why don't we go somewhere?" he says. "Take Martha to see some Christmas lights."

"Don't think Martha can really see, Pa."

I was hoping a joke about his car's eyesight would change the subject, but Pa still doesn't let up.

"Annika," he says, and it sounds weird to hear him use my full name. "Come on, be serious. Let's talk."

And hearing those words come out of Pa's mouth makes the hairs on my arms stand, the blood coursing through my body boil, the banging in my head even louder. Because when was the last time anyone in my family ever took me seriously when I asked them to talk?!

"Why am I not allowed to joke?" I cry out. "Why can't I laugh things off like you always do?"

He staggers back a bit and I've never seen this . . . crumpled look on his face. I wish he'd say one of his confusing proverbs, tell a corny joke, or even call me out for snapping at him. Seeing how hurt my dad looks makes me want to forget everything and sink into one of his hugs again.

Instead, he lets me be.

"I'll let you get some air then." He nods and gives me space. "You know where to find me."

I watch as Pa drifts and goes back inside our unit.

My hands gather my hair into my fists. Ugh. What did I just do?!

The nagging truth that I hate myself for feeling? I'm angry at Pa. Why does he keep insisting on leaving? Why isn't he trying harder?

And I don't know why I'm even allowing myself to feel this way. It's completely dumb and selfish! I've wanted Pa back for so long and I'm wasting time being mad at him.

My hand throbs after I slam the elevator button. Maybe getting some air can help me get rid of all these annoying feelings too.

The elevator gap is already closing when I see Seph rush out of our unit and squeeze himself between the doors.

"What are you doing?" I ask when his body narrowly escapes getting crushed by the elevator doors.

"The elevator's for all building residents, Ilagan."

I groan. "Forcing an elevator open can break its safety mechanism."

"Please. People force elevators open all the time," he argues.

And like some twisted joke, the machine rumbles to a sudden stop. Instead of showing the floor number, the screen on top flashes a red *E* for error. I press the elevator's emergency call button, but the line just keeps ringing and ringing. And no matter how high we hold our phones, both of us get zero signal.

"Just how I wanted to spend Christmas." My back slides down the elevator wall and I bury my face in my arms. *Great job, Nika. You get another Christmas with Pa and you mess it up so much that you get stuck in an elevator.*

Soon, I feel Seph move and take a seat beside me.

"Wanna talk about what happened?"

"Nope," I answer, my voice muffled and my head still buried.

"It might make you feel better if you talk about it."

Not answering him this time. From this point forward, I'm making a vow against talking, and everyone around me should respect my wishes.

"Do you wanna think of more nicknames for Dr. Derrick?"

That's when I look up at him. "What?"

"How about . . . One Derrick-tion?"

I scoff under my breath. "Didn't know he had plans of joining a boy band."

"Hey," Seph protests. "Derrick's a hard name to work with."

I'm about to resume sulking when an idea pops into my head. "Derrick-tor."

"Derrick-tory."

"Derrick-cula."

"Derrick-tion."

"You used the direction pun already," I point out.

"Yeah, I ran out, Ilagan."

His nose slightly scrunches when he hears me laugh. "Seems like the game made you feel better, though."

I focus back on scowling. *Don't admit that, Nika.* One boy shouldn't be enough to distract me from my misery.

When he suggests we play something else, I say, "What, you want to play the ice game again?"

Heat creeps up my neck when I realize how that sounded. "Stop," I warn Seph when he looks all smug.

"What? I didn't say anything."

"It was recency bias. Only thought of the game because the soiree just happened."

"Again, didn't say anything."

"I wasn't suggesting the game so we could hold—"

I catch myself before digging myself into an even bigger hole.

But he's still annoyingly smiling. "So we could hold what, Ilagan?"

Scowling for real this time. "Wasn't your whole mission about making me feel better?"

Seph finally drops it and mentions that we never got to play Never Have I Ever at the soiree. I only put up my palms so he doesn't tease me about the ice game again.

He follows suit and raises his fingers. "Never have I ever . . . gone through watching my mom move on with someone else."

I quickly drop my hands. "Nope."

"Have you talked to Auntie Beth about it?" he asks. "I'm sure she'd understand where you're coming from."

My mouth twists. "Moseph, I really don't like talking about this."

"You know, it's unhealthy to keep everything to yourself."

"Excuse you. I embody vulnerability."

He crosses his arms. "Yeah? Are you sure the vulnerability is in *this* body?"

I scowl when he looks so proud of his wordplay. "Fine, fine." I hold up my hands again so we can move on from talking about my parents. "Never have I ever . . . *not* eaten from the siopao boxes Ma gives you."

Seph pauses. "*That's* all you're giving me?" he asks, flabbergasted. "I ask for vulnerability, and you're giving me siopaos?"

"It was a struggle for me to eat all those siopaos," I point out. Ever since my Dr. Derrick boycott, it's been harder to chew with my right molars.

He then nods toward my hands. "Still your turn."

"I just went."

"That doesn't count."

I shake my head, not budging. "I don't see *you* confessing anything."

Seph considers this. "Confess something, huh?

"Never have I ever . . . ," he says, and takes a deep breath. It feels like an eternity passes while he considers what to say for his turn. I'm about to joke that it's already New Year's when he finally speaks.

". . . told anyone you were my first crush."

A moment passes . . .

Another moment passes . . .

Multiple moments pass and I still haven't said anything.

If not for my pulse ringing in my ears, I would think that I was having a stroke. Someone could write a love story about this moment. A boy tells a girl he had a crush on her; girl proceeds to have a stroke.

Seph was the first non-blood-related boy I was ever aware of. One of my earliest memories was our moms pushing the two of us to perform during Seph's seventh birthday. Maybe this "crush" thing he's confessing is all about proximity. I was the girl who was in his vicinity when he hit puberty. Of course his newfound horniness would latch on to the closest target.

And maybe it's not really *me* who he's attracted to. Maybe I'm an early sign for Seph to realize he's into talented women. Like, he doesn't find me hot. He finds talented girls hot.

I only snap back to reality when Seph speaks up.

"Your turn to confess something," he prompts.

"Th-that wasn't a confession," I argue, clearing my throat. "I—I was a very talented kid and had lots of admirers."

Seph's annoying grin pops on his face again. "How many admirers, exactly?"

"Lots," I insist. "Some might say I was a superstar."

For some reason, his eyes turn soft at that. "That's what your dad called you, right?"

The concern in his face makes my eyes prick.

He then says, "I miss my dad too."

"Did he get stuck in Amsterdam?"

Seph answers with a shrug. "Probably with his new family."

New family?

"Do you know my mom came up with the whole Moseph name because of my dad?" Seph says, his eyes lingering on the ceiling. "She thought they were having lots of problems because she had a hard time getting pregnant. So when I came into the picture, I was supposed to be the miracle baby, the one who'd make everything better.

"But then the night they brought me home," he continues, and takes a deep breath. "Ma was with your parents when my dad kept taking calls on his phone . . .

". . . Then my mom found out he was already seeing someone else."

Seph's eyes are welling up when he scoffs, "Turns out I wasn't the miracle baby."

This is what Pa meant when he said Seph's dad isn't around.

"My mom always talks about my dad like they're still in love. Talks about him like he's the best husband in the world," he says, shaking his head. "And I used to be like that too. I joined all those musicals, got into acting because those were the only times he'd actually pay attention."

I'm about to spit out some of the best curse words for Uncle Francis when Seph starts listing nice things about him.

"But my dad . . . I know some part of him cares about us." Seph then tells me stories of how in love he and his mom were, how his dad always contacts him during his birthdays.

I don't know why he defends Uncle Francis for the bare minimum. But I guess if either of my parents decided one day that they never wanted to see me again, I would keep loving them too. Even if Achi suddenly wanted nothing to do with me, I would still smack anyone who talked shit about her. Maybe love has no real limits when it comes to family.

"Shit, sorry," Seph curses while wiping his eyes on his sleeves. "This is what you call embodying vulnerability, Ilagan."

I try to nod while blinking back the tears burning in my throat.

"Are you . . . crying?" he asks.

I avert my eyes and kick his foot. "Seeing you cry makes me cry!"

It's annoying how he's even capable of laughing at this point. "I know what will cheer both of us up." His head turns my way. "Let's revisit that whole you finding me cute again."

I brush the sides of my eyes with my palms. "Um. You're the one who had the crush on me."

He bumps my leg back and then I notice his foot rests against mine. He's so close that I can smell his faint vanilla scent, see his eyelashes move when he blinks, feel his chest rise and fall when he breathes . . .

I have no idea what's louder—my heart racing or all the thoughts swirling in my head.

Another contender could be the alarm buzzing in my pocket.

"Oh!" I take out my phone and the clock reads twelve. "I think it's Christmas."

"Oh!" Seph moves to stand, and it quickly sets in that our situation at midnight has not changed from our situation at 11:59 PM. We are still very much stuck in this elevator.

He slides back down next to me and picks on the sampaguita

lei still hanging around my neck. "Any chance these flowers can give us a 'Christmas miracle'?"

"Hopefully," I say. "I didn't get to finish my buko pie."

"Come on. The real highlight of the night was the scrambled eggs."

My eyes narrow at him. "Seriously. What do you need from me?"

"Nothing." He puts his hand over his heart. "I really think they're good!"

I scoff and shake my head even though my insides did a little leap when he complimented the eggs' texture.

Silence stretches over us as we watch the red *E* flash on and off. Seph is the one who breaks the silence again.

"Did you really find me cute?"

I groan. "Moseph, so many girls in my class find you cute."

"Didn't know you did, though."

"Your mom did say, '*As a proper lady, you're not supposed to initiate.*'"

Seph rolls his eyes. "My mom gets a lot of things wrong."

A beat passes and I barely hear Seph when he adds, "I wish you would've initiated."

His words pulse through the air, and I'm reminded again of how small this elevator is. Seph's face always makes these goofy expressions when he's thinking something through, and I hate how . . . nice his face looks.

I hate how I like *looking* at his face, how my eyes are always drawn to how wide his shoulders are, how I wonder what it'd feel like if our bodies were pressed together in this elevator . . .

It dawns on me then.

Shit. Do I still find Moseph King cute?

"Why didn't *you* initiate?" I manage to ask, past the somersaulting in my chest.

"Would it have made a difference?"

"Maybe." I hesitate before admitting, "I could've told you that you were my first crush too."

He blinks; I blink.

My gaze follows him when he catches my eye. His look then travels over the rest of my face, and his hand moves from the sampaguita to gently lifting my chin. He inches closer and I brush my fingers through his hair. It's even softer than I imagined.

And when my lips meet Seph's? I also fully understand why Auntie Baby could talk about her first kiss for years and years.

"Merry Christmas, Ilagan," he breathes out.

And Auntie Baby did get that one thing right: Christmas is more magical when you're kissed.

32

I DIDN'T KNOW JOY COULD CAUSE INSOMNIA TOO.

My thoughts usually spiral when I go to sleep: What if I say the wrong thing to Ma again tomorrow? What if something happens, and my sister is all the way in Florida?

This is the first time I'm spiraling about something good happening.

"Never have I ever told anyone you were my first crush."

Seph's words keep ringing in my ears when I replay what happened in the elevator over and over again. Was that really me? Did I really get *kissed*?

I hear Achi snoring in the bed next to mine when my hand goes to my mouth, still tender from Seph's touch. It doesn't seem real—that I live in a universe where I get my first kiss then spend the night listening to my sister's snoring.

"Never have I ever told anyone you were my first crush."

Wait.

Were.

First.

Seph used words that very much imply past tense. I mean, I said that he was my first crush, too, but he confessed first! Ball was very much in his court. He had all the opportunity in the world to expound on his confession.

But he didn't.

Once the elevator got fixed, we were all so busy trying to console our mothers that Seph and I were all right that no one probed what happened while we were stuck. Pa was the only one shooting me suspicious glances for the rest of the night.

Even Seph was acting like the kiss never happened. After Auntie Baby had reached her wine quota, Seph took her home, thanked Ma for hosting, and left our place like it was any other Christmas.

If I'm his first crush, does that mean I'm not his *present* crush?

Lord. Look how quickly we resorted back to spiraling about sad things. I kick the covers and stumble out of my bed. Nope, nope. It is Christmas Day, and more importantly, the day I got my first kiss. I'm not going to waste my time decoding a boy's use of past and present tense. There should be no room for sad thoughts today. Happy thoughts only!!!

When I gently close my door and lunge past the two-step stairway to the living room, I find Pa lying down on the couch. Since Achi stayed over tonight, he insisted that he stay outside so we don't feel too cramped. He didn't budge even though I argued that a ghost doesn't really take up much space. I wonder if this is Pa's form of silent treatment. Is he mad about my comment that he always jokes around and laughs things off?

"You're still up?" Pa asks when he notices me.

It's the same thing he asked me before I lost him. The night before everything changed, Pa came into my bedroom to check on me. He always tried to help when I had trouble sleeping.

After he asked if I was still up, Pa tapped my wrist and knelt by my bed. "Let's make a deal, Superstar," he whispered. "If you try to get some sleep tonight, we can go somewhere fun after school tomorrow."

"Promise?" I asked Pa.

I remember Pa saying he promised before kissing me good night.

And then the next day, it was Ma who showed up at dismissal instead of Pa.

He never picked me up from school again.

Stop, stop! I internally scream at my brain. This is Christmas, and on Christmas, there's room for happy thoughts only!

I'm shaking away any memories of that day when I slide next to Pa on the couch. The stack he kept inside the piano bench is laid across his lap. We haven't really talked since I snapped at him after noche buena.

"Does your body still not sleep?" I ask him.

Pa shakes his head.

"Don't you get tired?"

He smiles my concern away. "I kind of like it," Pa says. "It gives me more time to look over things.

"Like . . . this photo."

Pa shows me the horrendous family Christmas photo where I have a triple chin from how hard I'm scowling.

He clutches it tighter when I try snatching it away from him. "I thought I destroyed all copies of that."

"But it's my favorite photo of you. It really shows off my beautiful daughter's eyes." Pa holds up the picture right next to my face. I scowl even harder.

"When I greeted you Merry Christmas that year, you stomped off and said it's not *merry,* Pa."

"Because you made me perform with your coworker's son."

"But you loved performing."

"He was a DJ, Pa."

Pa's partner in his warehouse business had an aspiring DJ son who now goes by the name DJ Tofu. Many Christmases ago, Pa suggested we do a song number together at our annual family Christmas party. DJ Tofu turned down my microphone because my voice was getting in the way of his "beats."

"Heard he's in the lineup for some summer festival next year."

Of course, I got this information from Auntie Baby.

"Really?" Pa asks. "You should check him out."

"Or maybe *we* could . . ."

I'm trying to gauge if he can see himself sticking around for that long, but Pa doesn't pick up on the hint. He's already gone back to looking at more photos.

"Remember this?"

Pa shows me a drawing of a coupon with the words *Valid for 1 gift* scribbled on it. "You gave me this when you were nine, I think."

I nod, remembering. "I felt bad when you and Ma gave me a Christmas gift and I didn't have anything for you."

"I can think of a perfect gift you can give me this year."

Pa then points his lips at the magic mic that Auntie Baby left behind.

"I'm still recovering from my performance with DJ Tofu."

He raises his finger. "One song?" he asks. "I miss singing with my superstar."

Once Pa switches on the mics, "Christmas in Our Hearts" by Jose Mari Chan is already lined up in the queue. The machine flashes different shades of red and green when the opening melody plays. He offers me the other mic attached to the side and I hesitate.

I was already sobbing by the end of our Battle of the Bands performance. Getting to sing again with Pa during Christmas in our living room . . . am I ready for that?

"Whenever I see girls and boys selling lanterns on the street . . ." Pa croons along to the classic Jose Mari Chan song.

He smiles when I move to pick up the second mic he left on the couch cushion. I wait until the pre-chorus before I start singing the lyrics that I know by heart. This used to be our family's favorite one to perform—I swear, I even caught Achi singing along once. I remember Pa and I would still be singing this song all the way until March, even when all the Christmas lights were taken down.

My voice cracks when I hit the high note at the ending chorus and I laugh when Pa copies the note, messing up too. God. I've missed singing.

I thought Achi was humoring me when she said that Pa would've been proud of me during the Battle of the Bands night. In my dreams, reuniting with Pa always happens in the far future when I have time to get my shit together. I figured that when I grow up, I'd find my way to become someone my parents could be proud of.

But sitting on our family's favorite couch, butchering a Filipino Christmas classic—I guess I never thought that my dad would enjoy spending time with the version of me now.

The two of us stop laughing when we hear footsteps coming from the area near the bedrooms.

I turn down the machine's volume and the melody plays in the background when Achi steps into the light.

Her eyes go straight to where our dad is sitting.

"It really was your voice."

Finally, my sister can see Pa too.

33

THIS MOMENT RIGHT HERE? THIS MIGHT QUALIFY FOR PLOT TWIST OF the century.

No one in their right mind could've ever guessed that both Ilagan sisters would get *this* worked up over prom. For a while, I thought that my sister seeing Pa and her joining in on the plan would be a good thing, a more likely win-win for everyone.

Then I remember that she is *impossible* to work with.

Prom and Pa's fortieth day are scheduled this weekend, and we can't even decide what dress to get Ma to wear for prom.

"You want Ma to wear *that* to Saint Agnes?" Achi gawks at me when I show her one of the options I picked out.

"It'll look good on her figure," I insist.

"With that cut, they'll see *all* of her figure." She rolls her eyes at the gown's very classy open back and points again at the mannequin in the long-sleeved dress covered with feathers. "I really think we should go with that one."

"Have you ever been inside the Saint Agnes gym? Ma is going to sweat right through that dress."

Throughout Christmas break, my sister dealt with Pa's situation in different ways.

There was denial: "How did you do this? Through the computer? Some new AI thing?" Achi said while patting down Pa's body like she was airport security.

Anger: "I can't believe you kept this from me! If the ghost of a dead parent appears, it's understood that you should tell your sister!"

And the last stage that's been going on ever since:

Indifference.

Achi has been acting stranger than usual since Christmas. When Pa asked if we wanted to watch the fireworks during New Year's like we used to do, Achi turned him down and said she'd rather stay inside and avoid the smoke. Even when Pa asks her about her job, Achi never goes into psych mode, and replies with mostly one-word answers. I keep having to confirm with Achi if she actually sees and hears Pa since she's sure not acting like she does.

So that leads us here, trying our best to not kill each other while we re-create the most magical prom night for our parents. Achi actually proved useful in that aspect since she proposed to the admin that our prom needed more parent chaperones and volunteered Ma for the list.

I really feel it in my gut that prom is the solution to everything. Getting crowned prom king and queen seems like the epitome of my parents' high school love story. If that all comes back to Ma while she's "chaperoning" our prom, then she should be able to see Pa.

And we can go past Pa's timeline of forty days.

Yet to re-create a night that changes everything, Ma really can't wear a dress that makes her look like a sweaty ostrich.

Pa butts in and tries to act as the mediator again. "Nika, maybe you can reach a compromise with your sister," he suggests. "Plus, your mom looks good in anything."

"I can handle her," Achi says curtly, then moves on to ask the shop attendant if they have a newer version of the dress in stock.

At first, I was trying to give my sister the benefit of the doubt and thought that she's still processing seeing Pa again, but this is just rude. She keeps avoiding eye contact, following me around whenever I leave her and Pa alone for one second.

You would think that she'd be a little more excited to see our dead dad back.

Hours later, after the staff at the store loses all patience with us, Achi and I still can't agree on a dress. We ultimately decide on letting Ma choose, and having the losing dress (most likely the ostrich monstrosity) returned.

Achi brings the two dresses to the counter, and I stick close by to make sure she includes *my* pick. Pa trails us and tries his best to spin this whole shopping ordeal into a great sister bonding moment.

"How was your shopping experience today?" the cashier asks as she scans the items.

"Stressful," I mutter.

Achi ignores me and takes out her credit card.

"Ah, Ms. Ilagan!" The cashier beams when she reads Achi's details. "Great to see you again. The dresses that you had altered are also ready for pickup."

When did Achi get dresses altered?

Wait . . . Has my sister been shopping for Ma without me?!

She can't even look me in the eye when she tells the cashier that she'll pick them up another time.

I tell the cashier to hold the purchase and hurry over to the women's section again. "Nika," Achi hisses when I go through the gown selection. "I'm not buying more than two dresses."

"If you're giving Ma more options, I should get more options too."

Each dress I remove from the rack, my sister grabs and puts right back. I clear a whole section out of spite, and my sister barks at me to stop causing a scene. "Those dresses aren't for Ma," she snaps. "They're for you and me."

Achi has never shopped for me. I mean, clearly, our tastes

are very different, and my sister never shops unless it's for necessity, like a school thing or fancy occasion . . .

I hold my breath when it registers. "These are for the wedding, aren't they?"

She can't even give me an answer.

When she's busy returning the dresses I took out, I get straight to the point. "You're still planning the wedding?"

I swear my sister was paying attention to me. After I repeatedly detailed how re-creating past memories has been making Pa more "human," she told me she'd go along with the plan. It's common sense that re-creating our parents' love story means forgetting about Ma's other wedding.

Her eyes flit from me to Pa. "I'm just not sure—"

"What?" I ask, stunned. "Aren't you happy that Pa is back?"

"Of course I am!" Her hands tense from how tight she's gripping one of the clothing hangers. "But you said his fortieth day is this weekend, right? What happens after that?" Her lip slightly trembles and she looks away from him.

Her voice breaks when she says, "Losing Pa was hard enough the first time."

"Jackie . . ." Pa tries reaching out to Achi, but she brushes him off *again*.

"So what's your plan?" I lash out at my sister. "You're going to cheer Ma on when she gets married to Dr. Derrick?"

"You're too young to understand, but there are a lot of things that go on in a relationship—"

"I know that!" I cut Achi off, annoyed that she's again talking to me like I'm clueless. "And Pa has been telling me all about their relationship. I'm sure Ma still loves him."

Achi scrubs her hand over her face. "I'm talking about Ma and Uncle Derrick, Niks."

My palms start to sting from how hard my nails are digging

into my skin. I almost hear something snap in my brain the longer I have to stand here and listen to my sister talk about how "good" Dr. Derrick is for Ma.

"He really gets what Ma's going through and knows how to help her . . ."

I *can't*. If I keep listening to this, I swear I'm going to hurl one of the mannequins out the window. Achi keeps calling my name while I stomp off to the fitting rooms. My body couldn't physically take hearing another word from her about "Uncle" Derrick. Like, did Dr. Derrick hypnotize Achi during her last dentist appointment or something?! She always uses that "too young" line—discrediting my opinions just because I'm the youngest, but I'm our parents' daughter too.

From the space under the dressing room curtain, I spy the shoes of different people walking back and forth.

Then the image of watching Pa's shoes pops back in my memory. It was during that last year we had with Pa. I woke up in the middle of the night because I heard Pa and Achi arguing outside our bedroom. I inched closer, watching their shadows under the door. When Achi came back inside, she turned on the music in her speakers, drowning out any noise that happened outside our bedroom.

"Nika?"

I look down and see Pa's shoes turned toward me.

"Can I come in?" he asks.

Pa crouches and kneels down in front of me when I unfasten the curtain. He did this when I was a kid too—when he wanted to have a "serious talk," he always lowered himself down, made sure we were seeing each other eye to eye.

"I'm still mad at her," I say, making sure that point is very clear.

He bows his head and sighs. "Jackie knows. She walked around the mall so you can have time to cool off."

When that doesn't move me, Pa adds, "Your sister has been through a lot."

"Couldn't be worse than *dying*."

Pa draws in a sharper breath when he takes a seat beside me on the fitting room's bench. I steal a glance at the mirror in front of us and notice Pa's body flickers in and out. At times, I'm the only one who's reflected.

Pa shifts when he says, "Maybe we should rethink this whole re-creating memories strategy."

"What?" My body tenses on my seat. "We already wasted so much time during Christmas. We can't stop now."

"But what if this isn't what's best for you girls?"

How can having my dad back not be what's best for us?!

"Don't let Achi get into your head," I tell him. "She always acts like she knows everything, but she hasn't witnessed how you've been coming back. You're almost *here*." I swallow down the emotion when I think of losing Pa again. "You're taking Achi's side when she's been ignoring you."

"There aren't any sides here."

"If there were, you'd be on Achi's," I grumble.

"It's complicated, Nika. You were still so young then . . ."

"I'm not anymore!" I snap at him. Ugh. I'm so sick and tired of my family using that excuse over and over again.

If my achi heard this, she'd already be midway into scolding me for being so disrespectful. She might never stop lecturing me if she heard how I lashed out at Pa during Christmas too. An apology is hanging on my tongue when I feel Pa squeeze my hand, his fingers tapping the side of my wrist.

"I should've handled it better." His mouth tightens, looking like he's struggling to find the words. "I'm so sorry I left you and Jackie like that. I could've done something earlier . . ."

Why is Pa apologizing?

"It wasn't your fault," I say, immediately trying to console him.

The narrative I heard has always been that Pa's collapse came out of nowhere. During his wake, the priest gave his whole homily on how to accept the things in this life that we may never understand.

Everything in me quickly deflates when I see Pa's faded reflection in the mirror. It's like his spirit is barely holding on.

"Pa, you can't give up on the sun when it's just about to rise."

He looks at me then like I'm speaking in some other language.

"It's one of your proverbs," I remind him.

"Oh. Right." He does a low chuckle. "Hard for me to keep track of all the stuff I make up."

I can almost hear the glass shattering in my head with the realization.

"Wait. You've been making all those quotes up? This whole time?" I ask. "The one about the heart in fancy, the fish in the ocean, that there's magic behind superstitions?"

My legs go weak when it registers that Pa barely remembers any of it. All his advice, the words I've been clinging to like my personal bible . . . I can't believe none of it was true.

"Whenever you and your sister were going through something, I'd think of some saying to make you feel better," he explains, but with a faraway expression.

I try to calm and steady myself when I ask Pa about my personal favorite proverb. "Remember that time I got my tonsils removed?" I wait for him to nod before continuing, "You told me that when something bad happens to you, the universe owes you something good in return."

Then out of nowhere Pa says, "That was one of the scariest days of my life."

My eyes dart to him to make sure he's being serious.

"You were . . . scared?" I clarify.

Pa puts his hands close together. "You were this tiny when you were rolled off to the operating room." The smile in his eyes dims when he remembers. "I was so scared something was going to happen to my bunso, and I didn't have control over anything."

"You never told me you were scared."

He waves that off. "I'm not supposed to show you stuff like that, Superstar," he says. "I'm your dad. I'm supposed to be strong for you."

I didn't even think that fear was in Pa's vocabulary. I mean, this is the same person who told me seeing a ghost would be like reuniting with his best friend. The same person who said he's mastered controlling his feelings and not letting emotions overwhelm him.

My hand reaches for his face, gently stroking the area near his scar. I wonder how many more times Pa lied and said he wasn't hurting.

The words come out so quiet when I admit, "Sometimes . . . it would've helped if I knew you were scared too."

Pa kisses me on my forehead before he pulls me in for a hug. His breathing slows and deepens as he wraps his arms around me. I almost don't hear him when he says, "I'm scared now, Superstar."

My whole heart aches and I wish there was something, anything, I can do to absorb some of what he's feeling. Are there any words I can say right now to make *him* feel better?

"Having you back is what's best for our family, Pa." I hold on to him tighter, wishing it were enough so he never has to let go.

34

THE MAKEUP ARTIST AT THE SALON EARLIER TOLD ME THAT USING powder on my face would help blur imperfections.

Every time I get nervous that prom is tonight, I pat my face with powder.

Pat. Pat. Pat.

Blur. Blur. Blur.

I shouldn't be this anxious. All signs so far point to tonight being great. First of all, it finally registered on my sister that Pa is back. Pa asked Achi if they could spend the day together and my sister actually agreed. They wouldn't be "bonding" if Pa actually plans on disappearing later, right?

Pat. Pat. Pat.

My face is starting to have a striking resemblance to a clown's when Ma opens my bedroom door. When we showed her what we bought from the most stressful shopping trip of our lives, Ma scolded us for wasting money on dresses when she has perfectly good ones at home. By this, it turns out she also meant I should wear Achi's red ang pao dress from the ting hun.

The dress makes anyone look like a walking red envelope, but I'm not so opposed to the outfit choice this time. We need all the luck we can get.

Ma smiles at my reflection in the dresser mirror. "The hairstyle suits you."

"You don't think I look like an egg?"

I always wear my hair down, but the makeup artist also said that an updo might work better for my body's proportions. It took me a second to realize that he was calling me short.

"A very pretty egg," Ma teases, and she tells me to face the mirror again. She pulls out a golden necklace from a small blue jewelry box and tries it on me. "Think it goes with your dress?"

That's when I notice the small butterfly pendant shining on my neckline.

"Your father gave this to me."

My heart twists at the mention of Pa.

I don't point out that I can feel Ma's hands tremble when she fastens the clasp. "I know you wanted him to be here for tonight . . . ," she says, and gazes at my reflection again. "Baduy ba? Everyone used to wear this style back then. Ton picked the butterfly, too, since I kept listening to that Mariah Carey album."

I adjust the butterfly so it's centered. "It's perfect, Ma," I tell her, my eyes prickling at our reflection.

When I raise my phone to take a selfie of us, Ma asks, "You're not posting that, right?"

"My account is private."

"Kidnappers do not care about privacy, Nika."

After I convince Ma that I'm not going to post our picture and will listen to her advice about how other people tagging me is a "security threat," she finally agrees to a photo.

Her eyes are glistening when she smiles back at me. But her expression quickly changes as she inspects my face. "Why do you have so many powder blotches?"

"I don't know," I say, and bump the face powder container farther away from me.

Ma wipes her hands and grumbles about how she paid for a makeup artist who doesn't even know how to blend. While she's dabbing a sponge on my face, I ask her, "Did Pa give you the necklace during your prom?"

"Alam mo naman, your father, the romantic," she says as she keeps dabbing. "He was worried at first that I'd get mad that he spent money on the necklace."

"Did you?"

"Of course!" Ma says, and I laugh. "Your dad already used most of his allowance buying siopaos from me and then he splurges on jewelry?"

She shakes her head, but I can see her smiling. "But I made sure I wore that necklace when Buns by Beth opened."

"For good luck?"

Ma does one last dab and scans my face to make sure the makeup is even. I think she didn't hear my question until she breathes out, "Because I missed him."

She keeps talking while she adjusts the bobby pins that are holding up my hair.

"Your sister keeps telling me to go for the franchising deal, but it doesn't feel right to do all that without Ton. He was the one who kept telling me to dream bigger." She sighs. "That man was always my biggest fan."

Then why are you marrying someone else?

The question gets lost in my thoughts when we hear Auntie Baby's voice from the living room. "Annika!" she calls out. "Your date is here!"

Which prompts my mother to make the most bizarre statement. "Going to prom with a manliligaw is a big step."

"Seph isn't my manliligaw," I repeat for the umpteenth time.

". . . Boyfriend?"

No, no. He's definitely not *that.*

Is he?

Ma's forehead creases. "What are you two, then?"

"Neighbors." I stop and correct myself. "Well, friends, buddies."

“Baby mentioned this to me . . .” Ma’s eyes narrow as she tries to follow. “That kids your generation have MOMOL buddies now.”

There’s no one in *any* generation who uses that term. No one!

My phone then lights up on the dresser and Ma notices the name of the contact calling me.

“I’ll just take this . . .” I excuse myself and escape another possible interrogation.

Seph and I already predicted that our families would make a big deal out of us going to prom together (not a date! a prom offer!), so he suggested that he call my phone to signal when he steps outside the unit so we can have a private moment without possible prying eyes from the Marie-tres.

I note the fact that my heart is racing from the rush of a well-organized plan, not from the excitement of seeing Seph.

In the grander scheme of things, being unsure if a boy likes me back is a blip, an event that’ll barely register when someone pens the biography of Annika Ilagan.

Now that I have the chance of getting Pa back, completing our family again, I’m not asking the universe to deliver anything else. This is it. Having Pa back is all I want.

I know firsthand that it’s dangerous to ask the universe for too many things.

When I open the door, Seph is standing there (in a suit!), waiting for me and cradling a red corsage in his hands.

He messaged about the color of my dress, but I didn’t realize he was asking so his corsage and tie could match. And I’m still processing the sight of Seph in a tie. I half expected him to show up to prom with his usual unbuttoned shirt and sando combo.

“New dress?” he asks, and I tear my eyes away from staring too long at his hair.

"Um." My hand fixes the red strap that slips from my shoulder. "I borrowed this from Achi . . . It doesn't fit so well in some areas . . ."

"It looks good." He puffs out his cheeks and clears his throat. "You look good."

My face immediately goes hot. "You look good too."

Remember, Nika. We're approaching things with logic today, not emotion.

God. But then the edges of Seph's eyes crinkle, and he's smiling at me the same way he always does—the smile that makes me stop overthinking and realize . . . *Wait. Am I happy?*

I close the front door behind us and he pulls me toward the emergency stairway beside the elevator. After we check that no one, not one family member (ghost or non-ghost), is lurking around, he pulls me in for a kiss.

While my forehead is pressed to his, I feel his hand graze my hair, then my whole body rings from his touch when he traces a path down my shoulders and arms.

"You know, I thought of a pun for your name too," he whispers.

"If you say harmo-nika, there's no way you're going to prom with me."

His chest rises when he laughs.

"Gusto Nika," he says after a beat. "Get it? It sounds like gusto kita."

"Disgusting."

I roll my eyes at him, hiding how much hearing him say "I like you" means to me.

Seph reaches for my hand and plays with the hair tie on my wrist. "You're always holding on to this."

"It calms me down," I tell him.

And I don't know why I said it. Seph wasn't even asking me

a question. I could've ignored his comment, moved along, and carried on with the kissing. But now he's looking at me like he expects that I have more to say.

"Whenever I had trouble sleeping as a kid, my dad used to do this." I flip his palm open and tap the side of his wrist three times. "I don't know why . . . It just made me feel safe."

"And the hair tie reminds you of that?"

I remove it from my wrist and try to play it cool when I say the hair tie clashes with my outfit. "Never have I ever told anyone this."

Seph dips his head to catch my eyes.

"Never have I ever thought we would actually happen, Ilagan."

Does that mean we're *actually happening? Does he want to be together too?*

The question is on the tip of my tongue, but then I think about ruining whatever's happening right now. What's so wrong about staying like this for a bit longer?

Seph asks if I'm all right and I answer him with another kiss.

Not to sound cocky, *but* how many people can say they're at the brink of beating death while also making out with a cute guy?

Maybe the universe is still capable of good things after all.

35

HERE IS MY PUBLIC SERVICE ANNOUNCEMENT: PROM ISN'T ALL THAT romantic.

Like some twisted joke, the theme for this year's Saint Agnes prom is "Heaven Is a Place on Earth." I really pray that heaven in real life goes beyond the Saint Agnes gym. No matter how much effort the prom committee poured into decorating the place, this is still the same ground where I skinned my knee during our third-grade kickball game. The stage lit by the paper lanterns and flameless candles is still the stage where Kayla tripped and flashed her panties in our grade school graduation.

All these girls who look stunning in their gowns and makeup are the same ones who wear their Saint Agnes uniforms every day and yell out at seven in the morning asking if someone has an extra sanitary napkin.

Yet, even the most cynical part of my soul finds it hard to persist alongside Kayla's excitement.

"Nika, Nika." Kayla shakes me. "Don't those lights remind you of the *Twilight* prom scene when Edward danced with Bella?

"Oh my god. Look, they made the middle of the gym a dance floor! Are they going to play *High School Musical* songs?"

Kayla discovered a new talent tonight: She has a movie reference for every single detail at prom.

"The stage is just how it looked like in *Carrie* too!"

Seph hesitates. "Isn't that the one where a girl gets drenched in pig's blood?"

"Yes!" Kayla agrees, even more excited. "Then she proceeds to murder everyone!"

He darts me a concerned look, but I shrug it off. These are the moments I find my best friend more endearing than frightening.

We follow the long carpet that directs us to the pathway while Achi keeps gaping at the stage centerpiece that looks like an actual waterfall. "The admin can't get our budget approved for more volleyball nets, but they can fund *this*?"

It really looks like an enchanted forest threw up all over our school gym. There are pastel-colored lights lining a tunnel to the gym entrance that shimmer when anyone passes through. There are more strings of lights that twist and turn through the ceiling like the gym has its own vines and branches.

Ma rode with Auntie Baby since they had to get here earlier for "chaperone" duties—which works out for us since I get more room to discuss the game plan with Pa. But he's been acting strange ever since he noticed the butterfly necklace.

"Is that from your mom?" he asked when we stepped outside the condo.

I expected him to share more about their prom night, some backstory about how he got the necklace, or crack some corny joke, but he left it at that.

His mind seems like it's far away this whole evening.

He still has a glazed look in his eyes while the rest of us are trying to take in everything the prom committee did to the school gym. "Everything okay?" I ask.

"Hmm?" Pa says, and it's like he snaps out of a trance. "Of course, Superstar. It's your prom night!"

Pa points to the event's centerpiece. "Did they promote that there'd be a waterfall here?" he asks. "That would've been *falls* advertising!"

He goes on to hum the melody to "Heaven Is a Place on Earth" while we make our way through the decorations provided by the questionable budget. I try not to read too much into it—that Pa isn't acting strange at all. This is Pa admiring the decor, not him freaking out that we're running out of time.

Seeing Dani in angel wings is almost a welcome distraction. In front of the stage, Dani is busy ushering everyone to their seats. As prom committee head and student council president (let's not forget!), Dani apologized to Kayla that she had an early-morning call time and couldn't get out of it to pick her up.

Judging by how Kayla's mouth drops open while staring at Dani, I don't think she minds.

Dani is dressed like a literal angel in a strapless tube dress, complete with actual wings on her back. Of course, Auntie Baby is by her side, ushering guests while wearing matching angel wings too.

"Nice outfit," I tell Dani when she greets us. "Surprised there are no rules against wings in the handbook."

The wings even perk up when Dani stands straighter. "The handbook is against cleavage, not against style, Nika." Her eyes turn soft when they land on Kayla. "Hi."

"Hi," Kayla says back.

After Auntie Baby takes note of our attendance, she asks, "Did you bring a date, Kayla?"

I'm prepared to explain that we came in a group when Dani declares, "She did."

Dani's wings stand taller when she moves to stand right next to Kayla. "I'm Kayla's date."

Kayla's mouth falls open, but she takes Dani's hand when she offers it.

"Oh!" Auntie Baby's eyes flicker between the two. "Kayla's the date you were waiting for?"

My mind is already prepared to stick up for Kayla and dispute any possible Saint Agnes regulation, but Dani speaks up first. "We're fighting the patriarchy."

Wow. I've never seen Kayla swoon this much over a nonfictional character before.

"How is this related to the patriarchy?" Seph asks, and I shush him. At this point, Dani can spin words to mean whatever she wants them to mean.

As Dani directs us to our table, she hands each of us a ballot for prom nominations. I can't help but laugh when I spot the footnote at the bottom: *Remember your vote matters, a reminder from your class president, Dani Bautista.*

Then Dani asks out of nowhere, "How did you pull off your campaign strategy?"

I stare at Dani's face, trying to decipher what in the world she's talking about. Damn. And I thought I was getting better at speaking her language.

"What do you—"

I don't get to finish my question. My brain's too overwhelmed from the horror of reading the list for prom king and queen candidates.

Moseph King and Annika Ilagan

Who the hell put our names there?!

Moments from earlier in the night start to make sense. A few girls from my class said "good luck" to me earlier, but I thought they were being nice and wishing me luck so that my feet would survive wearing heels. There were some guys who were shouting out "King" at Seph when we entered, but I thought they were just calling him by his surname.

I'm about to ask Dani if she can use her student council powers to investigate who turned my name in when I notice Auntie Baby in her angel outfit shoot me a thumbs-up. She huddles between Seph and me and lowers her voice. "My sources say that you two are ahead of Sean and Julia in the polls," she whispers as if we're discussing the forecast of a national election. "Be ready for the dance when they announce the winners."

I gape at Auntie Baby. "Did you . . . *nominate* us?"

It sounds even more ridiculous when I say it out loud!

Auntie Baby raises her shoulders, but I see her throw in a not-so-subtle wink. "Tell your mother that there are lots of perks from being active in the alumni association."

The blood in my body goes cold and my throat feels like it's closing in on itself. Oh god. Am I going to pass out? This definitely is what people feel like when they run out of oxygen. Everyone's going to remember prom night as that time Nika Ilagan fell to the floor in front of her auntie in an angel costume.

Seph taps my arm when I feel like I've gone catatonic. "Ilagan?"

This memory was supposed to be the easiest to re-create. I'm not as clueless as when we were at the soiree and I don't have to perform in front of a whole audience like at Battle of the Bands. Our strategy here was simple. Once they declare prom king and queen, Achi and I would make sure that our parents are both on the dance floor to witness it. I even swallowed my pride and asked Mercury Retrograde to play the song my parents danced to back at *their* prom.

There was never any mention of Seph and me dancing. I know my strengths as a performer, and dancing is not one of them!

What if Ma watches me bomb the dance, then she gets too distracted from being embarrassed for her daughter that she forgets to remember Pa? This is the event that's supposed to mark his fortieth day! What if Pa coming back hinges on this one dance?

"I'm good!" I hear my voice go up another octave. "Prom king and queen. Woot woot."

Oh god. Stress has made me utter the words *woot woot*.

I'm still massaging my throat and regaining the feeling in my legs when we position ourselves around the table. We all take our seats and I pull a chair for Pa, making an excuse to others that it's for my bag. The program soon kicks off, and my mind starts thinking about everything that could go wrong again.

The buffet runs out of rice, Sister Marissa keeps interrupting the prom host to remind us to make room for the Holy Spirit, and the Swifties Who Crochet club does a surprise a cappella performance. It's like a hurricane of things happening all around me.

In the midst of it all, I keep an eye on Pa. Every other second, my head swings in his direction, checking to make sure he's still there.

My hand instinctively goes to my wrist, then I remember that I left my hair tie at home since it didn't match my dress. While I'm mentally cursing myself for prioritizing fashion over my sanity, I hear Seph ask, "Sure ka okay ka lang?"

I nod and smile through my anxiety.

I'm convinced he buys it when we both focus back on whatever's happening onstage. But then he stands up from the table. "Hey, wanna go outside for a minute?"

A minute? Does he not realize how many things can go wrong in a minute?!

"It'll be quick," he adds while my insides are still swirling with nerves. "Just wanted to show you something."

My gaze drifts to Pa again. His eyes smile at me when he insists that he'll be fine. "You've been staring at me the whole night, Superstar," he teases. "Go have some fun with your date."

Achi is still standing with Ma by the chaperone corner

when I check. I already followed up with the band twice and they promised they would play my song request. Everyone else seems to be relatively calm and not acting like their lives are at the brink of falling apart. I guess we have some time left before they give out those prom awards . . .

While I'm in the middle of telling Kayla to message me right away if anything comes up, Seph keeps telling me that we will be back before I know it. He leads me outside the gym and I finally relent and follow him to the covered courts by the senior high building—the same place where we assemble every morning.

I'm checking my phone to see if Achi and Kayla left any messages when Seph tells me to look up.

"Come on, Ilagan, there's a better view up here."

I sigh. "What's so interesting about these covered courts—" Then I see Seph standing in front of me, his hands reaching out with the red corsage he bought for tonight. Back at the condo, I told Seph I wasn't into all the corsage, prom rite-of-passage stuff. The real truth? I was too self-conscious to do it in case Ma or Auntie Baby saw, and for them to see if I might actually enjoy it.

He unravels the corsage's ribbon and I reluctantly hold out my wrist for him.

"You learned this from your other crushes?" I ask, ignoring how my whole body hums when I feel his fingers graze my skin.

The corner of his mouth curves at the joke and he ties the ribbon around my hand. "There," he says when he's done. "More ties to keep you safe."

Thank god none of my family members are here. I'd be mortified if they saw how getting this red corsage made me smile.

I shake my head when Seph smooths out his tie, all proud of himself in his suit.

"Prom nominations freaked you out, huh?"

“The thought of dancing with you did,” I tease.

“Grabe.” He puts a hand to his chest. “I was an excellent dance lead for *High School Musical 3*. Direk Myka called me a natural.”

“When did you do the third one?”

“The summer after you left.”

I’m about to ask more questions when Seph puts his finger on his lips. He then motions for me to listen to the music coming from the gym. It’s the song Troy and Gabriella dance to on their school roof in the third movie.

His face lights up when it registers. “They’re playing the catching lightning song!”

“It’s called ‘Can I Have This Dance,’” I say, laughing.

With no shame whatsoever, Seph bows and proceeds to offer me his hand. “Can I have this dance, Gabriella?”

I just stare at his hand. “That’s disgusting.”

My disgust doesn’t faze him. He goes on to recite the lyrics of the song in the middle of the covered courts. “Take my hand, take a breath.” He does an exaggerated inhale and I scan the area in case anyone’s around and assumes that I’m with the guy who looks like he’s doing some bizarre spoken word poetry.

“Please don’t do this later if we have to dance in front of people.”

Seph responds by jiggling his shoulders in front of me. “Don’t you want the music to be your guide?”

I place my hands on his shoulders to stop him, then he slides them to the back of his neck. My breath quickens when I feel his hold move to my waist.

“See?” he says. The sides of his eyes crinkle when he holds my gaze. “Excellent dance lead.”

“Is this how you get the girls? Do you use your ‘My heart is yours’ catchphrase on them too?”

Seph makes a face at that. "Ilagan, that's disgusting."

The rest of the song plays and I let Seph's arms hold me as we sway along to the melody. I don't know how this always happens. How does everything suddenly feel okay when Seph's around?

Maybe my brain doesn't know how to process romance. I mean, even during this slow dance, I'm thinking about random online videos. There was this one night where I couldn't fall asleep, and for some reason, I got so fixated by this random video of a duck in a river. The duck looked like it was having a great time, gliding calmly through the water, living its best life. But when you looked beneath the surface? The duck was paddling furiously, like it was scared it would drown if it stopped going for even just one moment. Being with Seph is one of the rare times where I feel like things could still be okay if I stopped paddling.

I bury my head in his chest and imagine that all I have to do tonight is stay in this moment with Seph, dancing to some cheesy *High School Musical* song in the middle of our high school's covered courts. It's the first time that whole evening where I feel like I get to breathe.

But then hearing my sister's voice makes the wind go out of my lungs again.

"Nika." Achi calls my name and pops out of nowhere like she's some ghost (the actual terrifying kind). Seph and I spring apart when Achi catches us. "I've been looking all over for you."

"Are they announcing the prom awards already?"

A new, bigger kind of panic wallops my gut when I see Achi's expression. It's the same dead look in her eyes that comes out when she has bad news.

Then she tells me, "He's gone."

36

I CAN'T BELIEVE I DIDN'T SEE THIS COMING. JUST AS I LET DOWN MY guard, it was inevitable that all hell would break loose.

The second I get to the condo, I ransack the whole place, yelling out Pa's name. I check every bedroom, the bathroom, under the couch. "Pa?" I keep calling out, my voice sounding more and more hoarse. "Pa?"

My sister keeps telling me to calm down, but there's no time to calm down! As soon as she told me Pa was gone, I dropped everything and started running back home. My sister chased after me and insisted that I get in her car.

What if Pa turned invisible again? What if he's here somewhere, trying to call us, but we can't hear him?

I try lifting my heavy mattress and my sister is being zero percent helpful. "You're going to hurt yourself."

Ignoring her, I squat and use the momentum from my legs. This is what they say in those workout videos that also end up on my feed when I scroll through late at night.

"Pa isn't there," she tells me, which is getting very annoying.

"How do you know?"

Then Achi says, "He told me."

My chest constricts when I remember she and Pa spent the whole day together.

I drop the mattress. "What happened?"

"Did you even eat dinner?"

This has become my family's tactic. *If we distract Nika with food, then maybe she'll forget about all the things we've been hiding from her!*

"What happened?" I press harder.

Achi draws a sharp breath when I insist that I'm really not in the mood for her garlic rice.

"He thought that it was easier if the news came from me."

My sister's still talking when all the memories from that day five years ago flood over me. The moment Ma and I arrived at the condo, I rushed over to check if Pa was secretly waiting to surprise me. By the time I got there, my sister was standing in front of Pa's room, blocking me from entering, watching with the dead look in her eyes.

My sister tries to come nearer and I push her away. "What did you do?!" I yell, feeling the hot tears fall down my cheeks.

"Pa knew he only had forty days, Niks." She pauses. "H-he didn't want to go . . ."

Catching Achi's voice breaking and seeing her barely hold it together makes me sob harder.

"But *you* wanted him to go!" I wipe my eyes and force myself to look away from her. "You barely talked to him; you said all that stuff about Dr. Derrick being good for Ma—"

"I lost a dad too, Nika!" she cries out. "'Di mo ba gets 'yun?"

For a moment, the two of us stand still in our bedroom, the only noises coming from me and my sister trying to hold back our tears.

"He didn't want to tell us he was leaving before, either, Niks." Achi wipes her eyes on her sleeve. "The doctor gave him the diagnosis months before . . . I only found out because I picked up the phone by accident."

Snippets of their arguments from years ago suddenly get clearer then. Achi yelling at Pa for missing doctor appointments, Pa shouting that he's doing his best to protect the family.

Achi doesn't say anything when she grabs the tissue box and leaves it between us. Just as I'm considering grabbing one, she's already gained back her composure, safely locked up her emotions in a box again. "We should talk about how we're going to explain this to Ma."

My heart's still hammering when she keeps talking, moving at a pace that I can't follow.

"Maybe we can say you weren't feeling well so I had to bring you home early from prom?" she proposes. "I could say it was from something you ate at the buffet so she doesn't worry too much . . ."

The thought of lying, downplaying things to Ma again, makes me want to throw the sofa against the wall. I can't. I can't do this anymore. My time with Pa isn't over! I was able to get Pa back before, and I can do it a million times more if I have to. I'm *not* losing him again.

"Where are you going?" Achi calls while I storm out of the bedroom. You know what the problem was? Getting more people involved. I've never been a group-project person, and I'm going to solve this whole thing by doing what I do best.

Working solo.

37

THE ELEVATOR REACHES MY FLOOR AND OPENS TO SEPH STANDING inside. He's still wearing the suit and a stupid pink sash that has a glittered *Prom King* print on it.

Truly, the last person in the world I want to see.

"Hey," he says, the sides of his eyes crinkling again as if everything in the world is fine. "Did something happen with Achi Jackie? I was gonna go to your unit to check on you."

"Nothing," I mutter, trying to bypass him to the elevator.

"Whoa, wait, wait. Ilagan, hold on." He grabs my hand. "Talk to me."

If I wasn't so busy talking to Seph earlier, then I would've caught Pa leaving.

"You missed our crowning moment. Didn't get to use my dancing skills since Julia and Sean took over."

If I wasn't so busy dancing with Seph, then I could've stopped Pa.

"I also didn't have time to give you this . . ." Seph grabs something from his suit pocket and places what looks like a plastic egg in my other hand.

"It's supposed to be a surprise," he says, rubbing the back of his head. "Tried to be cute with the egg thing, like a reference to your scrambled eggs."

If I wasn't with Seph, Pa would still be here.

After I don't say anything, he taps my wrist. "Hey, what's going on?"

All words escape me when Seph stares at me like he's so desperate to help. He always makes me feel that things will be all right. What if he can fix this whole situation with Pa's ghost too?

But then my whole body tightens as I consider opening up to Seph about Pa. I drift back to the prom sash on his chest and everything that happened tonight. Being with Seph didn't fix anything.

You just made everything worse for your whole family, again.

"Why did you even go to prom with me?" I almost spit out.

He looks at me like the answer's obvious. "Because I like you."

"Why?" I try to blink away the tears I feel coming.

"Hasn't it been obvious over the past weeks?"

My shoulders bunch up. "I thought we were just having fun," I manage to say despite my throat closing in on itself again. "Being one of your MOMOL buddies."

Seph stops short. "How can we be MOMOL buddies when I have no idea what that means?" It all makes my vison blur with tears. *Why is he still here?!*

"Hey." He dips his head so he meets my eyes. "I like you. Just you, okay? And I have a feeling from how it's been going, I think you like me too."

". . . What if I don't like you?" I ask under my breath. "Will you go away?"

The way his face falls makes my heart twist. It's like a dozen eternities pass while we stand outside the elevator without saying a word.

Then I hear Seph say no.

"If that's what you feel . . . ," his voice rasps out. "I'll always be your friend, Nika. Your family has always been there for me and I'll always be here for you."

He doesn't know what he's saying. I'm so tired of people

giving me false promises. I'm so tired of getting my hopes up. Everyone I care about always ends up leaving me.

So I go for where I know it'll hurt.

"We're only here because I feel sorry for you," I blurt out. "That's the only reason why I went along with the soiree, the prom . . . Your dad isn't giving you any attention, so you're desperate for anyone to notice you."

My eyes prickle from seeing the look on Seph's face. He doesn't fight back or say anything else. He just untangles his hand from mine and watches as I step inside the elevator.

The elevator doors slide shut and it's too late for me to take all those words back.

38

PA WASN'T THERE.

He wasn't at the school, he wasn't at the bakery, he wasn't at the airport. I took Martha and I drove her to every single place Pa and I have visited the past forty days. I went back to Saint Agnes again, hoping that Pa has been waiting for me after prom this whole evening. No one was there. By the time I got back home, the sun was already peeking through.

Achi was waiting up for me and said she gave Ma the alibi that I was already sleeping. I didn't have any energy left to care. When I sank into my bed, my mind just kept screaming about all the ways I let Pa down—and it forced me to snap into action.

That all led me here: a crowded dentist's office first thing on a Sunday morning. To my right, there are kids arguing over a PlayStation console, and to my left, another kid is crying after hearing they needed to get braces. While all this is happening, there's a Pitbull song about hooking up in hotels and motels blasting in the waiting room.

While Pitbull is shouting out names of different women, the receptionist calls out, "Annika Ilagan?" When I look up, she adds, "Dr. Go is ready to see you now."

As she leads me to the designated cubicle, I rehearse the speech I have for Dr. Derrick. I realize that everything went from bad to worse ever since he came into the picture. Pa was becoming more real every time Ma remembered him, but how can she keep doing that if she's getting married to someone else?

Well, there's no wedding if the groom decides to back out first.

I'm thrown off when Dr. Derrick isn't in the room. "Sorry, he'll be with you in a moment," the receptionist says in a voice that's barely a whisper. "Let's get you ready so you'll be all set for your cleaning.

"Sorry," she says again as she guides me to recline in the dentist chair. Gigi carefully straps a bib on me with a smiling tooth that says, *Ready for my tooth-pics.*

This is fine. I can still confront someone from this position.

"Annika!" Dr. Derrick startles when he walks in. He straps on a face mask, then lowers himself onto a rolling chair and scoots until he's by my side. "I haven't seen you in the clinic in a while." He faces the receptionist. "Gigi, when was Annika's last cleaning?"

"Oh, sorry!" Gigi flusters at this with her big puppy dog eyes and frantically goes through the records on her tablet. How am I supposed to yell at Dr. Derrick when Gigi's around? The woman has apologized to me ten times in the past minute.

He then turns on an overhead lamp that assaults my eyesight. "Sorry, we're working on dimming that," he says, handing me a pair of goggles.

"Your wedding—" I manage to squeeze out before Gigi inserts a suction tube in my mouth with a small "Sorry!"

The rest of my words get muffled when Dr. Derrick switches on the drill.

"Were you talking about your last appointment?" he shouts above the noise.

I try answering him, but it sounds a lot more like "Mmmmrrrrpppphhh."

Gigi then informs him that my last cleaning was eighteen months ago.

"Eighteen months?!" Dr. Derrick's eyes bulge out of their sockets. Evidently, he's more pressed about my gum health than anything wedding-related. "Is our reminder system not working? Maybe our patients aren't receiving their alerts." He instructs Gigi to take notes and focuses back on me. "Anything you want us to address first?"

I pull out the suction tube before I speak.

"Can you not marry my mom?"

He opens his mouth to respond, then realizes that Gigi is still in the room with us. She's paying close attention to her tablet. "Sorry, sir, should I note that under the patient's medical history?"

Dr. Derrick dismisses Gigi and tells her to attend to checking the clinic's reminder system first. Once we're alone in the cubicle, Dr. Derrick shuts off the lamp and lowers his face mask.

"I feel like I owe you a conversation."

"Please," I start to beg. "Just focus on hating me and how much it'd suck to have me as a stepdaughter."

His forehead scrunches when he listens to me. "I don't hate you."

"Of course you do."

He immediately denies it. "That's not true."

"You don't need to protect me."

"I'm not protecting you; I'm telling you the truth."

"So tell me the truth that you hate me."

"But that's not the truth," Dr. Derrick still insists.

I rest my head back on the dentist chair. Why did Ma have to pick a guy that's so difficult?!

"Beth and I already talked last night about calling off the wedding."

. . . *What?*

He waits for me to sit up and fidgets with his striped purple tie as he explains, "She told me that she wasn't ready to get married again. When we proposed to each other, I already told her that we can always have that conversation."

The day Dr. Derrick asked her was, admittedly, the happiest I had seen Ma in years. Of course, I don't tell *him* that.

"What do you mean you proposed to each other?"

Dr. Derrick sighs and places his hands on his lap. "Your mom and I had a mutual proposal," he says.

I look at him, confused. "Who went down on one knee?"

"We were both sitting down," he says, smiling. "Beth wanted to make sure we were able to hear each other clearly, discuss the logistics, the practical side of things. Also, I have really weak knees."

"How romantic."

"Very," he agrees, not picking up on the sarcasm.

"If it's mutual . . ." I pause, trying to follow. "How does that go? You just decide to ask each other at the same time?"

"Well, your mom already knew I wanted to marry her. I was pretty sure very early on. I'd had a ring with me just in case, but I didn't want to rush things since . . ."

I nod when we both leave Pa unsaid.

"I've known your mom for many years. From the first time I asked her out, Beth emphasized that her children came before anything else," he adds. "Then one day, she asked me if I really saw myself marrying someone who already had two daughters. I told her yes. And then she asked me if I was capable of caring for you and Jackie like my own daughters; I told her I already did."

Something inside my chest twists when I hear how sincere he sounds.

"Then she said marrying could be a good move for her girls. More stability and she didn't want you to get affected about her being a single mom," Dr. Derrick explains. "Your mom was . . . worried na nagkulang siya sa inyo by herself."

Everything inside me immediately gets defensive. "Ma has done more than enough for us," I argue.

"I agree." He doesn't deny it. "Families with a single good parent are better off than families with two bad ones."

"So my mom asked you to marry her because of us . . . not because of you?"

"I'd like to think that I was a small factor." He fills a paper cup from the chair's faucet and leaves it by my side. There's still this reflex that recoils at the idea of Dr. Derrick taking care of me, but I accept the water anyway.

"What are you gonna do now?" I ask him.

"I told your mom I still want to be with her."

"Even if she never marries you?"

"As long as she'll have me." He sips from his cup, then adds, "Most importantly, if you'd have me."

"Me?"

"Like you kids say, this is a safe space." He sits with his legs crossed, ankle over knee. "I know you have some doubts about me and I want to improve."

"Doubts? I don't have any doubts?" I hear my voice getting increasingly pitchy.

Dr. Derrick keeps his gaze fixed on me.

"You promise you won't take this out on my mom?"

He shakes his head and promises, "Safe space."

That's when I ask if he can pass me my bag.

"Do you have a secret list with your complaints about me?" he asks when I pull out my phone.

"Yes."

His eyes widen at my answer, but he lets me go on.

"Point one: You take forever to make coffee."

"Making a good cup of coffee is a process."

"Yeah, let's speed up the process," I say firmly. "Point two: your gift-giving."

"You didn't like the Waterpik I gave you for Christmas?"

I didn't even know he got me a present. "What did you get for Ma?"

"Same thing."

He can sense me judging, so he adds, "They're great for flossing hard-to-reach areas."

"And you give the most boring-ass greeting cards."

Dr. Derrick flinches (not sure if it's from my criticism or my cursing).

"You could at least add a pun," I suggest, pointing at my bib with the cartoon tooth. The gift comment looks like it stung so I save my purple tie thoughts so I can address the most offensive item.

"Point three: your family," I read. "I don't appreciate your mom talking about me and my sister."

Concern floods his face. "When did that happen?"

"Before the ting hun. Auntie Baby and Auntie Grace overheard your mom. She warned you about us embarrassing your family and us not being proper."

I see the moment when it clicks in his head.

But then he says, "That wasn't about you and Jackie."

"Auntie Baby says her chismis is ninety-nine point nine percent accurate."

"This is the point one percent," he tells me. "That message was meant for my mom's sisters. I never told you that I'm sorry that my aunties were rude to you during the ting hun."

. . . What do I say to that? I've envisioned confronting Dr. Derrick a million times. Not once did I imagine getting an apology. "My mom wanted to keep my aunties in check because she wanted to make a good impression on Beth and your family," he explains. "She's scared I'd lose my shot at another wedding."

Excuse me?

"How many times do you plan on getting married?"

"Once." He takes a moment and sighs deeply. "I was engaged to someone else years ago . . . She passed away a month before we were supposed to get married."

A chill goes through my body when I process what he's saying.

"That's a lot of information, but I'm here to answer any questions you have too."

Did I hear that right or did the suction tube do something to my ears?

I scan his face. "You're okay with talking about it?"

"I'm supposed to be honest in a safe space, right?"

"My family never talks about my dad," I admit before even thinking.

He sighs and his eyes flit to the ceiling. Maybe I pushed him . . . maybe the conversation went too far. I never expected Dr. Derrick to open up even more.

"It was a horrible accident," Dr. Derrick shares. "She had just passed her board exams. Running on no sleep, she had some drinks, and was in no state to be driving." His voice shakes with regret. "I—I can't go through a night without seeing what the crash looked like . . ." He shuts his eyes and shakes his head. "I made sure her parents never found out.

"I told them I was the one who crashed the car," he explains. "Made sure it was a closed casket, asked my friend who was a doctor to say she didn't feel much pain. That it was immediate when she bumped her head on impact."

"And they believe you were the one who was driving?"

"Yes."

"Did they blame you?"

"They've refused to talk to me since."

I sit there, stunned. "But that's not what happened."

"She and her parents had suffered enough," he says. "People would have seen Bettina differently if they found out she had been drinking. All the good she brought into the world would have been reduced to a tragic mistake. Sometimes, we have to hide things to protect our families."

"So you never told anyone the truth?"

"Not until I met your mother."

My mind gets dizzy imagining how long he's kept that all in.

"Bettina loved talking about the moon and the stars, so some part of me thinks she's somewhere in the sky," he says, pointing up.

His moon obsession was number seven on my list.

". . . Do you really think Bettina hears you when you talk to the moon?"

He stares at the ceiling again, weighing his words. "If it's possible for the moon to control the ocean's tides, who's to say that our dead loved ones can't hear us?"

It sounds like something Pa would say.

"Dr. Derrick," I prompt, and he turns to me.

"Does it . . . ever stop hurting?"

He returns my question with a sad smile. "Your family lost the love of your life, Annika," he tells me without sugarcoating it. The fact that he doesn't make one of those promises that "you'll be okay soon" or "just give it time" tells me he really does get it.

"Was Bettina the love of your life?"

He considers the question. "A love of my life, yes," he answers. "Although, when I think about *the* love of my life . . . the title would have to go to your mother."

Disgusting, I almost say. It's a miracle that the statement doesn't make me puke.

"That's the kind of stuff that should go on your cards."

"Should I draw a tooth next to it?"

I bite back a smile. At least he's learning.

"Annika," he says. "This is still a safe space, correct?"

Lord, does he still have more trauma to unpack?

"The cavity on your right molar is very alarming," he says with such a pained expression. "Can you please use the Waterpik I gave you?"

After the most painful dental cleaning I've ever had in my life, Dr. Derrick sends me home with a card that has a cartoon tooth cradling a heart. On the bottom, there's an added pun: *It's okay to have fillings.*

39

I STILL COULDN'T FIND PA ANYWHERE.

Every single place I can think of, anywhere that I remember he's been to before—there were no signs of my father. The security guard at his old bank had to escort me out after I scanned the lobby area again for the tenth time.

After I came home with nothing to report, Ma told me that Achi said she was staying over at her own condo tonight. At least this means I don't have to face a night of awkward silence with Achi in our bedroom.

Although I doubt that being alone and dehydrating my whole body is any better.

God. *Stop crying. Stop crying!*

Why are you still crying?!

If I keep this up, I'm going to flood the whole condo with my tears.

You know, this would be respectable crying if it were entirely about Pa—but there's a small, tiny part of my brain that lingers on Seph.

It's better this way. You won't get hurt this way. I keep repeating the same thoughts even though I desperately want to call him and take back everything I said.

God. How am I still thinking about a stupid boy when my dad is literally gone?

If maturity means not feeling things anymore, maybe this is what being seventeen is all about—feeling sad and horny at the same time.

Once my eyes seem to finally run out of fluids, I grab for

the ice pack I store in my bedside drawer. Lesson learned from years of experience: If I don't ice my eyes after a night of crying, I'm going to wake up looking like mosquitoes assaulted my eyelids.

While my hand searches for the pack, it bumps into the book hiding Pa's phone. I haven't checked it ever since Pa's ghost showed up. I plug the phone into my charger, and moments later, it lights up with a ton of notifications.

Most of them are messages from the contact labeled *Sweetheart*

Still thinking about seeing our baby go to prom. Did you ever think she'd be this grown up? –Beth

Wish you were here, sweetheart. –Beth

The last message was sent an hour ago.

I take the phone, creep outside, and notice the light seeping in from Ma's bedroom. When I press my ear to her door, I try to listen for any signs that Ma's already sleeping.

Knock. Knock. Knock.

I'm contemplating walking away when I hear a faint, "Nika?"

When I slowly push open the door, I see Ma is lying on the right side of the bed with her tablet propped up on the left. The left part was always Pa's side of the bed.

Ma scooches to the middle as soon as I climb in. I peer over her shoulder and see she's watching the *Pagpag* movie. If Achi were here, she'd convince Ma to switch the movie to something lighter. I mean, the movie is literally about a woman making a deal with the devil to revive her dead husband—this *has* to be triggering for Ma.

"Are you sure you should be watching this?"

Ma holds up her finger and whispers, "The ghost knows where they are."

I keep watching as Kathryn and her little brother, the

character Macmac, hide underneath a white sheet at an abandoned house. Roman the ghost murderer creeps into the room and swats away the other hanging sheets in the room with a wooden stake. Kathryn hugs Macmac closer when the ghost slowly walks away . . .

"Ay!" Ma covers her eyes when the ghost catches them.

"Kathryn's not going to die," I assure Ma. "She's the best character here. Movies never kill off the best characters."

Ma still doesn't look at the screen.

Like I predicted, Kathryn and her brother are able to escape from Roman's grasp and run outside to the garden. But then the ghost catches up to them. Roman knocks over Macmac with his elbow and chokes Kathryn by the neck. He shoves her to the ground and raises his wooden stake . . .

No way. There's no way the movie is actually going to let her die.

Ominous music plays . . .

Macmac yells for his sister . . .

Kathryn screams . . .

A gasp escapes my lips as Roman lifts the stake over her body, when suddenly, a dagger pierces the ghost's heart. With very convenient and impossible timing, Daniel (who was completely passed out just a moment ago) miraculously kills the resurrected ghost.

I only remember to exhale when the screen shows Kathryn and her brother alive and well.

My mom peers at me. "You were scared too, 'no?"

"I was not," I lie. "Told you. They never kill the best characters."

She pauses the tablet and adjusts her body so she's facing me. "Niks." Her hand brushes the hair from my eyes. "Have you been crying?"

"No."

Ma purses her lips so I change tactics. "Allergies," I say instead.

She answers with a heavy sigh and silence stretches between us.

"I know I'm the last person you want to talk through things with, but if you ever need somebody to talk to . . ." She eyes me with a sad smile. "Offer's always open."

My sister would want me to lie and deny for Ma's sake. Tell her that everything's okay, that I really have nothing I want to talk about—but something tells me that she can see right through me.

So I show her Pa's old phone. "I saw your messages."

Ma fidgets when she scans the texts she's been sending the past few weeks. "You weren't supposed to see those."

"It's not like I saw the dirty ones."

"Nika."

"Ma, it's okay!" I tell her. "I send myself messages from Pa's phone and pretend like they're from him. That's more embarrassing."

Her eyes grow wide. "You message Ton?"

I nod. "Have you tried looking Pa up online?"

Ma's brow scrunches. "Isn't that dangerous?"

I type out Pa's name in the YouTube search bar on her tablet. "Promise. This won't lead to the kidnappers finding us," I tell Ma when she still looks concerned.

With a heavy sigh, she finally relaxes enough so I can click on the video of Pa playing the piano at the mall. I laugh at the part where the people surrounding him start calling out song requests.

"Of course I'm going with Mariah Carey," I say right before Pa says it.

"How many times have you watched this?" Ma asks me.

I shrug. "Achi watches it too."

She stays silent and I worry that I said the wrong thing again.

But I finally voice the question I've been too scared to ask. "Did Pa tell you he was sick?"

Ma then stiffens and retreats to her scary, quiet place. *Take the question back!* my brain screams. I need to change the subject, make Ma forget about losing Pa, do *something* so I don't hurt Ma even more. So many thoughts are tumbling in my head when Ma can't even look at me.

Her eyes linger on the screen when I hear her reply. "Your dad made me promise not to tell."

I'm holding my breath the whole time she speaks.

"Your angkong, your dad's dad, was diagnosed with . . . terminal cancer when Ton was around your age," Ma starts to say.

My dad's side of the family always said my angkong was "gone too soon." No one ever mentioned that he had cancer.

"His uncles told Ton not to tell your amah about the diagnosis."

I pause to make sure I heard that correctly. "Why would they ask Pa not to tell his mom?"

"They were worried that your amah might not be able to handle that information, that it was too much for her. So Ton did everything he could to mask your angkong's condition."

Ma goes on to rationalize this by saying his uncles trusted Pa since he was the eldest son of the family, and my mind can't shake the image of my dad at seventeen. How could he have handled a secret like that?

"Did you know that your angkong was a piano player too?" Ma tells me, a smile crossing her face when she reminisces. "He was the one who taught Ton how to play. Ton always used to call him his best friend whenever he'd tell me stories about his dad."

Then my whole chest squeezes when I remember why Pa wasn't scared about breaking the pagpag superstition. How Pa said that he wished his best friend's spirit would follow him home so he could catch his friend up on all that he had missed.

I never knew that Pa was talking about his dad.

How could his uncles do that to Pa?!

"So they made Pa lie to amah that whole time?" I ask, feeling the heat rising in my neck.

"He wasn't lying, Nika, he was protecting his mother," Ma lectures me instead of seeing my side. "Tsai ya kha tsio, huan ho kha tsio. My parents used to tell me that—the less you know, the less you worry. Talking about things like sickness and death? That can do a lot more harm than good."

There's a throbbing in my head as I try to process everything Ma's telling me. "Does protecting your family always mean you have to suffer alone?"

I'm worried I've lost Ma to the quiet place again when she doesn't answer. Her voice comes out soft when she says, "I guess, sometimes."

"It sounds so lonely." The words fly out of my mouth before I can think twice.

The way Ma looks at me then makes my throat sting. While Pa can smile with his eyes, I always see Ma's heart breaking in hers. Her eyes are so sad when she turns the question back on me. "Do you feel lonely, sweetheart?"

My mouth opens with the reflex to downplay things again, push back the building geyser in my throat, insist that I'm fine and have always been fine! But the moment I try speaking, the whole dam breaks apart—all the tears flood through and I can't catch up.

"I'm here, Niks. I'm here," Ma coos while trying to catch my sobs. I feel her hold me closer and I start bawling into her arms.

"I could hear you before when you would cry at night about Pa." I wipe the edges of my eyes. "Then I made it worse when I would sing and hurt you all over again. I keep doing the wrong thing, Ma, and I'm so, so sorry that I always make your life harder."

Ma rubs my shoulders when they rise and fall from my crying. "Nika." She cups my face and wipes my cheeks. "You don't make my life harder. Loving you is the easiest thing in the world." Her heartbroken eyes are glistening when she asks, "And did you really stop performing because of me?"

"I—I saw you crying to Achi before my last show," I confess. "I didn't want you to go through that again."

"But I loved watching you sing." A small smile crosses her lips when she brushes my hair with her hand. "You're so talented, just like your father."

My heart still braces itself whenever Ma mentions Pa.

"When I saw you practicing that day, I got overwhelmed with so many emotions, and . . . I don't know how to handle all of that sometimes. It breaks my heart when I see you hurting and I think I push you too hard because I want to help so badly." Ma then shuts her eyes as if she's reliving it all. "I worry that I don't know *how* to help you and Jackie," she admits, her breath hitching. "Before I go to the office in the morning, I usually walk a couple laps around the bakery contemplating all the things I could've done wrong. Did I give you too much space? Did I give Jackie the right advice? Did I tell you the correct thing?"

Based on all the worries Ma lists, she must walk the whole of Metro Manila every morning.

"That's why you have such nice calves."

"Diba?" Ma chuckles and stretches her legs. "Worrying is great cardio."

"But you really don't have to worry about us, Ma," I say, brushing off the tear sliding down her cheek.

She pauses and smooths my hair again. "Asking a mom not to worry is like asking her not to breathe," she says, then sighs.

Hearing that makes me want to swallow all the emotions back down.

"When you say that you get overwhelmed with a lot of feelings . . . ," I start to say. "That happens to me, too, usually when I get mad about things. I don't think clearly and I do some really shitty things I don't mean. I'm sorry I was shitty about you and Dr. Derrick."

"Nika, don't call yourself a shit."

"I'm not," I argue. "I was using shitty as an adjective."

Ma looks me in the eye then. "You lost your dad. People deserve forgiveness for the things they do when they're hurt."

". . . But what if I'm always hurt?"

The room grows quiet after that.

I then feel the need to add, "But I realize he's not . . . the worst guy in the world," I assure her. "Like you could've done way worse, especially with all the kidnappers lurking around the internet."

But Ma's face still stays serious despite the joke. "I should've been smarter about all of it," she says. "With everything that's going on, being with Derrick, it felt like he understood . . ." I notice how Ma's face brightens with each mention of his name. "I should've called off the wedding earlier when I saw how it was affecting you."

Then she ends with a wistful voice, "Maybe I got too carried away."

"You were happy, Ma," I tell her, and squeeze her hand. "I want you to be happy."

She wipes her eyes and clutches my shoulder. "I thought people only cried this much in the movies."

"Could be fun if they made one about us." My mind wanders and imagines an Ilagan major motion picture. "We could star in the *Pagpag* sequel."

Ma considers this. "That sounds too dark. Our family isn't going to be in a horror movie. I want a happy film."

"I think that's hard with the whole dead dad thing."

"Our family can still have a love story," she insists.

"Maybe Pa would've gotten a different ending in the movie."

I say it without really thinking—again. That part of my brain that's supposed to be in charge of filtering out what I say? Pretty sure that's nonexistent.

But then Ma nods like she understands. "Because movies never kill off the best characters."

She smiles when I add, "They would never kill you off, either."

Ma notices the clock on her tablet and tells me I should really get some sleep. "No more keeping everything to yourself, okay?"

Um.

Okay, from where I'm standing, I have two choices. One: Lie and basically cancel out the progress that Ma and I made in our heart-to-heart. Two: Tell the truth and risk getting sent to the hospital for grief hallucinations.

"Um. Ma?" I carefully ask. "There's something you need to know."

Ma looks at me and the words tumble out of my mouth. "When I didn't pagpag after Pa's death anniversary, his spirit came back. He was sort of a spirit, I think, but he felt real, Ma, so I thought Pa could stay with us permanently."

Then I recap everything from the forty-day superstition to everything that went down during prom night, to how I've spent the last day searching for any signs of Pa.

"I don't know if there's a way we can contact him. There must be experts who know how to get in touch with spirits. Maybe we can ask Father Melvin, like that should be something they teach priests . . . Wait. Ma, where are you going?"

Before I finish talking, Ma climbs out of bed and changes out of her pajamas. She snatches the car keys from her drawer and tells me to go get her bag.

Lord, did I just shoot up my mother's blood pressure?

She tells me to get dressed, too, and I repeat the same question.

And Ma says, "We're going to bring back your father."

40

FOR THE FIRST TIME IN LILIBETH ILAGAN'S WHOLE EXISTENCE, SHE chooses to buck superstition.

She called up my sister, told her we were picking her up and driving to the Memorial Park. Achi had a ton of questions, but all Ma said was that we didn't need to do the usual protocol.

Usually, once we set foot inside the cemetery, Ma gives us a red envelope and a pouch of rice that we're supposed to throw away as we exit. Even when Achi mentioned to my mom that she had an extra ang pao in her bag, Ma said we didn't need any tonight.

"We want the spirits to follow us this time."

You would think that forgoing all her beliefs would turn Ma into a jittery mess, but she's the definition of calm and composed.

She calmly led us to Pa's grave, calmly lit the incense, calmly walked back to the car, and is currently calmly driving us home. Plot twist: The one who's the actual jittery mess is my sister. From the back of the car, I can hear Achi's deep breathing in the passenger seat. She's been huffing and puffing like a woman in labor.

I bump the back of her seat with my knee. "Why do you sound like you're choking?"

Her voice is out of breath when she asks. "Can we stop for a CR break?"

"When we get back to the condo, you can go up to use the bathroom first," Ma answers, her eyes never leaving the road.

"What about food?" Achi lifts her chin so our eyes meet in the rearview mirror. "Niks, do you wanna stop at Potato Corner?"

My sister just initiated getting fast food. I thought the world would end before this ever happened.

Against my own cravings, I tell my sister that we can't stop for fries. "We're not supposed to pagpag. The whole point is that we're going straight home so that Pa follows us there."

Has my sister's mind been floating this whole time? Ma and I have been discussing nonstop about how if we can't find Pa anywhere, maybe breaking pagpag again will bring him back to us. I don't get why she's acting like she never received the point of our mission.

Unless . . . is she sabotaging the mission on purpose?

"Do you not wanna see Pa?"

She gaslights me in response. "What're you talking about?"

"You're distracting Ma with CR breaks and french fries."

"My bad for thinking you might be hungry," she says with a scoff. "Even before seeing Dr. Broso, you wanted pancit canton."

Achi and I yelp when the car suddenly swerves, and Ma parks on the side of the road. Since when did my mother drive like she's in one of those *Fast & Furious* movies?! "Nika is seeing Dr. Broso?" Ma darts her eyes at Achi and me.

"No!" we both deny while my heart is still pounding.

"It's what kids Nika's age say, Ma," Achi says.

"R-right."

Judging from my sister's silence, I'm assuming she's leaving it up to me to explain.

"When Achi said I'm *seeing* Dr. Broso . . ." I think and clear my throat. "It's not like seeing, like getting therapy. It's like when I'm seeing someone, I think they're cool."

Ma stays silent while Achi looks at me like I'm not the one salvaging her stupid excuse.

"Since Dr. Broso is so accomplished, 'I'm seeing Dr. Broso' is sort of a compliment," I ramble away. "And like you, Ma, with your bakery. My classmates would also say, hey, auntie, I'm *seeing* you."

The only thing I wish I'm seeing is an exit to this conversation.

A beat passes before Ma sighs. "You're really terrible at lying, Nika."

"I . . . I'm not . . ."

Am I supposed to defend my "I'm seeing you" explanation or the fact that I'm actually an excellent liar?

Then my sister, for no reason, throws me under the bus. "That's why I keep telling you, Niks, to not make up so many stories—"

"Isa ka pa." Ma cuts Achi off. "Don't pretend that you don't hide things from me too."

Achi stammers. "Ma, I never—"

"When you help out with the bakery, I know you don't charge the company. I know you've inquired about renting out your condo and asked the bank about my retirement fund planning. I know you borrowed my superstition notebook because you were nervous about your GRE exam.

"I also know that my brilliant daughter got awarded a fellowship to one of the world's best psychology programs but wants to turn it down so she can take care of her family."

My sister doesn't deny any of it. I don't remember the last time I saw her tear up without her shades on.

"And right now, you're scared that I'll break down again if your papa's spirit doesn't show up."

Achi's shoulders tremble when she answers. "I don't want to see you like that again."

Ma gives my achi space to cry and places her hand on top of my sister's. "You're the one who's been taking care of this family, Jackie," Ma says. "Let me take care of you too."

I lean closer to Achi's seat and stretch my arms to hug her when she bawls harder. "I'm always *seeing* you, Ach."

She laughs between her sobs. "That's such a stupid lie."

"Whatever. You like my stupid lies so much that you'd rather room with me than go be the smartest person with the alligators in Florida."

Ma shoots me a look that makes me feel like I'm in trouble.

"Sorry," I add, and wag my finger at Achi. "Make sure your housing is far away from the alligators."

"Annika," Ma warns.

"Promise, that was my last joke."

"Remember that you can tell me things, too, okay?"

"Ma, I'm not hiding anything."

Achi scoffs. "Please."

"What? Ma and I just had a heart-to-heart. I'm an open book!"

"Oh, you *are* an open book," Achi agrees. "It's so obvious when you're hiding something."

"When the two of you would turn on the ceiling fan to hide that you're arguing at the bakery," Ma prompts.

Achi and I gape at Ma. "You knew about that?"

Ma cocks her head at us. So this is where Achi gets her I-know-more-than-you-think head tilt from. "Why do you think you girls are so smart?"

My sister then adds, "How about all the times Nika used the upset-stomach excuse to get away from things."

"She was saying she was suffering from PMS even before she had her first period," Ma says, chuckling.

"Hey," I protest. "I was an early bloomer."

Ma nudges Achi. "How long do you think she's been trying to hide her and Seph?"

"The most obvious people alive." My sister rolls her eyes. "Was that ten years in the making?"

"I still think she's too young to date." Ma gives me a pointed look with that. "But at least he's a good boy, and they were always so cute together. Remember when she burned her bangs because she was ironing her hair out for one of their rehearsals?"

"She was always in a rush whenever we got in the elevator, but if Seph's there, she'd give this whole lecture about how it's common courtesy to hold the doors open."

My chest twists into knots the more they talk about Seph. God, I really miss him.

"Hey, can we move on from talking about me, please?"

"But isn't this your favorite subject?" Achi teases.

I place my hand over Achi's mouth, and face Ma's direction in the driver's seat. "If we're telling you our secrets, Ma, you have to confide in us too."

My words stretch on while Ma starts the car again and makes the turn to our condo's parking structure. Then she says, "Parents are supposed to protect their kids."

"But, Ma." My sister holds on to Ma's knee. "Who's the one protecting you?"

Ma doesn't answer and the car goes quiet when she switches off the ignition. Her hand hovers over the door handle before she steps out.

"The day you two saw me at Dr. Broso was my first appointment," she says, her voice shaky. "Derrick told me how much grief counseling helped him, and I think . . . I might need it too.

"Do you girls want to go with me for my next session?"

Ma's eyes glisten when the two of us agree with no hesitation.

41

IT WAS NAIVE OF ME TO THINK THAT MA LET GO OF ALL HER SUPERSTI-tions. The moment she sets foot inside the condo, it's like the superstitiousness switches to overdrive.

"Your father is a lost soul," she keeps repeating to me and Achi. "There are souls who roam around our world and then give up their shot at heaven. We need to help him find his way!"

For this to happen, Ma's big plan includes baking enough food to feed a small country. She's been making buns, rolls, pies, cakes—any pastry you can think of, it's currently being prepped in our kitchen. I don't know, maybe in Ma's mind, ghosts find their way more easily when they're well-fed.

An even more bizarre request she gave me: "Nika, go get a butterfly net!"

I've never owned a butterfly net and I have no idea where in the world to find one. When I mentioned that Pa first showed up as a butterfly, Ma said we should cover all the bases in case he comes back as a winged insect.

"Pretty good, right?" I ask my sister.

I used my half-broken badminton racket and tied a plastic bag to the head's frame. Ta-da! Makeshift butterfly net.

Achi doesn't give me credit for my resourcefulness. "You and Ma aren't thinking straight."

"A butterfly wouldn't know the difference between the real thing," I say, swooshing the racket.

She checks if Ma is still occupied with the pie in the oven. "Superstitious beliefs are Ma's coping mechanism," Achi stresses when Ma's out of earshot. "She wants to feel control over her life, so she believes in things like butterflies and lost souls."

Normally, I'd be on the same page. I still stand by science despite my spotty chemistry attendance. Yet my same rational brain feels better when I have my hair tie on my wrist. The same rational brain spent the past forty days with Pa's ghost that was invisible to everybody else. So maybe part of me sees where Ma's coming from and can understand why a butterfly flying into our home can mean so much more. I guess it can't hurt to believe in things that are bigger than our world.

That's the moment I start thinking of all the things that Pa believes in. If anything's going to draw him back here, it's not the food or Ma's buko pie.

I leave my sister with the butterfly net and ransack my bedroom for where he left the cards, photos, letters he stored in his piano bench. Together, I dig up my memories too—all the photo albums, the ticket from our Battle of the Bands performance, a snowflake sticker from the ceiling, Ma's necklace with the butterfly pendant—maybe gathering all this in one place will be enough.

Nobody notices me once I return.

After placing everything on the table in front of the couch, I call out to Achi, "By the way, I'm telling Pa you didn't believe in him when he shows up!"

She doesn't even give me a response.

Not a single word from my sister or my mother.

Actually, there aren't any of the usual chaotic baking noises coming from the kitchen. No signs of my ma yelling out instructions or my sister bouncing between the hundred dishes being made. I walk in their direction to find Achi and Ma standing still, staring at an upturned soup bowl on the floor.

"What's that?"

Still, nothing from them. They're frozen in place, mesmerized by the sight of the soup bowl. Maybe *I'm* the one who turned into a ghost.

But when I actually do something and nudge the bowl with the side of my foot, Achi suddenly grabs my ankle. I have to hold on to the edge of the counter so I don't fall and crack my head.

"Do you want me to *die*?!"

She just scoffs at that. "I barely touched you."

I turn to Ma to make sure she witnessed what just happened.

"A butterfly flew in and we placed a bowl over it," Ma explains.

"He's under there?" I gape at Ma and at the tiny bowl.

Achi stops me again when I try reaching for it. "He might get away!" she protests.

"Weren't you just saying that you didn't believe in the stuff about souls and butterflies?"

"I still don't want to hurt the animal."

"You should be more concerned if we're hurting our father."

Then a familiar voice chimes in. "Who's hurting your father?"

All three of us freeze when we see Pa appear on his spot by the couch. If he's some sort of mirage or hallucination, this time, my whole family is having the same one.

"Ton? Ton!" The bowls and spoons Ma was holding crash on the floor when she yells and rushes toward him. Ma keeps patting him everywhere, checking if he's all right.

Pa slowly moves his hand to Ma's face, eyes widening that he's able to touch her. Cradling Ma's face, he tells his wife, "I missed you so much, sweetheart."

"Sweetheart, you have no idea." Ma's eyes are glistening when she pulls Pa in for a kiss.

For a moment, I wonder if Achi doesn't see him. Unlike Ma, she hasn't moved or said a word. "He's right there." I help her and point in Pa's direction.

"Jackie?"

My sister's still frozen when he says her name.

"You came back," she says in one breath. "I can't believe you came back."

Before Pa can answer, Achi runs and wraps her arms around him. "I'm so sorry. I'm so sorry. I missed you so much, Pa," Achi chokes out while Pa sinks into her hug.

My heart swells to a thousand sizes when he meets my eye. "I had to see you all again."

This is it, right? Pa is *here*. He's back for good?

"Look, I gathered everything here." I spread out the photos on the table in front of Pa. "In case you feel yourself disappearing, we can keep re-creating any of these memories."

"Nika . . ."

The tone in his voice is not what I'd expect from someone who had just vanquished death.

"Or when that doesn't work, maybe we can always keep going back to the cemetery and breaking pagpag . . ."

"I only have a few hours."

All words escape me when I see the look on Pa's face.

"Beth, I promised you that I would take care of you, protect our family. That I would do anything to keep our daughters safe. I'm . . . so sorry for leaving you." His breath shudders when he wipes his eyes. "I was going to leave quietly, spare you all the pain again."

My throat tightens when Pa looks at me and Achi. "But I wanted to see my girls one more time."

My sister's the one who voices out my biggest wish.

"Then stay," Achi says, the words coming out so soft.

"That's not how the world works."

The look on my dad's face breaks my heart. "I tried . . . I really did try."

A buzzing, tingling sensation appears when my hand closes on Pa's skin. I can feel the weight of everything he's been carrying when I cup and cradle his face with my palm, graze the scar above his left eye. I was willing to do anything to bring Pa back for good, and I still would. Part of me wants to keep fighting. I desperately want to tell Pa that I'd commit to being stuck in the past if that meant keeping him around.

His voice is defeated when he whispers, "I hope you can forgive me one day, Superstar."

Out of everyone, I'm realizing that my father is the one who deserves to move on.

42

WE CATCH PA UP ON EVERYTHING THAT'S BEEN HAPPENING SINCE HE'S been gone. It's also kind of like boot camp to train my sister on how to relax and have fun again. We stay up late while Achi tells Pa how she feels like counseling might be her calling, the moment she was chosen to interview for the PhD program, all the details about the atrocious dental cake Dr. Derrick's sister made for the wedding.

Pa gets the idea that we can make an even worse teeth cake, but Ma said we already used up all the baking ingredients with the buffet she made to assist Pa's lost soul.

Achi suggests that we go to the 24–7 convenience store, which we all agree to. But then Pa backs out last minute.

"Go ahead first," Pa urges us.

"What about you?" Ma asks.

"I'll stay back to rest for a moment, sweetheart." He cracks the same smile he puts on when he's trying to make everything light again. "Gives me time to appreciate the new details around our home."

After assuring Ma that he's feeling fine, Pa tries shooing us away again. "It's getting late. You should get going."

My heart drops to the floor when I realize what he's trying to do.

"I'm not missing your last moments, Pa."

He stops short but gives me a small smile in return. "Who says you're missing anything, Superstar?"

"I can take it," I assure him, looking him in the eye so he

knows he doesn't have to hide behind his jokes this time. "We can handle the truth."

His eyes flit from Ma, Achi, me.

Pa lets out a long exhale before saying, "I'm not sure I can handle telling you the truth." Tears slide down his cheeks as he looks at each one of us, studying our faces. "I don't want my girls to see me go," he confesses. "It'll be even harder to leave."

Achi told me that during prom night, Pa excused himself and there was no one else around him when he vanished. None of us got to say goodbye the day he passed all those years ago, either.

Ma chimes in then. "I have an idea."

IT'S JUST LIKE THE MILLION CAR RIDES I TOOK AS A KID. SITTING IN THE back seat next to my big sister while Pa gets caught up with Mariah Carey playing on the radio.

"A one, a two, a one, two, three, four." Pa counts us down during the opening guitar riff and signals for us to sing along with the "doo-doo-doos" flowing through the speakers. Pa guides Achi to pat her lap with the song's percussion and Ma mouths along to the background vocals as we build up to the chorus. I catch Ma and Achi smile when I start singing in the car with my family for the first time in years.

Ma said she was going to keep driving in circles around the area, but I stopped noticing that we were passing the same streets and sights over and over again.

I take my dad's advice and only focus on the people I want to see.

Pa belts out the last notes and I can see the tears pooling around his eyes as Ma holds his hand through the ride. Ma suggested we stay in the back of the car, so that this way we get shielded from what happens to Pa. Still, I can sneak glances at Pa through the rearview mirror. My whole chest tightens when his reflection starts to flicker in and out again.

Then I remember what Ma said, about Pa giving up a shot at heaven.

"Pa . . . after this, you're gonna be okay, right?"

He looks over his shoulder at me and Achi.

"Like, you're still going to find a way to heaven?" I ask.

"I'll be okay, Superstar." He reaches for my hand and taps my wrist three times.

"It's easier to find places when you know what they look like."

"You know what heaven looks like?" Achi checks.

Pa's eyes smile as he gestures to our family gathered around him in the car.

"Must be something like this."

The second time our family lost Pa, he was far from alone.

43

FIVE MONTHS LATER

YOU WOULD THINK MY SISTER WOULD TAKE A BREAK FROM OUR therapy homework for graduation day. We're already fifteen minutes behind schedule and Achi thinks this is the appropriate moment to pull out her Wheel of Emotions. I made her a pocket-size copy that she can take with her once she leaves for Florida, but I really should've given it to her closer to her flight.

"What are we all feeling right now?" she asks.

Jackie Ilagan, everyone. My sister switched from Ms. Emotionally Constipated to Ms. Let's Talk About Our Feelings.

Dr. Broso introduced the Wheel of Emotions during one of our earlier family therapy sessions. She typically goes through us one by one, asking each of us how we're doing. My turn was usually the shortest. I always said the same thing, "Nothing much going on." We only get an hour, so I figured Achi and Ma needed all the time they could get.

But a few sessions later, Dr. Broso looked me in the eye and said, "Nika, if you're shoving your issues under the rug, that means you're shoving yourself under the rug."

She then showed me her Wheel of Emotions—this circular graph that's supposed to capture the range of human emotions. "Sometimes, we have trouble expressing ourselves because we don't have the words to describe what we feel."

After handing me the graph, Dr. Broso said, "Take a look at this. Maybe this could be a good tool for you."

Don't get me wrong. I've seen both *Inside Out* movies, so I was fully aware that people have emotions and can name the appropriate colors assigned to each one. Although under the sad category, the wheel branches out to other feelings:

Lonely.

Vulnerable.

Guilty.

Grief.

I didn't realize that there are so many ways a person can experience sadness. These are all the feelings I've never spoken up about with my family.

My sister shoves the wheel in my face again and I cry out, "Achi, we don't have time!"

Unfortunately, Ma also doesn't see the urgency of our current situation. "Didn't Dr. Broso say that our emotions are sending us important information? We should pay attention to them."

I sigh and land my finger on the wheel. *Stressed.*

Achi takes her turn and points to *Nervous.*

Ma's hand lands between *Sad* and *Happy.*

"Great! Now that we've gotten the wheel out of the way, let's move!" I start ushering Ma and Achi out of the condo when Auntie Baby greets us at the door.

"Look at our graduate!" she exclaims as she puts a dozen flower leis around my neck. Her face is fully made up and she's wearing a pin that says *Proud Saint Agnes Alumna* on her dress. "Half of the leis are for Kayla, but I'll let you hold them for now. Thank goodness I caught you. I thought I'd be too late to pick up my ticket."

I turn to Ma for help. Is Auntie Baby expecting a ticket from *me*? My quota for three graduation tickets was already used up by Ma, Achi, and Dr. Derrick.

But Auntie Baby answers my question for me.

"Did you hear about your classmate who got suspended for sneaking in alcohol on campus?" Auntie Baby lowers her voice and Ma's leaning in like she's saying, *Tell me more.*

"Grace found out because the student was one of the altar servers! Apparently, the girl was pouring tequila into the Mass wine. Father Melvin was rambling and slurring his words while delivering all his homilies last week!" Auntie Baby gasps with Ma as if she's hearing the news for the first time too.

"Tragic, really." Auntie Baby shakes her head. "But when life offers us tragedies, we look on the bright side. I figured that this girl's graduation tickets would go to waste, so I personally volunteered to take them."

"Very selfless," I say, and wince when Achi kicks the back of my leg.

"Of course." Auntie Baby beams at me. "I'm not missing seeing my two girls graduate."

Auntie Baby holds up her arms and I forget the time for a moment to sink into her hug. Big shout-out to my altar girl classmate who made Father Melvin drunk with tequila. She made me realize that it would feel like someone's missing if Auntie Baby weren't there at graduation.

Just when I thought we were finally ready to go, Auntie Baby tells me she needs to borrow my student ID to claim her tickets.

I sprint to my bedroom and grab my ID in record time . . .

Then my eyes land on the plastic egg that's still on my dresser.

Speaking of someone missing . . .

I never even figured out what was inside this plastic egg Seph gave me all those months ago.

When I twist open the lid and unfold the rolled-up paper inside, I find a long list of song titles.

"Torete"—Moira Dela Torre

"Always Be My Baby"—Mariah Carey

"Can I Have This Dance"—High School Musical Cast

"so american"—Olivia Rodrigo

At the bottom, he wrote, *worked hard to remember the titles of the songs that remind me of you.*

There's more when I flip to the back of the list.

my heart's always been yours, ilagan.

will you go to prom with me?

44

MY PLAN WAS SUPPOSED TO BE SMOOTH AND DISCREET. I PUT A NOTE inside the plastic egg that there's an extra graduation ticket for Seph if he wants it.

Step one: Leave plastic egg outside Seph's door.

Step two: Walk away to the elevator and message Seph that I left something for him.

Step three: Seph finds the egg, then decides what to do with it.

Just having completed step one, I'm backing away from the King unit when the door creaks open.

Seph is wearing another one of his shirts that's only buttoned halfway. His brow furrows when he sees me scrambling with a plastic egg on the rug outside the door. It's all very awkward as hell.

"Heeeeeey, you." I stand, not really sure what to do with my hands, squeezing the egg with my fingers. "Long time."

He's still looking at me like I'm a weirdo with an egg. "Aren't you graduating today?"

I nod and smooth out my dress. "Yeah, I was about to head out. Achi and Ma took forever, so I'm about . . ." I check the watch on my phone. Shit. "Thirty minutes late."

". . . Do you need a ride?"

"Oh, no. My family's actually waiting downstairs," I explain, my free hand continuing to flail.

Seph is about to go back inside when I blurt out, "Did you wanna go?

"To graduation," I clarify. "You've done a lot for the Saint Agnes community with all your performances. Didn't you volunteer for one of the game booths at the fair too?"

His face looks so lost right now. "I'm not a student at Saint Agnes . . ."

"I want you there," I say more clearly, and offer him the plastic egg. "I didn't know what was inside, so I had no idea you asked me to your prom."

Seph just stares at my hand.

"You have the right to say no, Nika," he says with a shrug.

It's like a punch to the gut every time he doesn't call me Ilagan.

"Like, you don't owe me anything, really," he adds. "You don't have to feel sorry for me anymore."

He averts his eyes from me then, blinking hard.

I keep turning the plastic egg in my hands. "I didn't think I was going to make it to graduation," I admit, then take a deep breath. "When I lost my dad, I thought that was it, you know? That it was all downhill from there.

"I—I thought I could never be happy anymore. How could I when I lost my favorite person?"

Seph's face softens at that.

"Then when I spent more time with you, it got scary because there were times that I forgot I was sad or angry," I say, trying to make sense of what I want to tell Seph.

"You remind me of what being happy feels like."

His gaze still lingers on the floor, leaving what I just said hanging in the air.

"And I'm trying out this new thing now, where I don't give up on all the good things going on for me . . . So I'd rather not give up on you." I pause and sigh. "And I really hope you haven't given up on me . . . yet."

A beat passes and I consider aborting my mission, giving up and doing the walk of shame to graduation from the sting of Seph's rejection.

Until the sides of his eyes crinkle when the smile I've missed so much appears.

"Wow." He puffs out the air in his cheeks. "So you *really* liked my promposal, huh?"

I groan and shake my head, trying to play it cool and hold in how relieved I am. "I give it an F-minus."

"Please. Easy A-plus. The way I reused the 'My heart is yours' catchphrase? Kahit ako kinilig eh."

My voice remains cool and unbothered when I ask, "The Saint Francis prom is next week, right?"

He nods.

". . . Maybe you can find a date at the Saint Agnes graduation?"

Still totally being cool and unbothered.

Seph juts out his lip. "Well, the girl I wanted to go with never got back to me . . . ," he says. "Not sure how she feels since she ran off after we were supposed to dance too . . ."

"Sorry we didn't get to dance."

I hope Seph can hear all the other sorrys that are laced in that apology.

All he does is shrug. "You can make it up to me during my prom."

"Yeah?" I ask, feeling my whole face lighting up.

"Just to clarify . . . you're offering not asking, right? Because you can't ask someone to *their* prom. That's not how it works, Ilagan."

He tells me he'll change super quickly when I warn him that I'm very close to missing the entire graduation ceremony.

"And, Seph?" I say before he goes back inside to his bedroom.

He turns around, his face carrying the smile that's in my top-ten favorite things to look at. It belongs to Moseph King, my neighbor, my first crush, the boy I'm pretty sure I've been falling in love with.

"My heart's always been yours too."

45

IT TURNS OUT THAT I COULD'VE KILLED MORE TIME BEFORE THE ceremony.

From how long Dani's acceptance speech is, we're about to break the Saint Agnes record for longest graduation in the school's history.

Dani already stood up before Sister Marissa announced the recipient of the Gold Leadership Award. She strutted up the stairs, carrying a whole journal with people she wanted to acknowledge for sticking with her through all her campaigns.

"This is for feminism, for allyship, for inclusion, for peace!"

She shouts out every single social justice cause to end her speech. I laugh under my breath when I spy Kayla mouthing along to Dani's speech like she's watching her favorite singer perform. Third-wheeling Kayla and Dani has made me warm up to some of Dani's . . . Dani-ness. I also figure it's a good self-preservation tactic in case Dani Bautista actually does rule the world one day.

After Dani takes multiple selfies onstage and steps down, members of the faculty march in to award diplomas. Achi already turned in her resignation, but the school still invited her to go up, so she can see off her last graduating class.

Our row gets called and I pull on the hair tie on my wrist when the names get closer to mine. The gap between me and the stage closes in and I force my feet to keep moving forward—it's too late to back out now. My eyes scan the gym filled with hundreds of people and I feel a tug in my heart when I find Ma's face.

Auntie Baby is ordering around Seph and Dr. Derrick to help raise the giant posters she brought, but Ma is oblivious to all the chaos. She blows me a kiss from her seat and mouths, *Go, Superstar.*

Pa once told me that the secret of the universe is when something bad happens to you, the universe then owes you something good in return. To this day, I'm not sure if my dad really believed in the saying or if he was just making something up so I'd feel better.

Would he think that this is the universe's way of balancing things out? The Ilagan family lost Ton, so Nika gets to graduate, Jackie gets to earn her PhD, and Beth gets to franchise her bakery.

I'm not sure how the world operates, but I'd like to look at it differently. If good things happen after the bad, I don't want to think that only bad things happen after the good. Because making it here after everything my family has been through feels like something good—and I want to believe that the universe will always be capable of good things.

"Annika Nicole Lee Ilagan."

Sister Marissa announces my name and my family's corner of the gym erupts in cheers, most audibly from Auntie Baby.

I shake hands with my teachers onstage and stop short when I see my achi openly crying at the end of the line.

"Lost your shades today, Ms. Ilagan?"

She lightly punches my arm and tells me to go pose for my photo before I hold up the rest of the graduates. "Don't hog the spotlight, Superstar."

The photographer guides me to where I should stand and I make sure my necklace with the butterfly pendant is visible and centered.

This time last year, I never would've imagined I'd end up

at graduation. I always thought that not having my dad here would make all this seem empty, that it would feel like losing him all over again. But being here surrounded by all these people who are my home and my family, it's when I feel Pa most of all.

I still see him everywhere I go—and I sometimes whisper to the sky, telling him to please take care of himself.

Because if the moon can control the ocean's tides, who's to say that our dead loved ones can't hear us?

Just as I make my way down the stage steps, I spy a small white butterfly land on my sleeve.

"We're doing okay, Pa," I whisper under my breath.

And I swear, I catch the butterfly smiling before it flutters away.

GLOSSARY

There are nearly two hundred different languages spoken in the Philippines, a country composed of over seven thousand islands. The characters in this book speak a mixture of English, Tagalog, and Hokkien. Tagalog and English are two of the most widely spoken languages in the cities of Metro Manila. It's normal for people to mix both languages, a practice that is commonly referred to as Taglish. This could mean incorporating English words into Tagalog grammar or switching in and out of both languages in the same conversation. For Chinese Filipinos, a majority can trace their roots to the Fujian province in China and speak a language called Hokkien. The use of all three languages in this book reflects the multilingual experience of these characters living in the Philippines.

abangers–someone who waits; slang for someone who's waiting for their crush to be single and available

achi–first older sister; also a title used to address an elder female, even outside the family, as a sign of respect

Ako na.–I'll do it.

Alam mo.–You know.

amah–grandma on father's side

Ang bastos mo naman kay Ma.–You're so rude to Ma.

Ang liit mo pa . . .–You were so small . . .

ang pao–a red envelope containing money, usually given during occasions like weddings or New Year's

angkong–grandpa on father's side

artista–celebrity; actor/actress

asado–sweet-savory pork or chicken stew

Ateneo—a university in the Philippines

Baduy ba?—Is it uncool?

Baka mapasma ka niyan.—*pasma* has no direct English translation but describes a condition that happens when the body is exposed to sudden changes in temperature

bangus—milkfish

banyo—restroom

barangay—smallest administrative division in the Philippines; similar to a neighborhood in other countries

barkada—group of friends

Beh khan tshiu pa tapos ang judgy na.—They're not even married and she's already so judgy.

bibingka—rice cake often cooked in banana leaves typically served during Christmas and traditionally sold outside churches for people who go to Simbang Gabi, predawn masses held for nine consecutive days before Christmas Day

bo le so—no manners

bola-bola—pork meatball filling for siopao that often comes with a boiled egg

buko—coconut

bunso—the youngest child in the family

Buti walang rain.—It's a good thing there's no rain.

Cebuanos—people from Cebu

chilimansi pancit canton—instant noodle dish that combines the flavors of chili and calamansi, a type of Philippine lime

chismis—gossip

CR—abbreviation for comfort room; toilet

demonyo—demon

Di ho se bo?—How are you?

'Di mo ba gets 'yun?—Don't you get that?

Diba?—Right?

Dinala ko dito.—I brought it here.

doktora—a woman doctor

EDSA—one of the major highways in Metro Manila

Feel mo naman.—You're assuming too much.

Fil-Chi—shortcut for Chinese Filipino; a Filipino of Chinese descent, often born and raised in the Philippines

Ganun pala.—So that's how it is.

Gets?—Do you understand?

grabe—wow

Gusto kita.—I like you.

Hard to get talaga ang mama mo.—Your mom is really hard to get.

hay—an interjection used to show exasperation or sighing

hirit—jokes or comebacks

hoy—informal interjection used to get someone's attention

Iba naman ang glow ng prom king and queen.—The glow of a prom king and queen is different.

Isa ka pa.—You're one to talk.

jowa—slang for romantic partner

Kahit ako kinilig eh.—Even I felt kilig.

kakanin—Filipino rice cakes

Kasya pa kaya sa akin?—Will this fit me?

Kawawa naman si Seph.—Poor Seph.

Kaya pala . . .—So that's why . . .

kilig—a swoony, butterflies-in-your-stomach type feeling from an exciting or romantic experience

Kumain ka na?—Have you eaten already?

Lakas mo, bro.—compliment based on context; could mean "You're the man, bro."

Libre ko.—My treat.

longganisa—Filipino sausage

lugaw—rice porridge or congee

made kwento—shared a story

Malay mo.—You never know.

Mang [Willie]—respectful title for older men; similar to "Mr. Willie"

manliligaw—suitor; someone courting or pursuing someone romantically

Marites—a gossip; someone who is up to date with the latest news and loves spreading rumors

Matagal pa?—Is it going to take much longer?

merienda—snack

MOMOL buddies—friends who make out with each other but don't have an exclusive relationship (Nika still insists that this isn't a thing)

na naman—again

Nagkulang siya sa inyo.—Didn't do enough for you.

naman—word that can be added for emphasis. Example: "Wow, how sweet naman!"

Nililigawan ka ba niya?—Is he courting you?

'no—a conversational filler used to punctuate a question. Example: "He's really into the moon, 'no?"

noche buena—feast held during Christmas Eve, usually around midnight

Oo nga pala.—You're right.

pa—a Tagalog particle that can sometimes be added for emphasis

pagpag—Filipino superstition that says you're not supposed to go home immediately after going to a wake to prevent the spirit of the departed from following you home

pamahiin—superstition

Parang kailan lang . . .—It seems like it was just yesterday . . .

pichi-pichi—steamed cassava dessert covered in shredded coconut or cheese

pogi—handsome

puto bumbong—steamed purple glutinous rice cake also typically served during Christmas and traditionally sold outside churches for people who go to Simbang Gabi

puto pao—a fusion of a puto and a siopao; a steamed rice cake with savory siopao filling

sala—living room

sampaguita—small white flower often sold as garlands

Sandali na lang . . .—Just a little longer . . .

sando—sleeveless undershirt

shobe—younger sister

siopao—soft steamed bun with a savory filling

sipsip—suck-up

Sira.—You're out of your mind.

sobra—used to describe something that is too much or excessive

Sobrang porma din ni Francis.—Francis had a lot of style too.

Sobrang selos mo, Pa.—You're so jealous, Pa.

Sorry nabigla 'ata kita.—Sorry, I think I startled you.

suman—rice cake often wrapped in banana leaves

Sure ka okay ka lang?—Are you sure you're okay?

Sweet mo naman kay Seph.—You're so sweet to Seph.

taho—silken tofu served with syrup and tapioca pearls; often sold by vendors while carrying big metal containers

ting hun—a pre-wedding tradition observed by Chinese Filipinos; also serves as an engagement ceremony

tocino—marinated sweet pork

"Torete"—song by Moonstar88 and covered by Moira Dela Torre that translates to "Head over heels in love"

totoy—young boy or kid

Tsai ya kha tsio, huan ho kha tsio.—The less you know, the less you worry.

Tshia dim.—Please drink.

Tsiah lo.—Come eat.

ube—purple yam often used in desserts

Wait lang.—Hold on.

White Lady of Balete Drive—refers to a famous ghost who appears as a woman dressed in white who haunts Balete Drive in Quezon City

Yun o!—There it is!

ACKNOWLEDGMENTS

When I was sixteen, I really wanted to write a zombie love story. It was going to be about a high school girl who falls in love with a zombie who wants to kill her (very obvious I had a *Twilight* phase). I had it all played out in my head—epic battle scenes, love triangles—but I let the idea go after I couldn't write more than four pages. That experience made me think that I wasn't a good enough writer to pull off stories with anything supernatural. I'm not sure if I pulled it off this time, but I'm so grateful for the people in my life who helped me believe I could try.

To my agent, Thao Le—I feel like I'm always flooding your inbox with my random story ideas. When I came up with this pagpag concept in the middle of the night, I immediately sent you an email. I would have never had the guts to pursue this book if not for you. To Jennifer Kim, Andrea Cavallaro, and the Sandra Dijkstra team, you continue to be the best people to work with. Thank you for all that you do.

To this book's wonderful editor, Anna Roberto—you took a chance on this story when all I had was a synopsis and three chapters. From deciding which parent would be the ghost, scrapping of Wattpad chapters, to figuring out the book's title, thank you for the trust and for sticking with me through this whole journey.

To the rest of the Feiwel and Friends team: Jean Feiwel, Kat Kopit, Mallory Grigg, Kim Waymer, Veronica Ambrose, Edmund Mander, Samantha Sacks, Carlee Maurier—thank you for welcoming this story and for making this book possible. To Emily Stone—I teared up when I saw the comment you left after copyedits. Thank you for giving this book its first review.

To Koalanov and Mallory—thank you for creating the most beautiful cover for this book.

To Layla S. Tanjutco—I'm so lucky to receive guidance from such a brilliant writer and editor. Thank you for your feedback and for flagging whenever I give my projects the wrong titles.

To PM Kaw and Kendrick Chua—whenever my family gets impressed by the Hokkien in my stories, I tell them it's because of you. Toh-sia!

To Joycelyn Te—thank you for helping me with the therapy and Dr. Broso scenes. Most of all, thank you for telling me to not shove myself under the rug.

To the writers I met at the Tin House Workshop: Beth Cho Little, Danielle Emerson, Elizabeth Johnson, Fin Leary, Jaimee Garbacik, Kay Amato, Jesaka Long, Kat Boyd, Michele Kirichanskaya—your comments helped me so much through revision. I'd gladly stay up until four in the morning again to talk about your stories.

To Nina LaCour—you are as inspiring a teacher as you are a writer. Our one-on-one really changed how I saw this book and my writing.

To Zakiya Jamal and Megan Scoma—thank you for being the groupchat I can turn to for anything writing-related. Maybe one day we can start a Swifties Who Crochet club too.

To Annica Siy Yap—even if you were in the middle of planning your own wedding, thank you for saying yes to my call and answering my ting hun–related questions.

To Ayet Tan and Nicole Sytin—my initial idea was that Nika would be part of glee club. While that plot line didn't push through, thank you for being willing to chat about your high school glee life.

To my FNB, Pauline Siy—when you checked up on me the

first time I got COVID, I asked, "Hey, wanna read this story pitch?" Thank you for always listening.

To my creative friends, Kara Pangilinan Tan and Rej Tee (yes Rej, creative ka na rin)—you've been inspiring me since we were twelve. I guess there's a reason why all our hangouts turn into work sessions.

To Lexi Tiutan—I don't know if this story would've made sense to me if we didn't watch *Rewind* at your AMS place. Thank you for always being a Telegram call away.

To Alex Martin and Christine Tiu—thank you for always pushing me to dream bigger. I promise I'm building up my stamina so I can keep up with your goals (and travels!).

To Samie Yap—you taught me the beauty of superstitions and pastries. When I told you about my first book deal, I remember you tearing up on the phone and my NR self asked, "Why are you crying?" Thank you for being my ride or die.

To my shobes, Issa Yap and Trisha Ng—I hope you like the shout-out to Steve in the book. The month I spent with you helped me fall back in love with writing.

To my first reader, Lea Lynn Yen—thank you for always reading my messy drafts and for spending your birthday with this story. My favorite kind of feedback is getting emojis and screenshots of your Kindle. This book's plot became clearer to me when you said, "You have to believe it to see it." I'm so grateful that you always see and believe in me.

To the Board—Riana Tan, Janelle Panganiban, Myka Cue, Shar Solis, and Pammy Moran—you were the first people I messaged as soon as things started happening with this book (and everything after). My dreams get to come true because I'm standing next to you five.

Myka, my star—I would have to make a hundred more

Instagram posts to fully express how grateful I am for all the times you helped me with this book. Like Shar said, you are the sunshine of our lives. Thank you for sharing your light with me.

To my ate, Jena Arellano—thank you for believing in me, whether I'm on the tennis court or sitting in front of my computer.

To my aunt Marge, uncle Khan, and Fern—thank you for bringing me to my book events and cheering me on every step of the way.

To my cousin Hannah Sy—when I told you about my story idea, you said that I can't avoid the sad, but I can still be funny. Your advice became my mantra while writing this story. Without you, this book would have no title. Maybe next time we can go for the A24 one.

To my ahia, Alex and Jam—thank you for enabling my *Twilight* phase and reading my stories back in high school.

To my achi, Stenie and Joseph, two of the smartest people I know—thank you for always being there to offer advice. You trusting me with your kids gives me hope that I can keep writing YA fiction.

To my dichi, Sofia and Ross—I'm not sure if I would've finished this book if I didn't stay at your place for two weeks. People always tell me that I need a change of scenery to get inspiration; I guess all I need is to third-wheel with you two. Thank you for letting me be your Steve!

Dichi, when I wasn't sure about this idea, you were the one who told me to push for this concept. I miss having you in the next room, but at least I can still go to your place when I need to talk to my best friend. I love you deep.

To Jet, Seji, Teo, Andre, Aaron, Jana, and Basti—you're the superstars of my life. I'm so lucky to be your aunt.

To my mom, Elena—thank you for raising me to be a reader

and a writer. Thank you for bringing me to bookstores, for signing me up for writing classes, for printing out my stories and showing me what they'd look like as books. This book (and most good things in my life) wouldn't have happened without you.

One of my favorite parts about writing books is getting to meet the best people. To those who work in bookstores, the librarians, teachers—thank you for helping our books reach their readers. I want to especially thank the book community in the Philippines, who have been so supportive.

To JB Roperos—I'm so grateful that our paths crossed. Thank you for everything you did for authors and their books. You are missed.

Lastly, I want to thank you, dear reader. Out of all the books in the world, thank you for spending your time with Nika's story. I hope you never give up on the good things.

Thank you for reading this Feiwel & Friends book.
The friends who made

GOODBYE AND EVERYTHING AFTER

possible are:

Jean Feiwel, Publisher
Liz Szabla, VP, Associate Publisher
Rich Deas, Senior Creative Director
Anna Roberto, Executive Editor
Holly West, Executive Editor
Kat Brzozowski, Senior Editor
Dawn Ryan, Executive Managing Editor
Kim Waymer, Senior Production Manager
Foyinsi Adegbonmire, Editor
Rachel Diebel, Editor
Emily Settle, Editor
Brittany Groves, Assistant Editor
Mallory Grigg, Senior Art Director
Kat Kopit, Associate Director, Production Editorial

Follow us on Facebook or visit us online at fiercereads.com.

Our books are friends for life.